FAUST

FAUST

being the *Historia Von D. Johann Fausten dem wietbeschreyten Zauberer und Schwartzkünstler*, or *History of Dr John Faust the notorious Magician and Necromancer*, as written by his familiar servant and disciple Christopher Wagner, now for the first time Englished from the Low German

by

ROBERT NYE

HAMISH HAMILTON

LONDON

First published in Great Britain 1980
by Hamish Hamilton Ltd
Garden House 57–59 Long Acre London WC2E 9JZ

Copyright © 1980 by Robert Nye

British Library Cataloguing in Publication Data

Nye, Robert
  Faust.
  I. Title
823'.9'1F   PR6064.Y4W/
ISBN 0–241–10202–2

*Printed in Great Britain by
Richard Clay (The Chaucer Press), Ltd.,
Bungay, Suffolk*

Angelus in majori plenitudine sapientiae conditus est quam homo.
Sed nullus homo, nisi omnino amens, eligit esse aequalis angelo,
nedum Deo.

Aquinas, *Summa Theologica*, I, lxiii, 3

Peccatum hominis non est gravius quam peccatum daemonis. Sed
locus poenalis hominis est infernus.

Aquinas, *Summa Theologica*, I, lxiv, 3

TO

CHRISTOPHER SINCLAIR-STEVENSON

CONTENTS

Part 1

The Tower

1 Happy Christmas

'Hey, Faust,' I said.

He didn't answer me.

He doesn't like it when I talk like that.

'Incense,' I said. 'I say we need a pinch of incense here. Incense is nice. Especially sandalwood. A little bit of *tone* to the proceedings?'

He crossed his eyes.

'You mean I stink,' he said.

This was last Christmas.

We were in the cellar.

We had this girl's body on the table.

There was a huge fire burning in the grate.

'I stink,' he said. 'I'm a dirty old man.'

Too true.

He's a stinker all right. I have to stick jam up my nostrils.

Magic to come. Adventures. Facts come first.

Facts about Faust.

1: He's got long black toenails and fingernails. There's this boil on his snout.

2: He smears butter on the boil, and candlegrease.

3: Sex and candlegrease. That's what the Herr Doktor smells of.

I looked at the girl.

She was nice. Hair the colour and sweetness of honey. Tits like plump apple dumplings.

The only snag was:

She was dead.

'Sir?' I said. 'Master?'

He likes that.

'Napkins,' he hollered.

The fuck-up.

'Is it true that Luther says?' I ask him politely.

'Napkins!' he hollered. 'And I'm sick of your Luther jokes.'

'This isn't a joke about Luther. This is what Luther says.

3

You can lead a fiend to water, but you can't make him take a bath!'
He stroked his boil.
'I'm not a fiend,' he said. 'I'm damned, that's all.'
He licked his bloodstone.
'More napkins, please,' he said.
I put hot napkins on the dead girl's knees.
She had very nice knees. With dimples.
He was wearing his black cloak. Trust him to wear his black cloak.
I was wearing my red cloak.
The girl was naked.
Christ, but it was hot in that cellar. The fire like a furnace.
I asked him:
'So why don't you dip your damnation in the tub?'
He started rubbing with the napkins. He started at her knees and he worked upwards. He didn't answer me.
'You could give up stinking,' I said. 'You could give yourself a nice hot bath for Christmas.'
He shook his head.
'I sold my soul to the Devil.'
Ha ha.
That's his excuse for everything. You'll see.
He'd reached her nipples. He was rubbing them through the napkins. She had nice nipples but they didn't prick.
'She's dead,' I said.
He went on rubbing.
'Her mother said she died at three o'clock,' I told him.
He took away the napkins. He folded them.
He can be terribly neat when he wants to be.
'How *do* you bring the dead to life?' I said.
He grinned his horrible grin.
'Brandy, my boy,' he said.
I handed him the bottle.
You know what he does then? He goes and pours brandy all over the poor girl's body! As if she's a Christmas pudding and he's going to set fire to her.
He slapped her about. He rubs all the brandy in.
'Nice work if you can get it,' I suggested.
He rubbed.
He grunted.

4

'I don't get it,' I added. 'I just don't get it at all.'

He's a piss artist, of course. But the filthy smell in that cellar made me think. Does Mephistopheles forbid a bit of soap and water? Are magicians to be reckoned by their armpits? Did Simon Magus never change his socks?

'Did Simon Magus never change his socks?'

That got to him.

Simon Magus always does.

'Man stinks,' he says, coming all Original Sin on me. 'You stink, my son. I stink. And she stinks too.'

He stopped that rubbing.

He was wiping his hands on his moustaches.

'If it wasn't for me,' he went on, 'she'd soon stink more than us two put together.'

He stared at the fire.

'It's the human condition,' he said.

He took off his cloak.

He was naked underneath.

I thanked Jesus for strawberry jam.

Even so, I was having to hold my nose.

He climbed on the table. He was kneeling astride the poor girl. His prick dangled against her. He put his feet with their toenails to her feet. She had nice toenails. Her mother would have been proud of her. He spread out his arms and he put his hands to her hands.

'Happy days are here again,' I said.

Well, he didn't like that much either.

He put his mouth on this girl's mouth.

He kissed it.

He must have kissed it more than twenty times.

I noticed that his member didn't stiffen.

'Anyway,' he said, stopping kissing, twisting his big mouth sideways, 'I took a bath once.'

'Seven years ago!'

'That first night with our Helen,' he remembered.

Then he was busy back kissing again, that poor dead girl.

I took a long look at the candles.

Necrophily has never turned me on.

I said:

'You didn't do much washing, did you, though?'

He kissed.

5

Kissed.

Like a sucking plant.

Then he said:

'I played with my ducks.'

'What did Helen play with?'

'We had a nice time,' he said.

I shut my eyes.

'There was too much splashing,' I said.

'I couldn't help that.'

He couldn't help that. But the water ran over the sides of the tub and came down through the ceiling. It rained in his library that night.

Now the table was creaking.

I opened my eyes.

He was clambering off the table. His knees have black bristles on them. Brandy dripped from his prick and his balls.

'Just a few soapsuds,' he said.

'Bathwater all over your grimoires!'

'That made me mad, Kit,' he remembered.

'You hit me!'

'Naturally.'

'On the head.'

'What with?'

'A book.'

'Which book?'

'*The Book of the Sacred Magic of Abramelin the Mage.*'

He frowned.

'I could have sworn it was *The Key of Solomon*,' he said.

'It wasn't. I'd remember. *The Key of Solomon* isn't so heavy.'

'I'll take your word for it,' he said.

He crossed his eyes.

'That's why we haven't done it since,' he said.

'Done what?'

'Bathing.'

'Hey ho,' I said. 'And there was me thinking it was on account of you selling your soul to the Devil.'

He ignored this.

He was holding a mirror to the girl's pale lips.

The glass clouded.

6

Slowly.

Faintly.

But it clouded.

'You old bugger!' I said.

He shrugged.

He put on his cloak.

'Perhaps *Helen* would like another bath?' I said.

'Then let her take another bath,' he said.

He sucked at his moustaches.

He's got these long moustaches.

The clock made a noise as if it was clearing its throat.

He sniffed at his hands.

'I stink' he said. 'Therefore I am.'

He seemed quite pleased with this remark.

He ate a peach and drank all the rest of the brandy.

The girl on the table opened her eyes. They were china-blue. She couldn't believe her luck, if you ask me. Having been dead, and then waking up and finding yourself not in heaven or hell, but just some lousy German cellar with two guys in cloaks.

The clock struck twelve.

'Happy Christmas,' she said.

2   The Trouble with Nuremberg Eggs

I hate it myself when a book starts and you don't know the time or where you are or what's happened before you came in or who anyone is.

Sorry about that.

What's the time?

Half past ten.

I have a reliable watch. One of these Nuremberg Eggs, with a fusée to jack up the mainspring. Too big for the pocket, of course. I wear it hanging from my belt around my waist.

Only trouble with these Nuremberg Eggs is they look bad on ladies.

Take Luther and Queen Marguerite of Navarre.

They could have got on like a church on fire if it hadn't been for Nuremberg Eggs.

That Marguerite's not just a pretty face. She got through two husbands while her mind was on higher things. She was trying to patch it all up between Jesus and Plato.

Then, widowed the second time, she turned to the Reformation. Her court was a refuge for anyone bugged by the Pope.

Queen M has the one little weakness: her Nuremberg Egg. It embarrasses the lady, a-dangle down there in her middle. So she always keeps it hanging from her girdle inside her drawers.

This great patroness of the Protestants meets our Martin Luther.

A marriage of true minds.

An elective affinity.

Well, everything's going like treacle, until Luther asks her: 'Sister in Christ, what's the time?'

Queen Marguerite turns her back.

She takes a quick peep in her knickers.

'Martin, dear brother, my watch stands at —

'*Stands*, sister? *Stands?*' Luther roars. 'Then you keep him too close to your cunt!'

End of a beautiful friendship.

They fry Lutherans now in Navarre.

3   Ash Wednesday

Today is Ash Wednesday, 28th February, A.D. 1540.

I call A.D. 1540, Faust Year 24.

Don't worry. I'll explain about Faust Years.

Ash Wednesday. The day some people tart themselves up in sackcloth and trot along to the priest to have the sign of the cross made on their foreheads with ashes. (In these parts, young Protestant blokes round up Catholic girls in a cart when they come out of church, and drive them down to the river for a scrub.)

Ash Wednesday. The start of Lent. Even the Lutherans still call it that. For the Latins it's called Quadragesima. *Quadragesima dies*, the 40th day before Easter. Lent lasts forty days, and while it lasts you have to fast. Poor you, if you do. One miserable meal a day, and that after noon.

I'm writing these words about Lent with a quart of hot ale at my elbow. I've just stirred in a nice dab of butter the size of a hazel nut. I'm eating with my left hand while I'm writing with my right – slices of pig's liver, wrapped in the fat of the caul, roasted brown. I've some cherries and cracknels for later.

4 Wagner

I'm Christopher Wagner. Never mind about my parents. They didn't give two fucks about me.

Just the one fuck. Ha ha.

OK. I'm a bastard.

I don't know who my father was. Some waggoner or other. My mother was cook at the Wartburg. The waggoner stuck his spoke in her soup and I'm the comestibles.

The Wartburg. That castle near Eisenach. Like a wart it is, too. A brown papillary excrescence on top of a hill. Built by Louis the Springer. Louis sprang for the last time in 1123, and from then until about a hundred years ago his Wartburg was the court of the landgraves of Thuringia. A wild bunch. Minstrels and wanderers streamed there. Noisy singing. Great crowds. All-night boozings.

By my time, the Wartburg was no more than a run-down old garrison full of suits of armour which nobody bothered to polish. Perhaps my dear dad was one of the soldiers? Junker Wagner? A pikeman? A dab hand with the halberd? Even, sergeant in charge of the canteen?

I doubt that.

They let mother stay.

I remember the Sängersaal best. The hall of the minstrels. It was vast. Hung with cobwebs. It had frescoes illustrating the Triumph of Christianity, or somesuch. Standing there in that great empty hall a boy's ears could imagine they caught the echo of quite different songs.

Too romantic. I only got into that Sängersaal once. They kept the doors locked on account of the beer being stored there. I slipped in one evening when the quartermaster was drunk. I got my arse tanned when he caught me.

9

I spent most of my time in the kitchens. Pots and pans. Lard and oil. Rats and mice.

I like food. But hell must be a kitchen.

Then, on the 4th of May, Faust Year 5 (1521), the Wartburg received this distinguished kidnap victim. Martin Luther, no less, the Great Constipator. On his way home to Wittenberg from the Diet of Worms, Luther was seized and bundled off to our garrison on the orders of the Elector Frederick 3 (known as the Wise to those who didn't know him).

It was a put-up job, of course. The kidnap.

Fred 3 was hiding Luther in the Wartburg to save him from the Holy Roman Emperor Charles 5, who's a great Christian gentleman but scared stiff of mice, spiders, and heretics. Luther stayed with us ten months, calling himself Sir George. I was five at the time, but remember him clearly. Who could forget that big apple-shape skull and that stare like a cow through a gate?

Luther's problem:

He farted more often than he shat.

It's not just his face I remember.

We called him the Constipator. The Reformation was born on our jakes, there in the Wartburg, when Luther prayed and his bowels were moved. He used to pray in the lavatory a lot. What he prayed for, I don't know. But the two activities were connected in his mind.

Praying and shitting.

Luther called our castle his Patmos. He said he saw the Devil there and threw his inkpot at him in the little room above the trees. He missed.

5   Angels

I'm 24. When I left the Wartburg's kitchen, I went to study Divinity at the University of Wittenberg. I was admitted at the age of twelve, thanks to the patronage of the Constipator (a resourceful lad, I supplied him with enemas), plus – blush, Wagner – certain qualities or deformities of the prodigy which I possessed.

I was a regretful pupil. I didn't like the mood at Wittenberg. My teachers were all Protestants, and if there's one thing

I find sillier than Catholics, it's Protestants.

They are all busy lecturing their heads off on Justification by Faith Alone, the All-Pervading Action of God, Necessarianism, Imputed Grace, Predestination, and so on – that is, when they weren't equally busy burning Papal bulls and smashing images and dragging Mass-saying priests from the altar by their hair.

I reacted to all this by specialising secretly in angels.

Is an angel an entirely incorporeal being? Is an angel composed of matter and form? Do the angels have different faces? If the angels all have the same face, whose face is it? Can an angel blush? Sneeze? Wink? Do the bodies assumed by angels function as living organisms? Can an angel move from one place (say, Paris) to another place (say, Constantinople)? Would an angel, moving locally, travelling from Paris to Constantinople, have to pass through an intermediate place (e.g. Venice)? How long would it take an angel to get from Paris to Constantinople without stopping in Venice? If he stopped in Venice for (say) the weekend, would those two days not count if he didn't want them to count? Do angels travel at different speeds? Is an angel's thought identical with his substance? If an angel's thought *is* identical with his substance, does this mean that he can add cubits to his stature by thinking about it? Do angels bite? Do angels eat? Does an angel know he is an angel? Do angels know the future? If an angel knew a future in which angels were extinct could he change his personal fate? What is the nature of the angelic memory? Does an angel lust? If an angel lusts, does he lust after other angels? And/or human beings? Animals? Orchids? Time? Where the angels created before or after grass? Stars? Whales? Fruit trees? Can an angel, once enthroned in glory, sin? Which sin do the angels favour? Was the sin of the first angel that sinned the cause of the other angels sinning? Was the sin of the first angel that sinned merely *a* cause of the other angels sinning? If the latter, what were the other causes? Are the causes of sinning angels material, formal, efficient, and final? Did the number of angels that sinned equal the number of angels that didn't? How many angels can dance on the point of a pin? Why do they dance? To what music? Is such dancing on pinheads innocent angelic recreation or proximate occasion of angelic sin?

Et cetera, et cetera, et cetera, et –

Angels were my hobby.

Angels were my passion.

I majored in angels. To my own satisfaction. While writing the required papers for my professors on the various differing views of what gives in the Eucharist.

Viz.

1: The Lateran Council of 1215, as later translated into Aristotelian metaphysics by Aquinas, teaches that the bread and the wine are changed in their whole substance into the body and blood of Christ for ever and ever. The word for this is *transubstantiation*. The consequence of this view is that if the priest drops the chalice he must get down on his hands and knees and lap up every drop of wine from the floor, otherwise Christ gets on people's boots.

2: Luther teaches that the bread and the wine remain bread and wine but that the body and blood of Christ is present 'in' or 'under' the bread and the wine at the moment the communicant eats and drinks them. The word for this is *consubstantiation*. The consequence of this view is that it doesn't matter if the priest drops the chalice, because the wine isn't even hiding Christ until it hits the digestive tract.

3: Zwingli teaches that the bread and the wine remain bread and wine all the time, and that you just have to *think* of the body and blood of Christ. There is no word for this but *imagination*, and no particular consequences except that you've got to keep your mind on the job.

(Zwingli stopped teaching anything in Faust Year 15, when run through with a sword by his opponents at Cappel, near Zürich. He was armed with a banner. The Papists then hung him and quartered him, just to be sure, and burnt his body with dung.)

As for me, I'd passed on to the composition of a private thesis concerning the 3rd article of Question 63 and the 4th article of Question 64 in the *Prima Pars* of the *Summa* of Thomas Aquinas ('Did the Devil desire to be like God?' 'Is this world of ours the place where the devils are punished?') when I first met Herr Dr John Faust. As a consequence of my secret studies, no doubt.

That was ten years ago. I was only 14, please remember.

Goodbye, angelology.

6 Low German

I'm five feet six inches tall. Never mind. Height is peculiar. Take Alexander the Great. Wouldn't you have thought he was some sort of giant? I did, until I read the truth somewhere. He was five foot *five*! Take the Virgin Mary. This is legend, of course, but I've seen old texts which give her height as six feet eight! If that's true, then she must have looked down on her son right up to his crucifixion.

My hair is the colour of florins and as straight as you like. I wear it not short and not long, with a parting in the middle. I'm beardless.

I can speak seven languages – German, French, Italian (both Latin and vulgate), Turkish, Persian, Russian, and English. According to more of the nice useless information I dug up for my own amusement while at Wittenberg, Adam and Eve spoke Persian. It's certainly the most poetical of tongues. Quite impossible to tell the truth in it. The same silly source insisted that the Archangel Gabriel spoke Turkish. Well, Turkish sounds menacing all right. But, in that case, if any of the story was true, how did the Virgin Mary understand what the angel announced to her? She would have spoken only Aramaic, the vernacular in Galilee then.

I'm writing this book in Low German to avoid poetry and rhetoric, and because I like it. I favour a plain, blunt style. Just the facts. Nothing fancy. Besides, Low German is my birthright, and High German has been done to death by the Constipator in his version of the Bible.

7 A Nice Story about Martin Luther

By the way, I'm not an *anti*-Lutheran. As long as he doesn't shit in my can, I don't care what he does. After all, I owe the guy my education. Up to a point. Or an enema.

Nice story about Martin Luther.

He was invited once, at Wittenberg, to sit in with one of the few remaining Papists just to refresh his memory on the subject of confession. Luther wanted to know the going rate for sins these days. 'Oh, we try to be fair,' says the priest. A woman comes in and confesses the usual stuff with her lover. 'How may times did you sin, my child?' says the priest. 'Three times,' says the woman. 'That's three Hail Marys and three Our Fathers for penance,' says the priest, 'and ten pfennigs in the bag.' A man comes in to the confessional. Sex with his mistress. 'How many times?' says the priest. 'Three times,' says the man. 'Three Hail Marys, three Our Fathers,' says the priest, 'and ten pfennigs in the bag.' Just then the priest is called away to give the last rites to a dying banker. 'You pop in the box,' he says to Luther. 'After all, you used to be an Augustinian, and I'm broad-minded. No one need ever know. Business is brisk tonight. Just be sure to get the ten pfennigs in the bag, right?' Luther sits in the box. A girl comes in. 'Sex with my lover, father,' she confesses. 'Three times?' says Luther. 'Just the once, actually,' says the girl. 'Sure it wasn't three?' says Luther. 'No, father, it was one time only.' Luther thinks hard. Then he says: 'Well, I'll tell you what, my child. You just say three Hail Marys and three Our Fathers and put ten pfennigs in the bag – and the Church will owe you two fucks.'

8   The Philosopher's Stone

Where are we?

At Staufen, in the Breisgau, where Faust has this Tower. Staufen's near Freibrug. Freiburg's some forty miles north of Basel and the Swiss border.

I weigh 134 pounds in my birthday suit. My eyes are grey. My nose is sharp and turns up at the end. I have narrow feet and hands. I've a scar on my left cheek, which I earned in the Herr Doktor's service. We were supposed to be making the Philosopher's Stone from bicarbonate of potassium, mercury, sperm, and zinc. The laboratory blew up. The Philosopher's Stone is very important apparently, but I don't know what for.

I believe in free will.

I'm employed in this Tower as Faust's familiar servant and disciple. Well, I like work: I could watch it all day.

9 High German

Here's how I met the old fart.

I was in this eating place in Leipzig called Auerbach's. It's a wine cellar. The Leipzig Fair was on, and the place was noisy. I ordered steak medium rare and a half-bottle of lachryma christi. I was anxious to lose myself in Aquinas. I had my calf-bound copy of Questions 50 to 64 of the *Summa Theologica* propped up against the little wine basket and was half way through my meal when I realised that the person sitting at the next table was watching me.

He was a long, lank, gangling fellow in a filthy black cloak. His face was clean-shaven save for drooping moustaches that hung down like the tusks on a walrus. High cheekbones. A prizefighter's jaw. Nose like the beak of a hawk. Complexion the colour of candlegrease. Hair, worn long, falling across his shoulders like a drift of dirty snow.

An ugly customer.

In contrast to my frugal plate and bottle, this stranger's table was decked out with an incredibly complicated dinner. He must have been eating from a dozen dishes, taking a mouthful of this and a mouthful of that, chewing with relish, making a lot of noise, mopping at his lips all the time with his moustaches.

His table was crowded with bottles and glasses as well, and his hands scuttled indiscriminately between red wines and white wines like big inebriate spiders.

I marked him down as some eccentric Jewish merchant.

Some of my best friends are eccentric Jewish merchants, but I don't like being stared at.

I went on gnawing at my steak and trying to concentrate on the angels.

Unfortunately my neighbour's position at his table was exactly opposite mine. He had a table to himself, which was not surprising. I was sharing a long table with a lot of other students, but the place was thick with people and there was no room for benches on the other side of my table. So there was nothing in between us but my meat, my wine, my book, and the ruins of his feast. And I was being made more uncomfortable every minute by the knowledge that his eyes never left me.

His eyes.

I see I haven't said a word about his eyes.

That's because they scared me.

The man had big deep-sunken eyes, as cold and blue as any I ever saw. They seemed to bore straight into my brain.

I looked up once more only.

Those staring eyes made the meat in my mouth taste like ashes.

I pushed the plate away. I threw down my knife.

The man started laughing.

It was a great belch of a laugh. Not really sinister or ill-humoured. But it scared me even more.

I knew that it was me he was laughing at.

'Sir, you will forgive me.'

The words were spoken in High German. The voice was deep and musical. It was a polite statement, not a request.

He was standing over me and looking down. Not laughing now. But with tears of merriment in those freezing blue eyes and trickling down his sallow cheeks.

'*Merde*,' I said.

The eyes concentrated on the remains of my steak.

'My name is Dr John Faust,' he said.

He still addressed himself to me in German. My French fugue had not fooled him for a minute.

'Alias George Sabellicus,' he said.

I glared at him. He grinned.

'What do you want?' I said.

'Nothing,' he said.

'So why are you wasting my time?' I said.

'Wagner,' he said, 'I will not waste your time.'

I finished my lachryma christi in one swallow.

'Good,' he said. 'You don't run away when you learn that I already know your name.'

'How do you know it?'

'I've had my eye on you,' he said.

'My God,' I said.

He came and sat down beside me. People made room for him. He's that sort of person. Or he was then.

He didn't smell so bad ten years ago. But he didn't smell so

16

very nice either.

'Faust,' I said. 'That sounds like Latin. Sabellicus does too. But you're a German.'

'I am a Samaritan,' he said.

'A Samaritan?' I said. 'You mean, you come from Samaria?'

'I am a Samaritan,' he said, grinning. 'I mean, I come from everywhere.'

'Got it in one,' I said. 'You come from everywhere, and you're going nowhere. You're the Bad Samaritan, right?'

He crossed his eyes.

'Not good or bad, my boy. I'm just the *best*.'

'I see,' I said.

'What do you see?' he said.

'An old faggot trying to pick up a not very pretty boy,' I said.

The eyes looked hurt.

'I regret the laughing,' he said. 'I laugh a lot.'

(He doesn't now.)

'I like to laugh, Kit,' he went on. 'Laughter is holy. Man is distinguished from all other creatures by the faculty of laughter.'

'Ha ha, bloody ha,' I said. 'Aristotle.'

'I know you are clever,' he said. 'That's not why I need you.'

'Hey ho,' I said.

He spat on the floor.

He said: 'Not your mind or your body.'

'What then?'

'Your soul,' he said.

I didn't like this kind of talk at all. I got up to go.

He caught my wrist. His grip was like a tongs.

'It was not you that I was laughing at.'

'What's so funny then?' I demanded.

He flicked with the dirty forefinger of his free hand at the copy of the *Summa*.

'Aquinas on angels?' I said, incredulous.

'Pure shit,' he said.

'Shit?' I said.

'Pure shit,' he said.

'Herr Doktor Samaritan,' I said, 'you've got to know. You're full of it yourself.'

He laughed.
He let go of my wrist.
'Sit down, son,' he said.
I sat down.
I didn't want to.
But I sat down.
He started to tell me things about the Devil.
My wrist hurt. Still, I listened.
I went on listening.
I've gone on listening for the last ten years.
It's my head hurts now.

10   Facts

Faust is 60 years old this year, so far as I can make out. I know
various stories of where, when, and how he was born. That
isn't important. Where, when, and how he will die is more to
the point. That's certainly what he thinks. And I think it too.

I want to get this quite straight before we go any further.
I'm not telling lies and legends. Lies and legends about Faust
are cheap. For the price of a beer, any tavern in Wittenberg
will provide you with someone who'll say that Faust was con-
ceived on All Hallows Eve when a bolt of lightning went up
the cunt of a witch (or more likely her arse), and that he was
born talking Greek and with a third eye in the middle of his
forehead about two hundred years ago and defeated the Turks
single-handed before he even invented the printing machine.
I'm not trying to compete in the tall story business. I'm talking
about a man so real you can smell him through oak doors five
inches thick. I'm talking about that poor drunk out there now
in the maze all covered in pigeon shit.

So let's stick to *facts*.

Believe me, the facts about Faust are stranger by far than
the fictions.

11 Promotion Material

I've just given you my true account of how I first met him.

Now here's someone else's.

Document one.

The first historical mention of Faust.

A letter written in Latin by the Abbot Trithemius of Würzburg, sometime head of the Benedictine monastery of Sponheim, near Kreuznach in the Palatinate.

Trithemius wrote some quite decent histories, e.g. *De Viris Illustribus Germaniae* (1495).

What I mean is: he wasn't an imbecile.

His letter is dated 20th August, 1507.

It's addressed to the mathematician at Heidelberg, Johannes Virdung.

I'll translate it:

'Greetings in Christ, etc.

'He's a con man! And worse! That evil creature you've written to me about ... The so-called George Sabellicus! He calls himself the prince of magicians. I call him a bum, a big mouth, and — just wait till you've heard what I know about him!

'Anyway, what he needs is a good thrashing. A taste of the whip might just make him think twice about prancing about in public babbling his blasphemies and — *doing what he does* ...

'The things he calls himself! What else can they be but the mark of an idiot? They prove he's a fool and no philosopher.*

'Have you seen his promotion material? *Magister Georgius Sabellicus, Faustus junior, Magus secundus, Master of Divination by Fire, Bachelor of Divination by Water (Second Class).* I've got his ad in front of me now. You see what a bragger the man is? A person who is, in fact, a schmuck would do better to keep his fat mouth shut.

'I'm telling you: I know what I'm talking about. Couple of years ago, on my way back from Brandenburg, I put up for the night at this inn at Gelnhausen. I was informed that there was

---

* *Fatuum non philosophum* – sounds better in the original Latin, doesn't it?

19

this screwball staying there. A great magician, they said. Claimed he could make roses out of snow, they said, and that when he felt like a drink he just stuck his hand out the window and it came back with a double brandy. Well, you know Geln-hausen. It's full of suckers. I didn't pay too much attention. But at breakfast I looked round to see who'd be getting his bacon and eggs served first. He wasn't there. Our black bird had flown in the night without paying his bill. Maybe he'd heard I was asking questions about him. The landlord said the crook had given his name as Sabellicus. Christian name, George. No idea where he came from. Foreign-looking, he said. Someone else said his real name was Helmstätter. I don't know on what evidence. Faust was his 'magical' name, so he'd told everyone. You get the picture?

'Well, I made a few more enquiries. The local priests told me that this man had badly disturbed some of their parish-ioners with his talk. I asked what he'd said. It was all crazy stuff. I'll repeat just one bit to give you the flavour. Our Faust and/or Sabellicus claimed that, if the entire works of Plato and Aristotle were wiped clean from human memory, he could still restore them. Like a second Hebrew Ezra! And by his genius, he said, Plato and Aristotle would be improved in the process!

'I heard no more about him for a bit. Then, one day last September in Speyer, I heard of a man who'd been going the rounds in Würzburg the month before. This man had made a deep and terrible impression on simple folk by saying that the miracles of Our Lord and Redeemer Jesus Christ are no cause for raised eyebrows even. He himself could do everything that Christ had done, as often as he wished and anyime he felt like it. I asked about to see if the blasphemer had dared to give his name. He had. Guess who? John Faust!

'Now, here's the end of what I know about him. I'll not mince words. You'd better believe it. Just a few weeks ago, he came *here*! *to Kreuznach*! He went about calling himself a magus, and all the rest of it. I was waiting my moment to get him arrested for blasphemy, but he played his cards carefully and before I could do anything about it Faust got himself a job as teacher in the local school. How? By Franz von Sick-ingen pulling strings for him, I'm sorry to say. Yes, von Sick-ingen, our local steward, who's supposed to look after our affairs in the name of the prince you, my dear Johannes, serve so well. A politician! A man in public office! Well, I can tell you privately that von Sickingen won't be running things round here much longer. Not when the Inspector's report reaches Heidelberg. Von Sickingen gave that job to Faust because he's a fool with far too great an interest in what he calls "the occult". He was duped. He was taken in by a trickster. But that's not going to save his neck. Faust was appointed schoolmaster. He lasted just three days. Now he's flown! Run away in the night! Disappeared – somehow – before he can be punished for his crimes. You see, he was caught in the act. Not black magic. *He was buggering the boys!!*

'Yours in Christ, etc.
'Trithemius ✠'

12   Faust Declined

I've other things like this. You'll be given the chance to examine them all at your leisure.

For now, note only that the Herr Doktor has gone by different names at different times.

George or Georgius Sabellicus. Herr Helmstätter. Faustus Jnr. John Faust.

All these are names for the one person.

Dr John Faust.

My boss.

Faustus. Fausta. Faustum.

A Latin adjective.

Meaning: happy, lucky, auspicious, favourable, fortunate.

He's six feet three inches tall, as thin as a rake, and no longer happy, lucky, auspicious, favourable, or fortunate. (Jesus Christ was also six foot three. I learned that at Wittenberg.)

13   Horse Barrel Myth

By the way, he got me so drunk that first night I met him that I was convinced we ended up riding out of Auerbach's wine cellar on a barrel. As if the barrel was a horse, I mean. I've heard that people claim to have *seen* this. Only in the popular version Faust is supposed to have been with 'some students' at Leipzig Fair, and then to have mocked these draymen who couldn't roll a huge barrel out of Auerbach's, and Auerbach offers to make a present of the contents to whoever can lift it out. Faust goes into the cellar, sits astride the barrel as though it is a horse, clucks his tongue, claps his heels, cries Gee Up, and rides it out. The host has to keep his promise, and Faust drinks the contents of the barrel with the students.

This story is a myth. I don't know who made it up. The facts are as stated. I was the only student. I was drunk. The barrel was a barrel all the time. Auerbach was too mean to make a bet like the one in the story. We did drink the contents, Faust and me, but that was *before* the riding, and he paid for it. Three silver dalers.

14   What's Happening Right Now

Faust's household here.

Faust's household in this Tower consists of eight persons besides him and me. The first seven persons are the seven girls (you haven't met them yet, but you will, don't worry). They blew in just three years ago. The eighth person is a different kettle of fish. Our Helen of Troy.

I'm sorry to say that the girl with the china-blue eyes 'resurrected' in my first chapter went back to her mother two days after Christmas. She was a simple soul. The different kettle of fish turned her stomach.

But I've run out of hot ale and pig's liver. And I struck a bargain with myself that I wouldn't draw a second quart or start on the cracknels and cherries until I got to King Henry the 8th.

More about the 7 girls, etc, later.

What's happening right now?

1: Faust is waiting for the Devil. (Well, he is and he isn't. You'll see.)

2: I'm writing this book.

3: You're reading it.

So! Cherries! Another nut of butter melting in the ale, as I turn a fresh page to tell you all about —

15 Three Drunks at the 3rd Wedding of King Henry the 8th

'Hippocrash?' he said.

'Hippocrash,' I said.

Helen got out her powder puff.

He filled up my glass again. He filled Helen's glass again. Helen hadn't finished the glass before. The hippocras ran down the side of Helen's glass. It made frosty patterns.

'Henry the 8th!' he said.

'Henry the 8th!' I said.

We toasted the English king.

Helen stared at her powder puff. She aimed for her nose. She missed.

We were all crocked out of our minds.

This was four years ago. Another Lent. We were at Ingolstadt.

'Hippocrash?' he said.

'Hippocrash,' I said.

He filled us both up again.

Helen glared at her powder puff. She looked for her nose again. This time she found it. Helen's got this thin nose. It gets red when she's drinking.

'Henry the 8th!' he said.

'Henry the 8th!' I said.

'God bless him!' Helen said. 'Though I'm not sure . . .'

She sipped. Then she giggled.

Ingolstadt is a fortified Catholic antheap. It boasts of its Catholic university, founded in 1472 by the Duke of Bavaria, Louis the Rich (known to his bosom buddies as Oofy Lew). We were there at the Catholic university, corrupting the Catholic students. We'd had a heavy day.

'What's this we're drinking?' Helen said.

'Hippocrash,' I said.

He filled us all up again.

'Henry the 8th!' he said.

'Hang on there,' I said. 'This could get boring. Let's drink to someone else.'

'Better not,' he said.

'Why not?' I said.

23

'Because this is *his* hippocrash.'

'This is *whose* hippocrash?'

'Henry the 8th's,' he said.

'I knew it,' cried Helen. 'I knew there was something –'

'*Henry the 8th's?*' I said.

'Henry the 8th!' he said.

He drank his in one go.

I hadn't touched mine.

Helen was glaring at me as if I was personally responsible for the Fall of Man. She likes to blame me for things.

I watched him. He licked his lips. It was like two slugs mating.

He filled up his glass again.

I said: 'This is the Defender of the Faith's hippocrash?'

'Yup. From his third wedding.'

'When was that?' I said.

'Today,' he said.

He drank it all down.

I held my spinning head.

'*Today's* wedding?' I said. 'How'd you get hippocrash from today's wedding sent here?'

'Special messenger,' he said.

'I just knew there was something *queer* about it,' said Helen. 'Is my nose red?'

I watched him. He winked at me. I drank half my hippocras.

'So who's our Henry marrying today?' I said.

'Someone Seymour,' he said.

'Someone Seymour!' I said. I swallowed the other half.

He filled us both up again.

'What happened to what's-her-name?'

He chopped at his huge Adam's apple with his forefinger.

'Yesterday,' he said.

'So he could marry this Seymour today and send you his hippocrash?'

'Is my nose red?' Helen said.

'Partly,' he said.

He kissed Helen on the nose.

Helen tried some fresh powder work.

'Also Anne Boleyn's incest,' he said.

He gulped down his hippocras.

'Henry caught her in bed with her brother,' he said.

24

I sipped my glass slowly.

'Go on then,' I said.

Well, he might have gone on. He might have been able to tell me what I later found out for myself. That Queen Anne Boleyn had been tried by 27 peers on the charge of incest with her brother, Lord Rochford, and by 45 commoners at Middlesex on further charges of adultery with four gents of the court. One of these gents, a violinist called Smeton, pleaded guilty. None of the others said anything until admitting their guilt when they got to the scaffold. Anne herself kept her mouth shut. Then she laughed with her head on the block. Then she looked up and said she was glad her husband had got a good headsman from Calais in for the job. She had such a little neck, she said.

He might have been able to tell me some of this.

I wonder.

I never found out.

I never found out because Helen had started her screeching.

She's a powerful screecher, our Helen. Her screech can bend candleflames. Her earrings fall off when she screeches.

'I *adore* Queen Boleyn!' Helen screeched.

One earring fell off.

'Queen Boleyn's got *style*!'

Then the other earring.

'Henry's cut off her style,' he remarked.

He was stroking his boil.

Helen went under the table in search of her earrings.

'Would you like to see it?' he said, looking at me.

'Her style?' I said weakly.

'Today's wedding,' he said.

'Do we have invitations?' I said. 'As well as his hippocrash?'

Helen, under the table, had violent hiccups.

Helen often has violent hiccups.

Especially when 'emotionally disturbed'.

Especially when drunk.

Helen can't hold her liquor.

He can't cure Helen's hiccups.

All those alchemical powers, and he can't cure the hiccups.

'Queen – hic – Incest –?'

Helen came up. Her face was as red as a beetroot.

'I can – hic – 't – can't –'

I looked under the table. I found them.

I handed the earrings back to her. She thought better of trying to put them back on. She also thought better of thanking me.

She was hiccuping now fit to burst.

'Hold your breath, dear,' I said.

She glared at me. Now it was like I had started the Reformation single-handed. Helen's a Catholic.

'Try drinking from the other side of your glass,' I said. 'No, dummkopf! I don't mean turn the glass *round* . . .'

He got to his feet.

He was swaying. He clutched at the table.

'Bring me water,' he said.

'For the hiccups?'

'For the journey,' he said. 'To the wedding!'

'We need water for that?'

'And a towel.'

He was looking quite dangerous. His eyes crossed and uncrossed each second.

'Get your finger out!' he said. 'We'll be late!'

I went out of the room. I fetched water and towel. Somehow. I can't remember taps or anything.

When I came back I was seeing two Helens, four earrings. All of them screeching.

'Insects – hic – Annie – !'

'Shut up,' said three hims. 'It's Queen Seymour now. Wash your hands.'

We plunged various hands in the basin.

The paint on Helen's fingernails flaked off. Some cheap vermilion.

He flicked with the towel.

'Now dry them,' he said. 'Here we go!'

I was holding the towel by one corner. Some Helens held another corner. Several hims held the middle.

I heard this flat virginal playing.

We were dancing a galliard.

'The king's composition,' he said.

I couldn't believe it was happening.

'*Green Sleeves and Pudding Pies*,' he said, grinning.

We were in a great ballroom, where men and women took each other by the hand and jigged up and down in triple time.

All the men wore ornamented cloaks which reached only as far as the hips. Their trunk hose were tight, but round the waist they were puffed out and padded. Bit like lettuces with legs. The women wore the skirts of their dresses very wide, pinched at the waist but open in front, displaying rich petticoats which reached to the ground, completely concealing their feet. Men and women alike had sleeves with puffs, falling in circles to their wrists.

Dancing in the dark.

Music played on tambourines and hautboys. And there was that flat virginal, with its jacks clicking, its quills plucking, hammering out the tune which he said was called *Green Sleeves and Pudding Pies*.

I say the ballroom was in darkness. Not quite true. Each dancer bore a lighted taper in the hand. The tapers were long. They moved about like fireflies in the gloom. The idea of the dance seemed to be to blow out other people's tapers while preventing them from blowing out your own. To gain this end, there was a lot of pushing and shoving and wrestling.

I saw a man in a parti-coloured tunic leaping in and out among the dancers. He wore a cowl which finished as a cock's head, winged with a couple of long floppy ears. He carried a bauble in his right fist, with a bladder on the end of the bauble. He was using the bladder to slap the backsides of the dancers.

'That's Will Somers,' he said. 'Henry's court jester.'

Will Somers smacked a lady with his bladder. The lady was drunk. She was dancing on her tip toes, trying to blow out a gentleman's taper. She tripped, collided with the man, and they both went down. The man got up and bowed. He remained in a bowing position, peering into the lady's ruffled petticoats. The lady was sprawled on her back, her feet in the air, her starched dress sticking upright like a cabbage. There was a lot of waggling and poking of tapers, lit and unlit, before anyone helped her get up.

'Hic – *icky*!' said Helen. 'English pigs!'

Jugglers and tumblers poured in.

The tumblers walked on their hands with their feet in the air, or with their heads twisted backwards so as to look out through their legs.

The jugglers were playing with knives, brass balls, silver

plates. They were quite good, but I have seen better in Bremen.

The dance petered out in confusion.

The tambourines stopped. And the hautboys.

People watched as the jugglers lit torches and threw them from hand to hand.

This, of course, made more light in the ballroom.

It was only a matter of time . . .

We stuck out a mile.

Three drunken Germans.

Him in his black cloak.

Me in my red cloak.

Helen in her blue gown from Dresden.

A tumbler looked at us from under his arse. With commendable dexterity, he pointed.

'German spies!' he cried out.

Swords were drawn.

It seemed everyone turned and confronted us.

The jugglers rushed up with their torches.

'*Ave* – hic – *Maria!*' screeched Helen.

The virginal player played on.

He was murdering that *Green Sleeves and Pudding Pies*. He kept making mistakes and playing the bad bits again until he got them right, or almost right, or less wrong.

We were seized and dragged up to the virginal.

King Henry the 8th struck the last wrong note.

He considered us.

I considered him.

He was tall, brawny, his complexion ruddy, with auburn hair combed short and straight in the French fashion, and a round face that would have suited a pretty woman running slightly to seed. His eyes were blue. His beard was red. He wore a white suit sugared with diamonds.

He turned back to the virginal.

He laughed very pleasantly.

'Hang them,' he said.

He bent over the keyboard. He played the last few bars of *Green Sleeves and Pudding Pies* again. This time he got them right.

Everyone clapped, except Helen and me.

He clapped, the great punk.

We were bundled outside.

There was a gallows in the moonlight in the garden.

The ladies and the gentlemen came out with flaming torches. They stood round the gallows. They chattered and laughed. One nice young girl kissed me. She tasted of caraway comfits.

'What sport!'

'Oh, I say!'

'String 'em up!'

He stood licking his bloodstone.

'Last requests?' said the hangman. It was Will Somers, the court jester. He was the hangman. 'Last requests?' he repeated, trying the ropes.

'Don't – hic – do it!' suggested Helen. She screamed this in German.

He grinned at Will Somers.

'We are Germans,' he said, speaking English (which he doesn't). 'May we wash our hands, please?'

'That the custom in Germany?'

'That's the custom in Germany.'

Somers shrugged.

He had water fetched.

It was in a gold bucket.

Helen and me washed our hands.

He stood in the middle. He was holding the towel. He gave one end to Helen. I held the other.

'Goodbye, England,' he said.

We were back in Ingolstadt.

He was toasting King Henry.

Helen wept and was sick.

I felt dizzy. Screwed up. I could still hear *Green Sleeves and Pudding Pies*. My mouth tasted like a worm had crawled through it.

Helen stayed with her hiccups.

She had hiccups all night.

'No more flying for me,' she vowed, when they stopped.

'Did we *really* go?' I asked him. 'Did we wash our hands in England, and dry them in Germany?'

He crossed his eyes.

'I didn't dry my hands,' he said. 'But then I didn't wash them.'

There was an ant in my hippocras.

16 The Pact

A few minutes before midnight on Good Friday, 1516, John Faust, being then about 36 years of age, possibly crazy, probably zonked, certainly already both daft and drunk enough to reckon himself an adept in what he likes to call the Art of Ceremonial Magic, took a small penknife and pricked open a vein in his left hand.

He let his blood run into a saucer. He set the saucer on warm ashes to keep the blood from congealing.

He picked up a pen. He dipped it in his blood.

He wrote on white parchment as follows:

'I, John Faust, hereby set down and solemnly record that I give myself body and soul to the Devil, and to his regent spirit Mephistopheles.

'I do this on one condition – namely, that they, the Devil and his servant Mephistopheles, shall instruct me, and fulfil my desires in all things, physical and metaphysical, as they have promised and vowed to do, according to certain Articles already agreed between us.

'Further, by this document, I covenant and grant with them, the Devil and his agent Mephistopheles, that at the end of the 24 years following its date they shall be empowered to do with me as they think best, body and soul, flesh, blood, and spirit.

'Hereupon, I defy God and his Christ, all the angels of heaven, and all living creatures made in the image of God. I reject all that lives in God's name.

'And to the greater power of this pact, I have written it with my own hand and in my own blood.

'And thus I subscribe to it with my name and my title,

                                        'John Faust,
                                        'Doctor of Divinity.'

Faust copied his pact out in ink.

He kept this copy.

What happened to the original, written in his own blood?

What are the 'certain Articles' he speaks of as already 'agreed' between him and the Devil and Mephistopheles?

Has he been 'instructed' as he demanded?

What does he mean by 'God'?

By 'the Devil'?

By 'Mephistopheles'?

I've asked him these questions myself. Maybe 100 times. I've had about 200 answers. All different.

But early this morning, I asked him again.

You'll have what he said this time just over the page.

I put his pact at this point – the time being just one o'clock, today, Ash Wednesday – to give a better answer to your wondering *What's happening right now?* Also to explain about Faust Years.

When I said Faust is *waiting for the Devil* this pact was what I was driving at.

Get it?

On Good Friday, 1516, Faust wrote this garbage which he thinks of as making a 'pact' or a 'covenant'.

The dope 'gave himself body and soul' (as he puts it) to the 'Devil' (as he puts it).

Under the terms of the pact or covenant he believes he was granted 24 years in which he would be served by a 'regent spirit' called Mephistopheles.

He measures – we measure (I humour him) – the years of his life from this year of the pact: 1516.

So that the year when I first met him in Auerbach's wine cellar, 1530, was Faust Year 14.

The year in which Helen turned up was 1533, or Faust Year 17.

The year the 7 girls came (I'll be coming to them) was 1537. Faust Year 21.

This year, 1540, is Faust Year 24.

His *last* year?

Good Friday this year falls on the *13th* of April, I see from my calendar.

Unlucky for some?

As you'll have gathered, I have my own thoughts on the whole stupid matter.

Besides, the Herr Motherfucker himself now has other plans.

But I won't spoil the story . . .

I'll give you today's events just as they happened.

17 Forty Days

'Forty days,' he said.

Dawn.

Here at his Tower.

We were walking in the maze.

The maze here is octagonal, with hundreds of parallel hedges and paths. The hedges are twelve feet high and three feet thick.

(I measured them one night.)

There are six different entrances to this maze, but only one way in to the middle and out again.

He says Mephistopheles made it. The hedges are privet. Lots of grubs in them. Caterpillars, maggots, cuckoo-spit, that type of thing.

He says that this maze is a microcosm of the world.

He was drinking from his bottle as we walked.

He's got this funny walk. He sort of stoops and lopes. I have to trot to keep up with him. When he's drinking it's easier.

'Forty days,' he said, over his shoulder.

He stopped to stare east at the sunlight. It was starting to poke through the hedges.

He said: 'I like the sun.'

I caught up with him.

'It's going to be a nice day,' I said.

He stood looking east. Then he spat.

'Ash Wednesday,' he said. 'Fuck the sun.'

He drank from his bottle, eyes shut.

He's got this good bottle. It's Saracen. Embedded gold leaf in the base.

He kept his eyes shut. 'Forty days!'

'Well, it's quite a long while,' I suggested.

He opened one cold eye. It glared at me.

I considered my boots. They're tanned leather.

'Take Noah,' I said. 'Look at that. Forty days in an ark in a flood. But his trip ended safely. The keel hit a mountain.'

He flicked out his left hand. He cuffed me.

'OK,' I said, nursing my ear. 'And we don't have the gopher wood.'

Brandy ran down his chin. A burnt amber dribble.

He went off through the maze at a lope.

I had to run to catch up with him.

When I did, he was swigging more brandy. He was sweating. He usually sweats, but not this much, and not so early in the morning. Sweat dripped from his eyebrows like grease.

I said: 'Master, Herr Doktor, you're drunk.'

He grunted. 'Not drunk enough.'

'Why not sit down?' I said. 'Do the job properly?'

I crouched on my hunkers. The grass was still dewy. I tugged at his cloak. He fell over.

'Spisser's Wood,' I prompted.

He sprawled on his back like an up-ended grasshopper, the bottle still plugged in his mouth. Pale sunlight played on the gold leaf in the bottom of it.

I waited till he'd had enough.

'Spisser's Wood,' I repeated.

'Spisser's Wood,' he said softly. 'I've told you.'

I chewed at a grassblade. I waited.

His hands were both shaking. His right hand was twined round the bottle, which he pressed to his cheek. He held on to the grass with his left hand, like a man scared he'll fall off the world.

He shut his eyes tight.

Perhaps five minutes passed.

I noticed the grime on his eyelids, like some filthy frost.

You'd have thought he was sleeping, except he was drinking.

A lark started to sing down in the valley below us. The maze goes right out on this ledge in the side of the Schlossberg. Freiburg's down there. You would see the great spire of its minster if it weren't for our hedges. That spire's very tall. 386 feet, they say.

All at once, without opening his eyes, he started.

I knew he would.

You could set your watch by his nightmares.

18 Spisser's Wood

'I knew what I wanted,' he said. 'Spisser's Wood is near Wittenberg. A thick wood. A dark wood. Near Wittenberg. I'd been there before. This time it was different. There's this crossroads of trees in the middle. Ash Wednesday it was. No one there. It was evening. Late evening. Ash Wednesday. I cut myself a hazel stick. A whitish-red stick. Two forks in it. It had flowers on it, leaf-buds, and stigmas. The stigmas were blood-red. I cut them. Then I drew with my stick in the leafmould. I drew this great circle all around me. I filled the circle with other circles. Characters. Numbers. Letters. The ten squares of the Crux Ansata. The Sephiroth. I knew what I was doing.'

He shivered, drawing his black cloak close about him with his left hand, clutching his bottle to his chest with the other.

'Mephistopheles,' he whispered.

He was grinning.

Then he said:

'I waited till the wood was very dark. While I waited, I prayed. I enflamed myself with prayers – of a certain kind. Time passed. There was no moon. No stars. Nothing. Then I heard the bell of the Schlosskirche ringing faintly in the distance. The midnight angelus. I stepped into the circle. I began. I used all the right invocations. The vocabula of Alhim, and Alim. *Mephistopheles!* I cried. *I summon you in the name of the Devil!*'

He roared these last words, lying there on his back in the maze in the early morning sunlight. He roared them with such power and conviction that I confess I looked over my shoulder . . .

I don't usually.

See, I've been here before, like I told you. I've heard every word of the story. It got boring about the third year.

All the same, I looked over my shoulder.

This 40-days-left rattling me?

I don't think so. But I looked over my shoulder . . .

I saw only a spider spinning its web in the hedge. There

was dew on the web. A perfectly ordinary spider. There wasn't a fly in the web.

'So? What happened?' I said, just to humour him.

'Nothing happened,' he said.

This was new!

'No Mephistopheles?'

'Not at first,' he said. 'No.'

Not at first . . .

Hey ho. Here we go.

But for a single heartbeat there I almost thought he'd gone sane.

19 Mephistopheles

'OK,' I said. 'So you gave Mephistopheles another call.'

'I did not. I knelt. I said nothing.'

He took a long pull at his bottle.

There was a butterfly fluttering along the corridor of the maze where we were. This butterfly hovered about him. It flew round his head. He didn't see it. His eyes were still shut. Then the butterfly settled on the pointed toe of his right boot. He's got high boots of black leather. I think they're Hungarian. The butterfly was warming its wings in the sun.

He went on in a quiet voice:

'I heard a wind coming. It was far off at first, just a rustle of leaves in the wood. It was coming towards me. Moving fast. Getting stronger and stronger as it came. Leaves started to tear off the branches. They flew through the wood. Then they were everywhere. Leaves. Like moths in the dark. I was sweating. And the leaves – they got stuck to me. Such icy wind! Branches ripped off! Trees crashing down in the dark! I was picking the leaves from my face. I was spitting leaves out of my mouth. I thought I would choke, or be killed by a falling tree. Then I heard this great roaring and rushing sound. And then, all at once – Mephistopheles!'

'You saw him?'

I was keeping my eyes on the butterfly. It was a nice creature. A cabbage white, I believe. Nothing unusual. But a rather good specimen.

35

Butterflies I like.

'I heard him,' he said. 'He ran round the rim of the circle. The noise was like chariots on stones. It made my head ring. Then lightning struck. A huge tree came down, all ablaze. It fell with its crown near the circle, burning there like a beacon. Thunder cracking! From all the four corners of the wood!'

'Excuse me,' I said. 'Did you shit your pants?'

He opened one raw eye and looked at me.

He said: 'I was irritated, actually.'

'For Christ's sake!' I said.

He drank brandy. He seemed rather pleased with himself.

At least, there were fresh touches to this version.

For some reason, they made it more real. Still applesauce and horsefeathers. But more real. As a taste of a mad state of mind.

'I was really pissed off,' he went on. 'I was annoyed at Mephistopheles just trying to impress me with noises and fire. I was disappointed, even. I wanted to *see* him. I wanted to *talk* with him. Lightning – I'd seen plenty. And you can't talk with thunder.'

'I couldn't agree more,' I said.

His eye poached as he glared at me.

I concentrated on the butterfly. It appeared quite content on the toe of his boot.

I was glad when the eye shut.

A pause.

I could hear the brandy gurgling in his throat. He's got an Adam's apple like a tennis ball. Except I hope I never see a tennis ball so thick with dirt. If you went and smashed a tennis ball into the nearest jakes and fished it out again with a tongs, that would be getting something like his Adam's apple.

'I heard music,' he went on. 'Girls' voices. A song without words. So I said, *That's better*. I said, *Now let me see you*. Immediately, the singing stopped, and I saw a globe of light. The globe was dancing. Then it opened. It split down the middle. The light sprang right out in the shape of a man. He ran round the circle. Round and round, round and round, very fast. The heat burnt my eyebrows.'

They seem to have grown again.

He's got these shaggy eyebrows. They sprout out from his skull like old seaweed.

Now I knew what was coming. And for some reason I didn't

36

want the butterfly to hear it. Which is silly, of course. But I get these sentimental attacks now and then. I've tried taking pills for them. No go. I just have to live with it. I daresay I felt sorry for myself, and wished I was the butterfly. Anyway, I clapped my hands softly. The butterfly flexed its wings. Then it went, zig-zagging, artless, like its mother never taught it a damned thing. That's OK. I watched it cut loose down the maze.

'A grey friar stood there,' he said.

'Franciscans always burn best,' I said.

'A grey friar stood there,' he said.

'Not burning?'

(Sometimes Mephistopheles keeps burning all through.)

'Not burning.'

(I was in for the uncooked version.)

'Not howling? Not thundering? Not singing like a girls' choir from Hamburg? Not even pelting you a little with spring leaves?'

He drank from his bottle, ignoring me. The bottle was a jewel in the sun. I noticed his hand was still shaking.

'Mephistopheles,' he said, dribbling brandy. 'He spoke to me. I heard him. Mephistopheles.'

'OK,' I said. 'This is where I always ask you what he said. What you think you heard. The first words spoken to you by your spirit.'

He said nothing.

'And you never answer me.'

'That's right. I can't.'

'Why not? Why do you think you can't?'

He wasn't going to answer that one either.

'Christ!' I said. 'Forty days and all that. Don't you think it's time I had this bit? Mephistopheles' first words to you. What were they?'

Those eyes snapped open. But they didn't look at me.

He lay on his back, gazing up at the sky.

I'd been right, by the way. It was turning out fine, the weather. Sun coming up all bright-eyed and bushy-tailed.

'His voice was very beautiful,' he said.

I sighed.

'I know that. You've told me that at least a thousand times. But what did Mephistopheles *say* to you?'

He shook his head.

He stared at the sun without blinking.

37

He can do that. His eyes are cold as hell.

(Not that hell's hot *or* cold. Not that I believe in it. Just a figure of speech, you understand.)

All the same, it's not good for you. Staring like that at the sun. Bad for the optic nerves, it must be. It was making his eyes water. I noticed that.

'I knew what I wanted,' Faust said.

20   A Chapter with 69 Fausts in It

Here! I've been dodging his name! Why? Am I frightened or something?

At the end of that last bit, as I wrote the words – *Faust said* – it crossed my mind what I'd been up to.

I've looked back. It sticks out like the balls on a bulldog.

All through chapters 1, 9, 15, 17, 18, and 19 (until the last line), I avoided the word, calling Faust *him*.

That is: Whenever I've had to put down what we've done or said together, I've left out his name. Other places, where I was writing about the Herr Doktor more generally, no such inhibition.

It's odd. I don't like it.

It's almost as if I've been scared to look Faust in the eye. When Faust and me are there together face to face on the page, I mean.

I can't understand or explain this. It seems superstitious. It smacks of black magic.

It worries me a lot more actually than this crap about Mephistopheles' first words. What do I care what the old fuck-up thinks they were? He *imagined* the whole scene, in any case. But doesn't Faust love his little mystery? Doesn't he just! Out there in the maze this morning, staring into space as though he could see something I couldn't . . . Pretending those first words hold the secret of the universe, or something. Words he never heard. Words that were only ever inside his own crazy head. Ach, the hell with it.

But this business of me avoiding the name Faust. That's not good.

I ought really to go back and change things. But I write in a rush. There's no time. So much to get down before nightfall. And

38

the ale's going flat. Not a cherry left. I shall start on my cheeses.

I write fast. But not fast enough.

Fast. For Lent! Faster!

Faust for Lent. Me, Wagner, Fauster.

Well, I'll write Faust all over the page now.

Faustus. Fausta. Faustum.

The happy old unhappy fart.

Faust Faust Faust Faust Faust Faust Faust Faust Faust Faust
Faust Faust Faust Faust Faust Faust Faust Faust Faust Faust
Faust Faust Faust Faust Faust Faust Faust Faust Faust Faust
Faust Faust Faust Faust Faust Faust Faust Faust Faust Faust
FAUST   FAUST   FAUST   FAUST   FAUST   FAUST
FAUST   FAUST   FAUST   FAUST
FAUST   FAUST   FAUST   FAUST   FAUST   FAUST
FAUST   FAUST   FAUST   FAUST

FAUST

Go back if you like and stick them all in for yourself.

21 The Devil's Scissors

Faust* was licking his lips.

There was this leaf from the hedge of the maze stuck to his lower lip. He picked away the leaf. He licked that too.

'I want my soul back,' he said.

'From the Devil?'

'From God.'

I smiled politely.

He started rubbing the leaf between thumb and forefinger. He was grinding it to bits.

'That's what I told Mephistopheles,' Faust said. '*I want my soul back.*'

This was new. This was news.

He's given me hundreds of reasons for doing what he did.

Power.

* There. Done it. No lightning. No thunder. I'll *Faust* him! Nice cheese this. Gruyère. The one with the holes in it.

39

Wisdom.

Lots of big shit like that.

But this getting his soul back was one I'd not heard before. Of course he was drunk.

He was flicking leaf-dust in my face all the time, and he was grinning, but his eyes didn't grin.

Then:

'What was the Devil's sin?' the clown demands suddenly.

'How the hell should I know?' I said.

'What was the Devil's sin?'

'I don't believe in the Devil,' I said.

'*What was the Devil's sin?*'

He was terribly drunk.

I had to keep humouring him.

'Pride,' I said, wearily. 'The Devil is supposed to have been an angel who wanted to be like God.'

'Who says so?'

'St Thomas Aquinas.'

'Is Aquinas right?'

'I don't know.'

'Well, I do.'

'You think he's wrong.'

'No. I *know* he's wrong. The Devil didn't want to be like God. The Devil didn't want any part of God. He wanted *his* soul back. You call that pride?'

'I don't call it anything,' I said.

'Well, I call it freedom,' Faust said.

'You call it freedom,' I said. 'So you get up off your knees in Spisser's Wood and you ask your Mephistopheles to come to you again the next night. Twelve o'clock. Your house. And, being a punctual sort of a devil, he turns up on the dot. And you have boring theological chats, you and your grey friar. And, finally, on Good Friday, you make up your mind –'

'My mind was made up long ago,' Faust said. 'Before Mephistopheles.'

'So why wait till Good Friday?'

'I was testing the Devil,' Faust said. 'A simple experiment.' He drank some more brandy. He was slurring his words now. 'Mephistopheles only came if I called him. I had to be sure of that. I had to be sure that he'd leave me alone if I wanted that. I needed to know that the Devil wasn't as evil as God.'

Nice one, Faustus.

This beetle fell out of the hedge. It crawled down my neck. I let it go crawl.

Faust said: 'You're right about one thing. My conversations with Mephistopheles *were* a bit boring. We'd sit in my room. Rain on the roof. The wind at the windows. Candles burning. They were beeswax candles. Mephistopheles smiled a lot. But he didn't tell me much that I hadn't worked out for myself.'

'What was his smile like?' I said.

'Religious,' Faust answered.

Beeswax smells nice. I was glad we were outdoors. I'd no jam. His smell has got worse since last Christmas.

This beetle crawled right down my spine to the top of my buttocks. It tickled. I let it keep tickling.

Faust said:

'Your old friend Aquinas says man is a rational creature composed of a body and a soul. What Aquinas avoids – what they all avoid – is that neither man's soul or his body belongs to him. I mean in the end. His body goes back to the dust that it's made of. His soul goes back to its proprietor – God. Where's the sense in that?'

He spat.

'Man's not born free,' he went on. 'Man's a puppet. Men dance on the strings round God's fingers. Their souls are the strings. Well, the Devil has scissors, son. *Scissors!*'

This beetle got down in my breeches. I wriggled about.

'Man can't cut the string on his own,' Faust said. 'But the Devil can cut it. What Aquinas calls pride wasn't anything so cheap or so obvious. The Devil is an angel. Don't forget it. The Devil just knew what he wanted. He wanted his soul back. He wanted to be a free spirit. He *is* a free spirit!'

Brandy ran down his chin.

'And I'm a free spirit,' Faust said.

He was shaking all over.

'A free man in this world that's God's joke! A free spirit in eternity!'

This beetle got down to my balls.

'Do you think that the angels that didn't turn their backs on God can possibly be free?' Faust demanded.

This beetle was itchy.

'What's heaven?' cried Faust. 'Another great puppet show!'

41

This beetle was nasty.

'What's hell?' shouted Faust. 'The absence of the presence of God. Who says so? The Church says so, that's who. And for once they've got it just about right. *The absence of the presence of God.* That's what I wanted. That's what I want. And that's what I've got and I'm going to get!'

This beetle was circumnavigating my left ball.

I'd had quite enough.

I reached down. I pinched it.

I abolished the beetle, but nearly castrated myself.

'You get it?' Faust said.

I was yelping.

'Yes! Yes!'

22 The Articles

He thought I meant his crazy scissors' talk. I meant I'd got this fucking insect, that's all.

Faust was drinking, and grinning his grin.

'Mephistopheles promised me 24 years of freedom from God on earth,' he said. 'After that – perfect freedom in eternity!'

He crossed his eyes.

'The Articles,' he said. 'You remember them?'

I tried to look sensible.

These 'Articles' are the things he says he worked out with his so-called Devil's agent in the course of that long-ago Lent.

They go like this:

1. Mephistopheles only to appear or to speak when Faust calls him, in the form that Faust names.

2. Mephistopheles to be Faust's servant, doing always what Faust wants.

3. Mephistopheles to attend Faust at other times, invisible to others.

4. Mephistopheles to bring Faust anything he asks for, and to do what Faust wants done.

5. In the end, Faust to be a spirit like Mephistopheles himself.

'The 5th Article,' Faust said. 'That's the best one. That's my ticket. The last little snip of the scissors.'

His eyes were like coals. He was laughing.

'So why all the doom?' I demanded, getting up irritably. 'Why all the moaning about forty days? You should be looking forward to your total freedom! Don't you want to be a devil like your pal?'

'You don't know what you're talking about,' Faust said.

Maybe not. But then neither does he.

And have you ever had an abolished beetle stuck to your balls?

It's not a nice feeling.

I jumped up and down on the spot.

The beetle fell out down the leg of my breeches. I inspected it.

This perfectly ordinary beetle.

I mashed it with my heel to make quite sure.

23   Hell Defined

Faust ignored my dancing.

He was now almost totally stoned.

He was staring at the sun again, eyes wide. This time they didn't water, that I noticed. Maybe if you get drunk enough, they don't? All the same, it can't be good for the optic nerves.

'I'm not frightened of what they call hell,' he said. 'Hell's freedom from God. I look forward to that. But I have to be *sure*. As sure as I've been here on earth. It's been good, Kit. It's been good being free.'

'So you think that the Devil might have tricked you? That God's still got your soul in his fingers?'

'No,' Faust murmured. 'I just like the sun.'

24   No Grave for John Faust

All this shit about liking the sun. It struck me as maudlin. Faust was fuddled and muddled. The brandy had got to his brain. In one breath he talked of damnation, in the next of salvation. I could see that his wits were fucked-up. I was sick of his talk.

It's gone two o'clock now. I'm sick of this Gruyère as well. Better start on the celery.

I think, to save time, I'll just give you the rest of the Mephistopheles hooey in summary form. There are other things, more important, I've got to get down. Important, that is, in view of the journey before us.

Well, I told him his pact with the Devil wasn't so bad. Not now he'd 'explained' it. He'd worked out the odds and he'd got a good bet for himself. I went on about *freedom*, to humour him. I quoted Tertullian, Palladius, Ignatius of Antioch, Justin, Jerome, and the Council of Ephesus. I chucked in Poly- carp and Basil for luck. Then a few moderns: Melanchthon, Erasmus, the Constipator. I even cited a bit of French John. Aim being to cheer him up with the fact that, Latin and Luth- eran, Church Fathers and contemporary sons of bitches, they all tell the same bloody story. That man is corrupt from his first breath. Unoriginal old Original Sin. That being so, the Devil and his scissors made sense. (Or not absolute nonsense.)

Result: Faust looked at me as though I was a maggot that had crawled out of the apple in the Garden of Eden.

He didn't want any more theology. He wanted to tell me about his final parley with his grey pal Mephistopheles, and how the spook played postman for his pact.

He claimed he spent the whole of Lent, 1516, conducting his experiment. He reckoned that if Mephistopheles was tricking him, if he was telling him lies, then our friendly Franciscan fiend wouldn't be able to leave him alone. He'd have to pop up, barking and wheedling, and that would

(a) break the 1st Article of their agreement (i.e. that Mephistopheles should only ever appear when Faust called him);

(b) prove that the big boss, the Devil, was just as bad an interferer as God.

So Faust laid low, kept mum, waited, walked about with his hands behind his back, making a point of sitting often in Spis- ser's Wood, just to see if they'd interpret this as a sign that he was already theirs. If they'd done that, he said, then he'd have known he wasn't master of his own fate at all.

Not a squeak from behind the trees.

Not a single cloven hoofprint in the leafmould.

The weather improved, even.

44

Faust sat in the sun and he slept. He had sweet dreams, he says.

He finished his experiment on Good Friday. (Wouldn't he just? The old melodramatist!) He went and sat on a tombstone in the graveyard at Kundling. He had a bottle of some cheap Rhenish. It was morning. Nice day. People passing by him on their way to church. As each little religious caterpillar crawled past, Faust raised his glass high, said good morning. None of them answered, of course. Most of them crossed themselves. Some of them spat. He already had a certain reputation.

When they'd all gone inside, and the door shut, Faust strolled around the graveyard. He inspected the tombs and the urns. He kicked an urn over. It rolled into a hole. There was this newly-dug grave. It was empty, gaping, green jaws wide open, just waiting to swallow some mince-pie Christian body. Well, his mind was made up. No grave for John Faust! He filled his glass with Rhenish and he drank a long toast. '*To the Devil!*' he cried. And then: '*Mephistopheles!*'

Mephistopheles appeared immediately in the bottom of the grave. He was lying there, smiling his religious smile, wrapped in a winding sheet.

Faust dropped his glass and his bottle. They smashed.

Mephistopheles got up and bowed. He apologised profusely, his head sticking out of the grave. He explained that he hadn't meant to startle Faust. It was just that spirits usually materialised in forms that suited the places where they were invoked, and he hadn't allowed for Faust being human and not liking to see a body drop by in a newly-dug grave.

Faust reminded him of the second clause of their 1st Article. That Mephistopheles should always appear in a shape or form of Faust's own choosing. Mephistopheles pointed out reasonably that Faust hadn't named any particular shape or form on this occasion. So Faust said that until further notice Mephistopheles was always to appear as a grey friar, with a bell in his hand like St Antony.* What's more, Mephistopheles was always to ring the bell twice before appearing, so that Faust didn't drop his bottle, die of heart failure, etc.

Mephistopheles said OK.

He stayed on as a corpse for the time being. But every time after

* Hermit. Born near Memphis, about 251 A.D. Died (aged 105) on Mount Kolzim. Underwent some famous temptations in his time. His other emblem is a pig.

that, Faust said, he appeared as a friar, and rang the bell twice.

They chatted a bit about nothing, chiefly Mephistopheles' abilities. The corpse was in a jolly mood. He told Faust that he was Number One go-between for the circuit of the world from Septentrio to the Meridian. (Whatever that might mean!) All on behalf of the Devil, of course.

At last, Faust told the corpse his decision.

Mephistopheles didn't say anything. He just smiled. Like a patient confessor, no doubt. Then he went away. Faust says he didn't pop back in the grave. There was this funeral. A burying party came out of the church. Faust didn't stay to watch it. But Mephistopheles joined up with the mourners. He skipped in and out among them, winding sheet kilted. He sat on the bier. Then he vanished.

Faust says he saw Mephistopheles do this stuff, but the buriers didn't see anything because Mephistopheles just wasn't there for them.

That night, Faust made his pact.

When he cut his wrist and the blood trickled out it wrote words on his hand.

O homo fuge.

That's what Faust says the blood wrote.

I'll translate —

25 Knock Knock

I broke off because there was this knocking at my door.

'Who's there?' I said.

No reply.

Then a lot more knocking. Quite hard.

I put all these papers away out of sight.

I got up. I unlocked the door. No one there.

Somebody playing tricks on me. Probably Marguerite or Gretchen. I'll be coming to them, and the rest of the 7 girls, later.

Meanwhile, back to the blood.

26 Good Friday, 1516

O homo fuge means *O man, don't.*

Faust did.

He made his pact.

It was that night – the night of Good Friday, 1516 – and
(yup! of course!) the bell was ringing for the angelus. *John.
John. John.* He thought it rang for him. There was this cracked
bell in the Schlosskirche. *John. John. John.* It sounded like his
name, Faust says. It echoed through the streets of Wittenberg,
across the rooftops. *John. John. John.* A solitary broken bell.
The last nine strokes of the midnight angelus.

Faust was sitting in his room. He had this house in the
huddle of steep little streets near the university. He'd just
finished making a copy for himself of his pact with the
Devil. When he realised that the bell was the midnight angelus, he pushed inkhorn and candle aside. He crossed his
eyes. 'Bugger it,' he said. 'Now and at the hour of our
death.'

Well, that's what he says he said. I don't disbelieve that
bit. I must say it sounds like him. The way he used to be
when I first knew him. I'm glad he wasn't howling, anyway.

Then he says he heard this singing in the street.

He went to the window and looked down. The street was
empty. The singing stopped.

Some drunk on his way home, no doubt.

Faust stood there looking down into the street. It was quite
narrow. I know those streets. The houses lean together.
Women can sit at the windows on one side and gossip with
their neighbours on the other. You could just about touch fingers with anybody opposite, if you both had arms like spiders.

Suddenly, Faust says he heard this rushing sound. Like
armed men coming. Like soldiers marching. There was a
trampling of horses too. He heard their hooves. But no one
came. The street was empty.

(1516: it was a time of civil disturbances. I expect the Elector kept men on the move around curfew time.)

As Faust stood watching, he says he saw a peacock walking

47

down the street. It spread its tail. The eyes in its tail were like fire, he says. They blazed in the moonlight. The peacock sauntered slowly down the street. It passed his house. Then it disappeared. He says it was there one minute – burning eyes, feathers. Next minute, it wasn't. Well, I say that it went round the corner, as peacocks do. There's often a circus in Wittenberg round about Easter.

A mist came next. Despite the moonlight! The moonlight was all shining in the mist, Faust says. Like a little cloud. So a ball of mist comes rolling down the street. Faust says it bounced. He swears that he saw it bounce along the cobbles. He opened his window. Vapours drifted up from this bright mist. They smelled of violets. They smelled of everything sweet he had ever smelt. Faust took deep breaths of these vapours. They made his head swim. Then the mist passed by. The street was clear again. Quite deserted. Then Faust heard music.

Now, bands in the town at that time of the night are out of the question.

Faust says that it wasn't a band, anyway. Nor the girls' choir from Hamburg.

It was instruments. Clarigolds. Lutes. Viols. Citterns. Flutes. Harps. His ear made out those. There were others he didn't know. But all *indoors* instruments.

Faust shut the window.

The music was in the room with him.

He must have been drunk at the time.

He was certainly zonked by the time that he told me all this. I got him up off the grass and made him keep walking. We had to go somewhere so we made for the heart of the maze. He was shambling and staggering. I had to keep picking him up.

Faust says that this music was *infinite*. It made the tears run down his face. He couldn't see anyone playing it.

Faust thought the music must be coming from another world. He sat on the floor and he listened. He was sure now he'd done the right thing. If the Devil had music like this then Faust wished to belong with him. He says that he knew he belonged with the Devil, because the Devil *was* that music. And while the music lasted, Faust became it. It played through his body and soul. It made him feel free. If anyone

48

had come into the room while the music lasted, Faust swears that they wouldn't have seen him.

(Music can ravish the senses. I'm tone-deaf myself. But I've heard people speak of quite earthly music in similar style.)

Faust says Mephistopheles came when the music ended. He was ringing his bell like St Antony. He came through the door, not the window.

Faust says he went down on his knees. He went down on his knees to his friend Mephistopheles. He kissed the hem of the grey Franciscan habit.

Mephistopheles held out his hand.

Faust gave him the pact.

Mephistopheles said there was even hotter music where that music had come from.

Then he left Faust in peace.

27   A Vision in the Shrubbery

I left Faust at war with himself in the heart of the maze. He had finished the brandy. He was lying dead drunk by the fountain that plays in the middle. I noticed he took care to fall out of reach of its spray.

Faust lay curled like a snake on the turf. His cloak was stuck to him with sweat. His legs were all bent as if broken. Dribble ran from the sides of his mouth.

The last thing the Herr Doktor said before passing out was: 'Kit, go and get me more brandy.'

I went.

I was glad to be rid of his company.

I looked back as I went round the corner.

A pigeon was perched on his head.

It shat on him.

Faust didn't budge.

He was sucking his thumb like a child.

A madman of sixty, blind drunk.

It was quiet and good in the maze. Nice shadows falling in regular patterns from the straight lines of the hedges. I enjoyed my stroll back. The time was not much before seven.

Coming out of the maze, I met Helen going in.

49

My head was down. She must have had her nose in the air. We collided. Helen fell. She lay on the grass in a pool of blue silk.

Helen got up, refusing my hand.

'Where is he?' she whispered.

She looked like a saint in a tizzy. Her face was all flushed, her hair loose. She held herself stiffly, self-consciously. You'd have thought she had eggs up her cunt.

'In there in the middle,' I said.

A thick cloud of scent. Also julep. Helen made to brush past me. I grabbed at her.

'Don't touch me! I must not be touched!'

I looked at my hand. It was so-so.

Her hands were pressed together just under her chin. Red fingernails pointing to heaven. Her nose was red too.

'You've been drinking,' I said.

She blinked at me. Long eyelashes. Pupils dilated.

A rosary dripped from one paw.

'Was he drinking all night?' I demanded.

Helen flicked at my face with her rosary.

'My message,' she snapped, 'is for John.'

She spun round on two silver heels. She hurried off into the maze in a flurry of silk, scent, and julep.

I shrugged.

'Happy hunting,' I called.

I came through the shrubbery, back to the Tower. The shrubbery's horrible, wasted, quite gruesome with weeds. The roses are never cut back. No one does any gardening.

I went down to the wine cellar. I got what Faust wanted. Then I strolled back, enjoying the sun. I was taking my time.

Half way back through the maze, I heard Helen.

There was this scrabbling and praying from behind the hedge.

'How you doing?' I said.

More praying. Soft swearing.

'I think I'm lost,' she said.

'Go on,' I said. 'Astonish me.'

I retraced my steps, giving Helen directions, until she found a hole in the privet she could scramble through.

'It's a small world,' I said.

'What?'

'This maze. It's a small world. That's what the Doktor says.'

Helen shook her head angrily, as if she had other and more important things in it. Her eyes were green and hostile. Her mouth had a sulky curve. Lips carmined to look like the worst sort of strawberries.

She seemed in a bad-tempered dream. It couldn't only have been the twigs in her hair-do that made her look quite so spaced out.

'You all right?' I enquired. 'We could sit down and talk about microcosms.'

'Take me to him,' Helen said.

I bowed.

I led the lady through the maze to the middle.

Faust was just as I'd left him.

Correction: There were now *two* pigeons. One was squatting on his chest.

Helen gave a shrill squawk of rivalry. She knelt down. She shooed the birds away. She took Faust's head in her lap and smoothed his hair. 'O my darling, what is it?' she cried piteously.

'Pigeon shit,' I said.

'Horrid boy! I don't mean that.' She was wiping her fingers on the grass. 'What's the matter with him?'

'It could be damnation,' I suggested.

I plugged in the brandy. 'Let's try this.'

Faust woke, gulped, and winked. He was sober on the instant. That's the way it goes with him. He can drink himself through drunkenness, and out the other side.

'John,' Helen said.

Faust stayed plugged to his bottle.

'John,' Helen said again. 'I have a Message for you.'

Faust looked at her kindly.

Then he took another drink.

Helen whispered in his earhole:

'Send Wagner away, John.'

Faust shut his eyes. He swallowed. I watched his Adam's apple.

Helen starts praying over him. It wasn't nice to see. When she prays she pets this crucifix. She wears it round her neck. There's a relic in the crucifix. St Mary Magdalene's tooth.

Helen finished praying. She's a very snappy prayer.

She snatched Faust's brandy.

51

'You must send that boy away, John.'

'What gives?' Faust demanded.

'I have Orders,' Helen said.

'Orders? Whose orders?'

'Wagner's not to hear it.'

'What's Wagner not to hear?'

'The Message,' Helen said.

She was smiling as sweet as a mare with a mouthful of thistles. Her powder was caking. Her breath came like steam.

'Will you pass me back my brandy?' Faust requested.

'Get rid of that boy first!'

Faust grinned a helpless grin.

I walked off through the maze, kicking at the turf, doing my best imitation of a spare prick at a wedding.

As soon as I passed out of sight I got down on my knees and wriggled right under the hedge. I dodged this way and that. I doubled back through the maze until I was on the other side of the hedge, not more than six feet from where they were. I could hear their voices.

'Jesus Christ,' Faust was saying.

'No, dear,' Helen said. 'His Mother.'

I could hear the Herr Doktor slurp-slurping at his bottle. And the clickety-click of Helen's rosary.

'What did she look like?' Faust said.

'Indescribably lovely,' said Helen. 'She was wearing this gown of forget-me-not blue, with a turquoise kerchief and cuffs turned up with just a whiff of lace. She had a little cambric collar with a goffered edge, and seven pink pearls in her girdle.'

'Go on,' Faust said.

'Well,' Helen said. I heard her take a very deep breath. She went on in a piercing dainty whisper: 'I was praying at dawn, my dearest, for you. O my angel, I know how distressed you must be. I was praying for you, all fifteen decades of the Most Holy Rosary, saying them for you, John, and praying and praying that those terrible things you speak of will never come true – and then – oh, and then – then just as I was saying the last *Gloria Patri* there was this sort of *melodious twang* and Our Lady was there!'

I had to stuff my cloak into my mouth.

'She was *where*?' Faust demanded.

'On the top of the evergreen,' I heard Helen whisper. 'I was praying in the shrubbery. O rejoice, dearest heart, your Helen has been *visited*. I have witnessed a piece of Eternity!'

'You saw the Virgin Mary on top of an evergreen?' Faust said.

'She was ever so lovely,' Helen said. 'She was wearing sapphire slippers.'

'And she was standing on top of a plant?' Faust said.

'Not so much standing, dear. *Hovering*.'

'Go on,' Faust said.

There was a pause.

Then I heard Helen say firmly:

'John, Our Lady has answered my prayers for you. She spoke to me. She gave me the Message.'

'What message?' Faust said.

'She said that you must go to Rome, John!'

'*What?*'

'To the Pope! To the Holy Father himself!'

'Jesus Christ,' Faust said.

'Our Lady,' Helen said. 'Our Lady's very own words, my angel. She said that you must go like a pilgrim to the shrine of St Peter's in Rome. Only the Pope can absolve you! Don't you see?'

'Jesus Christ,' Faust said.

I heard Helen cross herself. You can always *hear* her cross herself. She smacks her tits so. They're like pimples.

She said: 'You'd better stop blaspheming for a start. The Blessed Virgin Mary doesn't like it any more than I do.'

'She tell you that too?'

'I've told you what she said, John. She said that if you go to the Pope before Easter you will be saved.'

I heard Faust groan.

Then I heard him drink some more brandy.

Helen said: 'I understand your surprise, my beloved. I was surprised too. But you must go to the Pope and make your Confession. You must tell him *the lot*! Only he can save you . . .'

'From what?' Faust said.

'From the Evil One,' Helen said. 'I have Our Lady's word for it.'

'The Pope?' Faust said.

'He has *the Keys*, my darling. The Keys that can unlock Heaven and Hell. I said to the Vision, "Is this the only way?"

53

And she said, "Helen," she said, "it *is* the only way." She said, "He must go to the Pope and confess all his tremendous sins and be saved from the Evil One."'

'Are you drunk?' Faust said.

I heard Helen snort with dismay.

I heard her fan clicking. Then more rosary beads.

'It's you that is drunk, John,' she said.

'You were drinking last night —'

'I am perfectly sober,' Helen said.

'All those juleps —'

'I was never *more* sober,' Helen said. 'I can tell you — Eternity is *very* sobering. Our Lady was wearing her halo. "Deliver my Message," she said. Then she went.'

'From the top of the evergreen?'

'Upwards. With a second melodious twang.'

I heard a bit of a scuffle.

'What —?'

'Water!'

'I don't —'

'It will help you to *see*!'

Helen was evidently trying to scoop water out of the fountain and throw handfuls over him. Or perhaps she had holy water concealed on her person. I wouldn't put it past her.

'John! It's the way!'

'To Rome?' Faust was saying.

'We'll be pilgrims!' Helen cried.

'Forty days,' Faust was saying.

'We shall ride!' Helen told him.

'I hate horses,' Faust said.

'You'll be rid of your sins, John! You'll not go to Hell!'

As for me, I'd stopped laughing.

28 Helen of Troy (and Elsewhere)

I think there's a rat in the wainscot. I keep hearing this scratching.

First, I thought it was Akercocke.

It can't be.

Akercocke's asleep.

54

He's my monkey.

I'll write about Akercocke later. I suppose that I must.

Meanwhile, a bit about Helen.

Helen came here just seven years ago. Faust said she was Helen of Troy. That particular bubble didn't last long. He soon dropped the Troy stuff. Helen's not exactly the most beautiful woman the world has ever known. Not by a long shot. Blonde hair, green eyes, like I've told you already. But her face would stop a clock.

Talking of which, it's just half past three now. Not bad going. And I'm nearly up to date with the story so far. One more chapter should do it. The chapter after this one.

To be fair to fair Helen, *she* never exactly claimed to be what Faust said she was. She just sat there simpering over the candles when he went on at dinner about Paris and Achilles and all that. She never winked, or denied it. That's not our Helen's way. But she never actually claimed an acquaintance with Troy.

Just as well. One day I asked her to spell Agamemnon and she couldn't. She had a go at Troy. It came out Try.

After Helen of Troy, it was the Simon Magus fantasy. Simon Magus is this magician in the Bible. He lived at the same time as Christ and the apostles and he tried to bribe the apostles into selling him secrets of how you do miracles. (*Acts*, 8, verses 5–24.) Then he tried to fly to heaven in a car pulled by demons. The car was going fine until Peter and Paul knelt down and prayed below. Then it crashed, and Simon Magus broke his neck. (See St Cyril of Jerusalem, 6th of his *Catechetical Lectures*.)

You get the crime of simony from the name Simon Magus. Simony is buying yourself a bishopric, etc.

Now, according to Irenaeus (*Against Heresies*, 1, 16), Tertullian (*De anima*, 34), Hippolytus (*Refutatio omnium haeresium*, 6, 19), and a lot of other chaps, this Simon Magus had a girlfriend who was called Helen.

Simon Magus started off by saying that she was the same Helen who had caused the Trojan War.

Then he said she was his 'first Thought', meaning that he had *created* her.

But according to the references cited above – and I forgot the most important, Justin Martyr (*First Apology*, 26, 1–3) – Simon Magus had in fact got this Helen out of a brothel in Tyre.

55

So —

Copying this, the Herr Doktor starts saying that our Helen is the same one Simon Magus had!

Which makes him Simon Magus, I suppose.

Simon Magus having been, incidentally, a Samaritan.

I mean: a native of Samaria.

Well, to be fair to Helen again, she didn't like that line of talk much better than the Trojan crap.

Helen's very religious.

So when Faust starts claiming she's the ex-paramour of a first-century magician and a gift to him (Faust) from Mephistopheles, our Helen gets distinctly miffed.

The crockery flew for a month.

Most of it hitting me, as you'd expect.

Then Faust shut up on the whole subject of her origins.

Not so, Helen.

Our Helen, as well as being religious, is a monumental liar.

Her own story varies.

One version:

Helen says that she started life on the sea coast of Bohemia. Her mother died and her stepmother hated her, so her dad deposited her in a wood to be eaten by wolves. However, she was rescued by doves. The doves led her to a castle. It was the castle of a friendly knight. This knight brought her up as his daughter. When he passed on – knocked off in a tournament – Helen became the queen of the castle. But she fell asleep when she pricked her hand on a spinning wheel, and she didn't wake until one fine day Faust came in through the bedroom door (spinning in the bedroom?) and kissed her.

I never much cared for that story.

She knew it.

She came up with another.

Helen's 2nd history:

Wicked stepmother, depositing dad, ditto. But she was found in the wood by a hermit. He was wonderfully holy, she says. They prayed together in the nude a lot. Then one day the hermit said she was getting too old for this sort of thing, and rather than having her lead him into temptation he took her to Avignon. At Avignon there was then the antipope, Benedict 13. Helen had to dress as a boy to travel with the hermit. To save her from rapers, she says. The hermit dropped dead of heart disease when they got to the French Pope's palace. Helen entered and became the Pope's page. The antipope's page, that is. It was a hard life, she says, and she hated it because he wasn't the True Pope. She left Benedict 13th's employment when her periods began, she says. This version doesn't take any account of Faust's coming.

3rd version:

Helen, the daughter of a count in Valence, was kidnapped by Saracens and shipped out in a galley to Saracen land. She had a really rough time protecting her virginity in the harem of Suleiman the Magnificent, the Sultan of Turkey. She did it by telling him stories. (I can believe this bit.) The stories were so boring that Suleiman always fell asleep before he got round to fucking her. Helen escaped on a camel across the Arabian desert. She was captured by slavers, and sold to a travelling circus. She was scared of the lions, and a terrible flop on the trapeze. So they let her sell tickets. When the circus came to Cracow, Helen escaped. She was only standing *outside* a brothel in Cracow, and wondering what to do next, she says, when Faust came along.

That version at least contains a few half-truths.

Helen *is* a born storyteller.

Helen *is* frightened of lions and heights – and lambs and depths. And just about everything else.

She might very well have been standing about in Cracow outside a whorehousse 'wondering what to do next'. She would be too stupid to go in, too stupid to know why others were going in, and Faust might just possibly have been coming *out*. He has been to Cracow. He went there to brush up his Water Divination. (He had only a second class degree in that subject, in the days of Trithemius, remember.) There's supposed to be this good school of magic in Cracow.

But there's a 4th Helen story:

Stepmother cruel, father and wolves, etc, only this time she's found in the wood by an artist out sketching. The artist is struck by her beauty (?). He's Italian. His name is Leonardo da Something. He takes her back to his studio and gives her a home. She helps him to mix his paints, sharpen his pencils, that sort of stuff. Then one day she sits for him. There's this lady called La Gioconda, a portrait job. The lady gets bored, because the artist is taking too long. She storms out of the studio. Panic. How can the picture be finished? The artist tells

57

Helen to strip and dress up in La Gioconda's gear. (Did the lady storm out in the buff? You've got it. Helen says she was going to meet her lover!) Helen does as she's told – blushing, of course, and changing behind a screen. The portrait is finished, and Da Something gives her 2 golden ducats. The picture – which Helen says does her no justice – they call the Mona Lisa. It's famed for its Enigmatic Smile, Helen says.

Now this last story also has one element of truth in it. (Helen's lies, like all good lies, usually have one such element embedded in their fantastic ingredients.)

Helen has bad teeth. Thin and yellow.

She smiles in this shadowy way, her lips never parting, so the bad teeth don't show.

That would explain the Mona Lisa's smile, I guess.

But 2 golden ducats is flimsy.

Faust has 44 flasks of trebbiano wine. (I'm drinking one now.) They cost him a ducat a flask.

Unless Faust was swindled?

Or this L. da Something was *mean*?

Anyway, that's enough about Helen.

I'm a tit man myself.

29   The Virgin Mary's Hind Leg

There they were in the maze, Faust and Helen, talking the hind leg off the Virgin.

I crouched listening behind the hedge.

Faust would say: '*Rome . . .?*'

And Helen would say: '*To the Pope, dear!*'

Faust would say: '*Confession . . .?*'

And Helen would say: '*You'll be saved, dear!*'

Faust would say: '*Mary . . .?*'

And Helen would say: '*Who else, dear?*'

Faust would say: '*Message . . .!*'

And Helen would say: '*For you, dear!*'

Faust would say: '*Jesus Christ . . .!*'

And Helen would say: '*Amen, dear!*'

And so on.

Well, I thought I'd throw up.

58

It went round and round, this malarkey, like the maze does, but making less sense. A double-tongued song for two singers. Returning always to the theme of Helen's 'vision' in the shrubbery, and the burden of the 'message' delivered to her from the top of an evergreen.*

The funny thing is – I couldn't work out from the tone what game the Herr Doktor was playing now.

He'd *got* to be kidding, of course. But was he spouting this stuff with a grin or a glare on his face?

That stewed voice gave no indication.

He just sounded blind drunk, that's all.

As for Helen, she sounded like Helen. The world's Number One Liar, full of bullshit and passionate conviction.

I stared at a worm.

The worm wriggled out of the grass and ran over my boot.

It was a pink worm. An earthworm.

I picked up the worm.

It was something to do. You have to have something to do.

'Helen?' Faust said.

'My beloved?'

'You never before –?'

'No, dearest. I never ever had a Vision before in my whole life. O my darling, I pray that I'll have one again. It's such a *fantastic* experience. I'm sure, as a matter of fact, I shall see Her again.'

'What makes you say that?'

'Well, the Blessed Virgin didn't say Goodbye in any sort of a way you'd call *final*. She just went up from the top of the evergreen with this friendly wave of her hand – she has such petite hands, pet. As if she was saying – well, *hinting* – that We'd Meet Again.'

The worm was cold and slimy.

I put it back down in the grass.

I heard Helen sigh. Like a pious wee bagpipes.

'If I see Her again – *when* I see Her again – I want you to be there, my darling. I desire you to *share* in my Visions.'

I heard a cuckoo. And Faust drinking.

'No doubt that glorious Togetherness will have to wait until you've been *absolved*, though,' I heard Helen prattle on. 'Our

* I think it must be our *azinheira*. 4 feet tall. Glossy leaves. Prickles like cactus. I inspected it on my way back to the Tower. A perfectly ordinary shrub.

Lady simply couldn't appear to you in your present state. I mean, all unshriven, and – and –'

'*Damned?*'

'I didn't like to use that word, dear.'

There followed a long pause.

I wanted to shout out: 'Where's your Devil's scissors now?'

I didn't.

I was holding my breath. I stared at the light on the leaves in the hedge. I prickled my cheeks against their barbed edges.

Then I heard Helen ask him:

'You'll go, dear?'

And I heard John Faust answer:

'Why not?'

30   Rat

I wish that damned rat would stop scratching.

Scratch. Scratch.

I can't hear myself think.

It's not in the wainscot. It's everywhere.

I mean: It is here in this room.

It must be a small rat. The bastard.

Can't find it. I've looked up and down.

This Tower, of course, is infested. Mephistopheles built it, Faust says.

Well, it's cold and it's damp and it's draughty.

And the plumbing's infernal all right.

Scratch scratch, fucking scratch.

At least, Akercocke's sleeping. Small mercies.

But I'll write about *him* later on.

I'm setting a trap. Getting out.

Herr Rat, you can have the Gruyère.

31 The Rest of the Virgin Mary's Hind Leg

Half past four.

I'm out here in the grotto. Very nice.

Shells and rock crystals, that's the grotto, with a slow stream running through it.

I'm dabbling my feet in the stream.

It's quiet.

Kingfishers, that's all.

Here's the rest of chapter 29 – interrupted by the rat –

When Faust said yes he'd go to Rome, Helen cried *Ave Maria* and I made a small secret meal of the hedge.

Then when he went on to say that *I* should go along with them, Helen stopped hailing Mary pretty sharpish and fell into some kind of fit.

'*That boy!* He'll spoil everything!'

'He'll be useful,' Faust said.

'He's so yukky!'

'There's the Alps to cross,' Faust said.

'He's a scoffer!'

'Bandits,' Faust said grimly. 'Wolves and rapers.'

'God forgive me, I just wish that that Wagner was dead!'

Charming.

Still, like most liars, Helen's swayable. She gave up her objections in the end.

'But no Black Magic!' she insisted. 'And Wagner's not to be a real Pilgrim like us!'

'Kit can think it's a caper,' Faust assured her. 'Kit likes a good caper.'

Well, I ran.

32 Motive

I ran back through the maze to my room, and I locked myself in. I started to write what I've written.

OK, then.

So here's how it is.

That Helen's a fox.

And Faust's crazy.

I've been here ten years. I've never seen any grey friar.

And this journey to Rome?

This journey to Rome is no caper. No pilgrimage, either.

This journey will keep the old fart busy. Maybe he won't drink so much. He'll be *moving*. That's good. If Rome's the direction he moves in, who cares? It might just as well be that New World which was found by Columbus. Or Cathay. Or Antwerp. Destinations don't matter. It's the going that counts.

All aboard for the journey!

To hell? heaven? Rome? or a death on the road in between?

Rome, maybe.

Death, sometime, most certainly.

Not the other things.

I'm writing this book to prove that.

33 Spy

I'll be glad to be shot of this Tower.

Back in my room.

Eight o'clock.

No rat in the trap. Cheese untouched.

But someone's been in here. I know it.

Someone clever with keys. They unlocked the door I left locked. They came into this room and looked round it. Then they went out again, locking the door.

I know this. They made one mistake. A quite stupid one.

My chair has been moved.

Not much. But enough for me to know someone's been here. There are these four marks on the carpet where the feet of my chair have dug in. When I came back – just half an hour ago – I noticed immediately that my chair wasn't sitting where I left it. I could see the four marks distinctly. Whoever came in here must have moved that chair six inches to the left.

Who was it? And what were they after?

Nothing missing. I've gone over the room.

Not a thief, then. A spy. Someone's spying on me. Which would explain that knocking on the door this afternoon. Whoever it was wanted only to know if I was in here. When they found out I was, they went away. Later, they came back, knocked again, found I wasn't here, and came in. But what in Christ's name were they after?

This book.

It's the only thing possible.

That explains my chair being moved. The spy sat down at my desk and went over the drawers. Then, when he couldn't find what he wanted, he pushed the chair to one side and knelt down to search underneath.

In which case, I fooled him. Ha! Ha!

This desk has a secret compartment. It's — No, I shan't even write down where it is, and how you work it! I can't be too careful now, can I? So, Herr Spy, if you ever read this – get stuffed! Enough to say that I have a foolproof way of knowing if that compartment has ever been opened. That tells me you didn't find it today. As for tomorrow: these papers won't be here then, any more than their writer. I must work out a way of protecting them from this unwanted reader of mine on the road to Rome. Well, I think that I have that already . . .

But it's curious.

It's crazy, in fact.

Because nobody knows that I'm writing this book, do they? Because I didn't know myself till this morning, when I came back from the maze, wrote *Hey, Faust*, and got going. Nobody knows. And even if somebody did know, why should they want to be reading it?

Only nine persons here beside me.

Helen. The 7 girls.* And Faust.

Our Helen can't read! (Deprived childhoods.)

The 7 girls — What a good job I'm writing Low German! If it's any of those lovelies tampering with my things (!), then I doubt if they'd make sense of the lingo. Jane *might*. Jane's clever. But on even that English intellectual I think the real nuance would be lost.

That's a nice word, that *nuance*. I'll drink to it. Some few sips of his trebbiano.

* OK. I'm *really* going to come to them tonight!

63

Him? Faust?

The most likely, all things considered.

So I'm grateful to that rat whose perpetual scratching annoyed me earlier on. Because the rat drove me out to the grotto. And it was only in the grotto that I scribbled down the reason why I'm writing this book. That motive stayed safe in my pocket while the spy was wasting his or her time in this room.

Bad luck to you anyway, Spy.

May you dance at your death – on the end of a rope!

And without an erection.

At least that damned scratching's stopped.

Did the spy catch the rat or the rat catch the spy?

The hell with this whole bloody Tower!

I'll be glad to be rid of it tomorrow . . .

Akercocke's awake. In his cage. Playing tag with his fleas. And smell-finger.

Did Akercocke see the spy? Now, if Akercocke could talk . . .

What the fuck am I writing? I must be shagged out of my wits by the pair of them. Faust and the fair Helen, I mean.

Thank Christ Akercocke can't talk.

Please Christ he never will.

Of course he never will!

Akercocke. He's just a rotten monkey and a millstone round my neck. I'll write about Akercocke last thing.

Meanwhile, I've this screwy new development to report.

34 V.V.V.V.V.

When it got cold in the grotto and the kingfishers went, I strolled over to the temple for a nap.

The Temple of V.V.V.V.V.

It's out beyond the maze, on the edge of the ledge that looks to Freiburg.

The Vs are Faust's motto. They stand for *Vi Veri Vniversum Vivus Vici.* 'By the power of truth, I, while living, have conquered the universe.'

No comment.

Faust used to use this temple for his Ceremonial Magic, in the old days. He did that to impress himself, I'd say. Also to impress me, when I was younger. Not that I was ever particularly impressed. Nothing ever materialised. Nothing ever came – except the Doktor. He'd come all right, when we'd done our chanting and prancing exercises, and waved a few swords about, and I'd sucked him in the middle of the Circle of the Great Work.

Ceremonial Magic!

Great Work!

A fine excuse to get a boy stripped off!

All that caper stopped seven years ago, when Helen turned up. I think he tried it on with Helen too. But Helen's too religious to mix sex and rituals. No doubt she sucks him off, but not out there. 'A creepy place,' she calls it. So it is.

So, the temple isn't visited any more. You go in through the pillars between the brambles and you cross the downstairs floor where he's got all this V.V.V.V.V. cut in the marble, then up the stone steps to the moon chamber. The moon chamber's not so bad, so long as you don't count the skulls and pentacles.

I don't count them.

I curled up in some skins and soon dropped off.

I slept for more than an hour. All that writing on top of this morning's nonsense in the maze had worn me out.

When I woke I came back to the Tower, went to the kitchen, and fixed myself some grub. Beef, cucumbers, and white and red chick peas. Tasty. I felt better for the sleep and the food. Also no doubt because I hadn't seen Faust or Helen since this morning.

I wasn't in any hurry to come back up here to my room. As a matter of fact, I didn't think there would be much more I'd have to add to these papers today. Just the promised account of the 7 girls, a note explaining Akercocke, one or two other historical documents I've dug up concerning the Herr Doktor's past.

Don't get me wrong. I was quite looking forward to rounding off the first part of my book with these things. Especially the 7 girls stuff, which I knew would be nice stuff to write. What I didn't allow for was any new twist to *today*. I supposed that I'd see Faust this evening and be told about Rome. I'd a modest proposal of my own all prepared in my head about that. Meanwhile, I put off this writing. I fished out my kite from the storeroom and climbed up to the top of the Tower.

35 Another Vision in the Shrubbery

I've this kite in the shape of a dragon. I made it myself –
slivers of wood covered with strong silks of many colours.

Kite-flying I always enjoy. When you hold the long string in
your hand you can feel the kite sing.

The breeze was just right. I got the kite up over the trees
down the side of the Schlossberg.

I was standing there on the parapet, minding my own
business, thinking my own thoughts, when the Doktor appeared.

Don't read any mystery into the fact that I hadn't heard
him making his way up the spiral stair to the top of the Tower.
He can tread like a cat when he wants to.

Faust wasted no time. He announced we were leaving tomorrow.

'Anywhere special?' I enquired.

'Rome,' he answered.

He was eating an orange. He likes eating oranges. He makes
a performance of it, picking the skin off the orange with his
teeth. Then he bites out big bits of it, and spits all the pips in
his palm. The juice gets clogged in his moustaches.

'Not likely,' I said. 'Count me out.'

Faust stared at me, dribbling. He hadn't supposed I'd say
that.

Which was why I was saying it.

'Rome's too far,' I added.

'Don't talk nonsense,' Faust said. 'Rome's just 500 miles as
the crow flies.'

'Auf Wiedersehen, old crow,' I said.

I tugged on the kite string. My kite zoomed, then dipped.
The string sang in my fingers. I could feel the great music.

Faust sat up on the parapet, one arm round his boots. He
sucked on the orange, rubbing his lips with the pith.

'Please come, Kit,' he said.

I admit this surprised me. I'd expected commands first.
Then wheedling entreaties. That's the usual order.

'Why should I?' I said.

Faust looked round. There was nobody up there with us, of course. He was totally pissed. I know all his stages by heart. I could see he'd been drinking his brandy all day, passing out, coming round, passing out again. Just now he was halfway to Ash Wednesday's penultimate oblivion. He would drink himself senseless, wake up once, fuck Helen, then drink himself off for the night. I might be a bit out about Helen, but the rest is for sure.

The bottle was stuck in his belt. Two thirds empty.

'If I tell you,' he muttered, 'you promise not to mention a word of it?'

'Tell what?' I said.

'*Why* Rome,' he said.

'The Inquisition isn't hot around here,' I pointed out. 'And I'm not in the pay of the Constipator.'

'I mean Helen,' Faust said.

I concentrated on the kite. It climbed high in the evening air. Up over the Glotter Tal.

'Go on then,' I said.

Faust munched a huge chunk of his orange. He got juice on his boil.

'I've seen him,' he said.

I said nothing.

'This afternoon,' he said. 'In the shrubbery.'

I let out more string. My kite needed it.

Faust said: 'I was reading Paracelsus at the time. Then I heard him. Two definite rings of the bell!'

'Dear me!' I said. 'I mean – *Wow!*'

'He was there in the fishpool,' Faust said.

'The grey friar?'

'Yes. Him. Mephistopheles.'

'Had you called him?'

'I was reading Paracelsus.'

'That's not quite the same . . .'

'I'd been thinking.'

'His name?'

'Yes. His name. *Mephistopheles!*'

I made the kite dance. It was glorious.

'In the fishpool,' I said. 'Was he swimming?'

'He was looking up at me out of the lily pads. Just his face in the cowl, do you see? Fishes swimming over his face. Coming out of his nostrils, some were.'

I said: 'Didn't the bell sound funny? I mean – being rung under water?'

Faust scowled up at the kite. 'No different than usual,' he said. 'It was just like it always sounds. Then he spoke to me, Kit.'

'That's against the first Article. You hadn't summoned him.'

'His message was *urgent*,' Faust said.

'Ah. I see. What was his message?'

'That we journey to Rome.'

'Rosaries all the way?'

'The Devil has work for me there.'

'Work, eh? What type of work?'

'A great work!'

'What type of great work?'

Faust spat all his pips in his palm. He always does this most carefully.

Then:

'Murder,' he said.

I wound some string tight round my hand. I let the kite bite me.

'Assassination,' Faust said.

He flicked away orange pips. He always flicks his pips away by striking with his forefinger against the index of his thumb. Left hand. His left hand forefinger has a particularly nasty long nail.

'Who do you assassinate?' I said.

'Not just me, my son. Us.'

'Who do *we* assassinate?' I said.

Faust looked over his shoulder. He was sweating. He was shaking. His neck is even filthier round the back.

'You wouldn't tell Helen?'

'I can hardly wait *not* to tell Helen.'

Faust came leaning close. He grabbed me by the collar. He pressed his mouth right to my ear.

'Paul,' he said.

I clutch at the parapet. Insufficient strawberry jam. His breath was disgusting.

'Paul 3,' he said.

'I heard you the first time,' I said.

36 A Modest Proposal

Faust leaned back. He was sucking his fingers.

'You'll come then?'

'No thanks,' I said.

Never keep your kite on too tight a rein. Let it go when the wind wants it. There was more wind now. My hair was being blown into my mouth. Faust's was streaming out behind him. A long and dirty white. He looked like a gargoyle.

I let out some kite string.

I said: 'Alessandro Farnese doesn't bug me. Why should I help you kill him?'

'Because he's the Pope,' Faust said.

'You don't say? Is that a good reason?'

'The best reason there is,' Faust said.

I managed my kite.

'Remember this morning?' I asked him. 'First of all, you kept chanting *forty days* like some poor sod in the wilderness. Then you gave me a pep talk on freedom. I found that quite inspiring, except –'

'This morning,' said the Doktor, 'I was drunk.'

'And this afternoon you weren't drunk?'

'Helen sobered me,' Faust said.

'That figures,' I said.

'She put my head in the fountain,' Faust said.

I looked at his boil.

As much candlegrease as ever.

The best butter.

I'll say this much for him: He always uses the best butter on his boil.

'We'll have to zig-zag through the mountains,' Faust was saying. 'Say it's 600 miles at the most. But the roads and the passes aren't so bad in the spring. A man could *walk* it in thirty days. Not that we'll be walking.'

'We fly there?' I said.

'Helen won't fly any more,' Faust pointed out. 'You know that.'

'I know that,' I said. 'So Helen's coming along for the assassinating too?'

'See here,' Faust said. 'This is serious work, boy. I've had more than enough of your capers.'

'I enjoy a good caper,' I said.

I shouldn't have said that. Too dangerous.

But Faust didn't remember.

The big lug.

He was licking his bloodstone.

'We ride to Rome,' he said. 'Riding fifty miles a day, we'd do it in less than two weeks. I'm allowing for three.'

'That's sensible,' I said.

'Just so long as I'm there for Holy Week,' Faust said.

'Holy Week's more than five weeks away. You should do it with time to spare.'

'*We* shall,' Faust said.

'I don't really like Rome,' I told him. 'I've only been there twice, admittedly. The first time there was a snake in my soup. It was a small snake, but it left a nasty taste, you know. The second time, this cardinal buggered me. He had the pox. It wasn't nice at all. They never sweep the streets in Rome, either. And remember what Martial says about the wine from the Vatican vineyards? That it beats vinegar. Poison as well, if I recall it right.'

'We're not going for a good time,' Faust said.

His voice was getting hairy and quite mad.

'All right,' I said. 'You're not going to Rome for the sex or the booze. You're going to Rome to kill the Pope. Tell me what you think your grey friar said. Exactly.'

'Mephistopheles,' Faust said. 'Mephistopheles has promised me that if I kill Pope Paul 3 before my forty days are up, then my forty days aren't up!'

'You get a reprieve?'

'Yes.'

'Sure?'

'As sure as eggs are eggs.'

'But these are Devil's eggs,' I pointed out.

Faust looked up at my kite.

He crossed his eyes.

'Mephistopheles has promised me that if I kill the Pope before this Good Friday then I get another 24 years,' he said.

'And you want that? You don't want perfect freedom any more? A little soul-cut with the Devil's scissors?'

'I like the sun. My soul's my own already.'

'OK,' I said. 'Another 24 years' sun, give or take the rainy days. But what then? Will your fishy friar require you to kill another Pope, and get another 24, and then another, and so on, and so on, until the end of time? Will John Faust be sunburnt and soul-free for ever on this earth – so long as he goes on bumping off Popes?'

Faust jumped me.

He snatched my wrist. He bent it hard.

I had to let go of my kite.

The bastard had hold of the string higher up.

'This is the Devil's business!' he shouts. 'We leave for Rome tomorrow!'

'You don't need me,' I muttered.

'I do. You are part of the plot.'

'What plot?'

'I'll tell you when the time's right. Not before.'

I examined my wrist. It was red from the bite of his fingernails. It was marked with his dirt.

I said: 'What about Helen? She can't be a part of the plot?'

'No.'

'Then why are you taking her?'

'Private reasons,' Faust said.

Him and his private.

'She'll get vertigo in the Alps,' I pointed out mildly. 'She'll waste time hearing Mass all the way. Besides, assassination is no job for a woman.'

'Helen wants to come,' Faust said.

I sighed.

I whistled.

'Hey ho,' I said. 'Can I have my kite back?'

'Listen,' Faust said. 'This is important. Helen doesn't know why we're going.'

'Of course not.'

'Not just that,' Faust said. 'Helen thinks we're going to Rome for quite a different reason.'

'What different reason?' I asked.

Faust chuckled.

He was playing with my kite, making it crash down towards the trees of the Black Forest, then letting it climb again with the wind.

71

'Helen thinks I'm going to Rome to be what she calls "saved",'
he whispered. 'Helen thinks I'm planning to confess all my sins to
the Pope, and be saved from hellfire, so-called. Me, John Faust,
free spirit, down on my knees in front of the Bishop of Rome,
begging him to let me off, absolve me, cancel my pact with the
Devil. Me, John Faust, shriven! Can you imagine it?'

'What a laugh,' I said. 'But you're kidding her along? Can I
have my kite back?'

'I'm kidding her all right,' Faust said. 'I'm humouring
Helen. You've got it.'

'I haven't got anything,' I said. 'I'd just like my kite.'

Faust toyed with the string.

'Very well then,' he said. 'Are you coming?'

I shrugged.

'Do I have any choice?'

Faust crossed his eyes.

'As a matter of fact, no, you don't. But I do like to offer you
one. I know you believe in free will. I'd prefer it if you would
say yes, without any magic.'

'Spare me the magic,' I said.

'Rome then?' Faust said.

'On one condition.'

(Here comes my own modest proposal!)

'What's that?' Faust said.

'That my 7 girls can come too!'

'Are you mad?' Faust said. 'Why should they come?'

I shrugged.

'Private reasons,' I said.

He laughed. The old fuck-up. He actually laughed.

It was nice.

The prospect of killing the Pope has done wonders for his
expiratory muscles.

'Very well, Kit,' he said. 'You can take the whole pack of
them. We've plenty of horses.'

'We'll need them,' I said. 'Hey, Faust, you hate horses!'

He groaned, looking worried.

'I'll manage.'

'You'd better,' I said. 'You're not riding on *my* back, I promise you. Now – if you don't mind – my kite!'

'To Rome?' Faust demanded.

'I'll go with you to Rome,' I agreed.

Faust patted me on the head with one stinking paw. He put the kite string back into my hand with the other paw.

'That's my boy,' Faust said.

37 The Archangel Gabriel

Faust shuffled away down the staircase. I stayed where I was. I didn't know what to think really. So I gave all my mind to my kite.

Kite-flying is nice. It absorbs the attention.

The sky was nice too. I like dusk.

The Black Forest was horrible.

I turned my back on it.

I crossed to the other side of the Tower, swinging the dragon-kite round in an arc high above as I went. If you tend the string carefully, winding, unwinding, dragging this way then that, you can outwit the wind. I got my kite just where I wanted it, out over Zarten.

This Tower is massive, its walls two men thick. From the battlements where I stood now I looked down the slopes of the Schlossberg. A few vineyards hanging on to the side of the mountain. To the right, over the Merzhausen defile, Zähringen, Beltzenhausen, Gundelfingen. To my left, dwarfing Freiburg, the giant's shoulder of the Schönberg.

A few stars in the dusk. Moon picking out the Dreisam's bright rush. The Dreisam flows into the Rhine, which goes on down to Basel. The road follows the river. That's the road that you start on for Rome.

I heard footfalls behind me. They were echoing up from the stair. A figure appeared in the archway. Our Helen, of course.

She stood blinking doubtfully, head cocked. Helen's short-sighted. She ought to wear spectacles, but she's too vain. The change from the gloom of the stair to the star-shot dusk on top of the Tower was giving her problems. She squinted.

I saw she was wearing a wide floppy blue hat with an emblem of two crossed keys on the brim.

Pilgrim gear.

'Nice evening,' I said.

She flounced over.

73

She was holding her right hand outstretched. Pale blue glove on the hand. Even paler blue rings on the glove.

Did she want me to shake hands?

Kiss her rings?

As I was wondering how best to achieve the first act with my hand full of kite string, or the second while perched on a parapet, Helen solved my dilemma by opening her fist.

She turned it palm upwards.

Full of sparkles.

'What's this?' I said.

'It's a handful of diamonds,' said Helen.

I didn't fall over the parapet.

See, I know Helen's ways. Most of them.

So I looked for the axe in her other hand.

There wasn't an axe in her other hand.

She was holding a kite in her other hand. This kite was a very odd shape. It looked like a broken-down vulture.

'I suppose that John's told you,' she said.

She poured all her 'diamonds' on the parapet. They didn't shine much in the moon. One of them rolled off the edge and straight down the rock-face.

I crouched on my hunkers. I touched them. My finger was stung.

'These aren't diamonds,' I said. 'Just glass.'

Helen sniffed at the stars.

'About *Rome* . . .' she said.

I sighed.

'Yes, I know about Rome.'

Helen took a sachet of gum from a bag hanging on the silver cord about her waist. Her waist's small. Helen diets a lot.

She held up the kite in her left hand.

'It's the Archangel Gabriel,' she said.

38   War in Heaven

I considered the Archangel Gabriel.

'I made it myself,' Helen said.

She stroked the silk mess with red fingernails.

'This pilgrimage, Wagner . . .'

74

'Hi, Gabriel.'

'You're not going to spoil it?' she said.

'Pilgrimage? Isn't it a caper?'

Helen looked at the archangel, pleased.

'Well, yes, it is that, of course. I use the word pilgrimage lightly.'
She patted her hat.

'Wagner . . .'

'I like your hat,' I said.

'Do you really? It's been blessed, you know.'

'I still like it.'

'Wagner . . .'

'Rome,' I remarked. 'It's just something to do.'

Helen smiled without showing her teeth.

'Wagner, I've thought of a game!'

'Rome-going?' I said.

'No! Not that! *This!*'

She held up the paralysed vulture.

I say that she'd smeared about a yard of the string, immediately below the kite, with some of the gum. She'd smeared it on thickly. There was cut glass stuck there in the gum.

The glass looked like her teeth, but not yellow.

'I don't get the meaning,' I said.

Helen giggled. Her earrings were jangling. Only once before have I ever seen her looking so playful. That was the morning after Faust bought the ginseng from the man from Baghdad.

'Let's have a kite fight!' she cried.

'A kite fight?'

'It's something I learned in my childhood,' Helen explained.
'When I was a girl in Cathay we would often have kite fights. You just barb your string as I've done, with some of these diamonds. Then you –'

'Hold on there,' I said. 'On the subject of childhoods –'

'You get your kite up wind, and let the string drift towards the other one. Then you give a quick jerk and snip! snap!'

'Like the Devil's scissors?'

Helen looked even blanker than usual. So Faust hasn't told *her* that one.

'Snip, snap,' I said. 'One of your games with the antipope?'

'Of course not. That was later. I told you. When I was a child in Cathay –'

'Look, I'm not hot on antipopes,' I said. 'But it happens I

checked out your Benedict one night and guess what?'

'My father was a merchant,' Helen said. 'We travelled the silk road to Kanchow.'

'Benedict 13 kicked the bucket a century ago!'

Helen coloured.

Some powder flaked off. A small snow.

'I have no sense of time,' she complained.

'So what was Cathay like?' I asked her.

'Quite quite indescribable!'

'I thought it might be,' I remarked.

Helen re-muddled Gabriel.

I hummed. I watched the lamps lighting in Freiburg.

'A kite fight,' I said. 'Sounds OK.'

'Well, bring your thing down,' Helen said.

I wound in the string. When the kite came back on to the Tower, Helen gave me the sachet of gum. I coated the string with it thickly. I pressed bits of crushed glass in the gum.

'Good gum this,' I said. 'It dries quick.'

'John got it for me,' Helen said.

'Arabian,' I said. 'He's not lost his powers, then. Just as well. We're going to need them.'

'Oh, we'll be all right,' Helen said.

'You think so?' I said. 'Alps? Wolves? Robbers?'

Helen shivered.

She addressed herself to the Schönberg.

'God,' Helen gabbled, 'Most Gracious God, Who of your great Graciousness made Abraham depart from this country and preserved him safe and well on his journey, I beseech You, preserve your children Helen and John in the same manner, O Lord. Protect Us from all dangers and make our travels light. Be our Shield in Battle, O Lord, our solace on the way. Be our shade in the heat, our protection in rain and cold. Carry us when we are tired. Be our support in adversity, our Staff when the path is slippery. So that with your Guidance, blessed Lord, we may successfully reach Our Great Goal and safely return home again. Through the Merits of Your dear Son Jesus Christ Our Saviour, and His Most Holy Mother Our Lady. Amen.'

The glass had stuck in the gum.

'That was nice,' I said. 'Thanks for including me out.'

Helen sniffed.

'I've prayed for safe passage,' she said. 'Wagner, I know we hold

76

different opinions. But we do have the one thing in common.'

'Faust,' I said.

'His soul's safety,' Helen said.

'Just Faust,' I said.

I shoved at the glass. It was stuck firm already.

Helen said:

'You don't even believe in John's magic really, do you?'

I said nothing.

'You don't believe in *anything*,' Helen said smugly.

'This is excellent gum,' I said.

'*Christopher*,' Helen mused. 'You know what your name means . . .?'

I let my kite out in the wind.

'Christ-bearer,' Helen said. 'Funny name for an infidel!'

'My parents weren't to know,' I observed. 'Call me Kit, if you like.'

My kite in the shape of a dragon rode high above Zarten.

'Oh, I couldn't! I wouldn't!'

Helen was struggling hard to get Gabriel into the air.

It wriggled.

It flopped about.

'John tells you things?' Helen said.

'This and that. Now and then.'

A sudden gust did Gabriel a favour.

The tangled mess shot out about twenty yards from the Tower, not aloft, but level at least with the battlements.

'We can never be friends,' Helen gasped, holding on to her kite string with both hands. 'But let's not be enemies either.'

Gabriel hesitated.

'Jerk it,' I said. 'Here, I'll help you.'

'I'd rather you didn't,' Helen cried, skipping away.

The archangel caught in a good gust.

It soared.

Briefly.

'See?' Helen screeched. 'I've done it!' She swirled round and round with the string. 'The idea is – to get your kite – up wind . . . Then let the string drift and –'

'Snip snap,' I said. 'Happy Devil's scissors childhood days.'

'I don't know what you're talking about,' Helen said. 'But I wouldn't believe it all.'

'Cathay?' I enquired.

77

'His story,' Helen said. 'John's.'

'I don't believe more than a quarter of anything he tells me,' I told her.

'I wouldn't go that far!'

'A half then?'

'That's wise,' Helen said.

She pulled frantically hard on her kite string.

Gabriel wasn't having any.

'I wondered when you'd start on my name,' I said.

'It's a *good* name!' Helen said. 'Oh, this is *impossible!*'

She was wrestling with the string, trying desperately to get Gabriel to climb with the wind. But the kite was so ill-made, it wouldn't. Slowly, not ungracefully, the archangel sank to the ground at the foot of the Tower.

'Life can be so unfair,' Helen said.

I said:

'So much for symbolism.'

'I don't understand you.'

'The Book of Revelation, isn't it?' I said. 'War in heaven. The dragon against Gabriel. The Devil against the other lot. You should have won this particular caper, by rights.'

Helen stamped her foot.

'Well, *you* didn't win it,' she said.

'No. Nobody won it,' I said. 'Would you like a shot of my kite, since your archangel's such a dead loss?'

'It was only a game,' Helen said.

She stood there on top of the Tower as if she was fishing, with the string going down in slack loops in the deepening dark.

'*Ave Maria,*' Helen said. 'That's what I say.'

'Amen,' I said.

Helen blinked.

'I mean – Rome will make a better game, won't it?' I said.

39   Beauty

I think we need a little light relief here.

About the 7 girls.

They came three years ago. Faust Year 21.

78

At that time, the Herr Doktor used to go on a lot about Beauty.
'Beauty is,' he'd say.

Then a lot of definitions. I mean a different definition each
day. Such as? Such as:

'Beauty is a virgin's pinch.'
'Beauty is blasphemy.'
'Beauty is a sick rose.'
'Beauty is a circle.'
'Beauty is the beginning of terror.'
*'Beauty is the first and last word in the Gospel According to St Judas
Iscariot.'*
'Beauty is truth.'
'Beauty is measles of the soul . . .'

etc, etc. Mostly crap, OK. But I like that kind of crap. I used
to like it when he talked like that.

I didn't like it that I was his bum boy.

True, by that time he had given up the Ceremonial Magic.
But there was still the odd occasion when he'd make me touch
my toes in the shrubbery, or suck him off in the middle of the
maze. When I first came here, he used to say I was his angel.
He meant I had an arse that suited him. 'Son,' he would say,
'I must inculcate you with black science.' This inculcation was
always via the fundament, or my mouth. I'd had enough of it.
It wasn't black.

Then one night, in the laboratory, he said:

'You know what we need around this place?'

(He'd been chasing me round the furnace. I'd refused.)

'More Beauty,' I suggested.

'You took the words right out of my mouth,' he said.

I'd taken the words right out of Faust's mouth.

Well, I was fed up with taking *him* in *my* mouth.

I wanted a change, and the old bugger must have known it.
He can be decent enough when he wants to be.

'More Beauty,' Faust promised. 'I'll see what I can do.'

He loped off in the direction of Kolmar, his face to the setting
sun.

Our Helen was furious when she asked me where Faust had
gone and I said that he'd just gone to get something for me.
She retired to her private chapel. 'A retreat,' she called it.

Faust didn't come back for a month.

When he did come back up the Schlossberg, there was this

79

vehicle behind him. Faust wasn't pulling it. It was pulled by six horses. Black horses. Black harness.

This vehicle was interesting. He told me its name was a char.

Yup. A char was a sort of a carriage.

It had a red canopy, red sides, and was long and quadrangular. Little windows, two on each side, that were star-shaped and round-shaped. Faces peering out of the windows. They were beautiful faces.

There was a small door in the side.

Faust opened the door with a bow. His hat swept the ground.

The 7 girls stepped out.

Faust introduced them.

'Marguerite, Gretchen. They're Walloons.'

'Salome. Persian.'

'Jane. She's from England.'

'Nadja. She's Russian.'

'Zuleika. From Turkey.'

'Justine. An Italian Jewess.'

Well, I was impressed. Also flattered. He'd gone to the trouble of finding me females whose languages I can speak.

I think I shook hands with him.

I certainly made the girls welcome.

Marguerite and Gretchen were identical twins. They had long blonde hair and speaking eyes. I'll tell you what their eyes said in a minute.

Salome was small. She had blue eyes, a full-moon face, and hair of the glossiest black.

Jane was tall and proud. Her gown clung to her. My first impression was of the defiant tilt of her chin, and the outline of long aristocratic legs under silk.

Nadja, the Russian, looked sulky. She had tapering fingers that plucked at the fur of her muff.

The Turkish Zuleika was giggling. When my eyes ran over her breasts, she blushed. I couldn't help noting the way that they bounced as she stepped from the char. And I knew that she knew what I'd noted.

The last of the seven, Justine, was perhaps the most lovely. Neither too tall nor too small, and she walked like a queen. Her lips were deliciously sensual. She smiled as she looked at me, and her little pale tongue flickered over her smile as she looked. It wasn't my face that she looked at.

As for me, I felt weak at the knees.

I'd lived this odd life, please remember. First angels. Then Faust. Never females. Yes, I was a virgin with females.

Helen burst on the scene.

She was raging.

She glared at the girls. She flicked at her nose with her rosary.

'It's all right,' Faust said. 'These are Kit's.'

Helen wasn't persuaded. She gave me her Medusa look.

'Prince Charming!' she snorted. 'I don't reckon he'll know where to *start*!'

She turned and flounced back to her chapel, her head in the air.

'Say a prayer for him then,' Faust called after her.

I escorted my seven new friends into the Tower. Faust leered as he loped by my side.

'Are they really all mine?' I demanded.

'If you think you can cope?'

'Well . . .'

'Good lad.'

They were all of them laughing. Excited. All save the English girl, Jane. Jane looked disdainful. I remember the glance that she gave our poor cobwebs. If I'd been a spider, I'd have died.

There was this enormous fire burning in the grate in the hall. The crucified goat hangs over that mantle. I saw Nadja inspect it with interest, hands clasped in her muff. The others looked elsewhere. That goat is plain stupid. It isn't a real goat, of course. Just wretched pink plaster. Helen likes to pretend it's a hind. In honour of St Giles,* Helen says.

Faust lined up the 7 in a row.

He was fussing and fretting about. A pimp in a filthy black cloak.

I whispered:

'Christ! Where did you get them?'

'I told you already,' he said.

'Not the countries,' I said. 'I mean, *how*?'

Faust rolled his eyes.

Then he crossed them.

'Ah! We have our methods, my son!'

This was the only hint he ever dropped that his so-called Mephistopheles had been helpful. Otherwise, I guess that I was supposed to believe that the Herr Doktor had rounded up

* Patron saint of cripples and beggars. Dates unknown. Had a pet hind.

these beauties in his travels, and persuaded them into the char, and brought them to live for my delight here at the Tower, all by his own sexual glamour.

Frankly, in this case I almost find it easier to credit the existence of Mephistopheles.

It was four years since Faust's great bath with Helen.

Granted, his boil was in its infancy.

Just a butter-smeared pimple, then.

Still and all.

Maybe he paid for the seven? Bought them for money, I mean.

But none of the girls was a whore.

As a matter of fact, all were virgins.

'They're maidens, like you, Kit,' Faust said.

I've forgotten to give you their ages.

Going from left to right down that line of them there in the hall then:

Marguerite and Gretchen were 14.

Salome was going on 13.

Jane was 17.

Nadja was 18.

Zuleika was 16.

Justine was $15\frac{1}{2}$.

I found this out later. At the time I just thought they all looked most incredibly young. Young and beautiful. A row of amazing young chicks.

'Which would you like first?' Faust enquired.

I gulped as I went down the line.

I looked at their fronts and their backs.

I pondered. It was difficult. I wouldn't have minded the lot!

Then I pointed to Marguerite and Gretchen.

They giggled. They stood holding hands.

'Do you mind if I ask why?' Faust said.

'Well,' I answered. 'Two heads are better than one.'

Faust nodded.

Marguerite and Gretchen grinned at me.

The others looked pretty pissed off.

Jane said:

'I've not come all the way from Northumberland just to be insulted.'

(She said this in English, of course. A posh accent.)

Faust patted her bottom. He doesn't speak English, but

Jane's annoyance didn't need a translation.

'I'm sure you're Kit's *second* choice,' he said.

Jane raised her eyebrows.

I nodded. I smiled at her. She'd understood Faust's High German. A clever girl, this one, I reckoned.

Jane perked up a bit after that. But she still gave me nasty looks, all through our dinner. Yes, the Doktor insisted on dinner. It was tasty. Roast peacock. With mushrooms.

The twins didn't eat very much.

When our meal was finished, Faust yawned. He was weary from wandering, he said. Taking a torch in his fist, he showed the seven girls to their rooms. Five of them had a room each, on my floor. This Tower is enormous. Many mansions. But Marguerite and Gretchen had the one room between them. The one bed. And I wondered at this.

Things became clearer when Faust shut the door behind us.

Marguerite.

Gretchen.

And me.

Like I say, they were 14 years old. Virgins. Blonde hair to their shoulders. Grey eyes full of mischief. Twin mischief.

Marguerite wore a white gown.

Gretchen wore a black gown.

Clothed, it was the only way I could tell one from the other.

Unclothed, as I found, it was different.

The sisters were Walloons – that is, from the French-speaking part of the Netherlands.

I addressed them in French:

'Now, girls, will you take off your gowns, please?'

They stood looking at me, hand in hand, in the torchlight. They were smiling identical smiles.

They said nothing.

Then they turned face to face, sideways to me.

'Shall we?' Marguerite whispered.

'Oh, let's!' Gretchen answered.

Very swiftly, they undressed each other.

Something – it must have been the eagerness of their hands peeling off each other's dresses and undergarments – half-prepared me for what happened next.

Marguerite and Gretchen starting kissing each other.

The kisses were quick, but not sisterly.

They got longer, and even less sisterly.

I stripped off as they fell on the bed.

Marguerite was the active one. Her hands stroked her sister's small tits. She tweaked and then sucked at the nipples. Gretchen wriggled. She sighed with delight. Then Marguerite rolled over on top of her twin. They were rubbing their pussies together.

My little Walloons were young Lesbians!

They were virgins where men were concerned. But not to each other.

I found the scene strangely exciting.

Two lovely young girls making love on the bed. And me nude in the torchlight beside them.

I daresay the challenge appealed to me.

I could see that these two little sisters were perfect accomplices in the pleasures of Lesbian love. Marguerite was the dominant partner. She lay there on Gretchen, her sweet rounded bottom going up and down and grinding from side to side as she worked on the other girl's cunt. Gretchen moaned with approval. But her eyes were wide open. She craned up to peer over her sister's freckled shoulder as I climbed on the bed. Grey eyes, soft dishevelled blonde hair, cheeks flushed from Marguerite's nimble attentions. Marguerite, in her present position, might be quite careless of me. Gretchen certainly wasn't. Her eyes opened wider. She reached out both hands for my prick.

I didn't let her have it.

Marguerite offered more of a challenge.

I drove into her, hard, from behind.

Marguerite couldn't believe it, I think. Don't forget, however accomplished a Sapphist, she'd never had a man in her life. She cried out as I pushed my prick into her. She squealed. Then she started to buck.

I found this delicious.

Like breaking a mettlesome filly.

I gripped tight with my thighs round her thighs and just stayed there in place.

Of course, with each buck aimed at dislodging me, Marguerite got me deeper inside her. She soon found she liked it. The bucking got more furious then.

Gretchen groaned. The weight of the two of us bumping up and down between her outspread legs must have been considerable. But it wasn't a groan of complaint. As I came down,

I kissed her. I was kissing the one little sister and fucking the other. My tongue went in and out of Gretchen's mouth. My prick went deeper and deeper into Marguerite's virgin cunt. It would be hard to say which was more greedy – the mouth or the cunt.

Of course, I know now that it wasn't such a marvellous fuck, as fucks go. For a start, Marguerite's cunt was so small, even after I'd broken the hymen. Also, I came far too quickly. Well, it was my first time.

But we had a nice orgasm, the three of us.

I came, as it happened, in the middle of a long kiss for Gretchen. Marguerite gasped.

Then she came, with a ferocious buck. I think it must have been the feel of my spunk shooting hot up inside her that caused her to come.

Gretchen came on the next kiss. Our comings inspired her. She wrapped her legs around the two of us, where we lay panting and heaving on top of her. As I later discovered, Marguerite has an uncommonly big —

40 Stone

Clit.

Clitoris.

I mean: the female equivalent of a penis.

Marguerite has a big one. That's how the two sisters had satisfied each other until Faust brought them here.

I didn't leave the word out because I am shy of it, or anything. I don't leave words out. You don't leave words out in Low German.

Someone just threw a stone at my window.

That's why the last chapter broke off.

(I'm not writing Literature. A chapter, to me, is as long as it takes me to write it. One chapter, one subject, more or less, just as long as it takes me to write it. And I'm writing as fast as I can. I'm writing as fast as my hand moves. This is my 85th page. 85 pages in one day, Ash Wednesday! Well, you'll see I'm no Rabelais. Just facts. Nothing fancy. And there's more I must write, though I'm tired. Once on the road to Rome, tomorrow – today! just gone

85

midnight! – I can't hope for as much time to myself.)

(Time to myself? Was an author ever so interrupted? First the knocks, then that rat, now the stone!)

I have very good windows.

Perpendicular. In painted grisaille.

Just as well. Or that stone would have smashed them!

Who the hell can have thrown it?

The Spy?

That doesn't make sense. Why should the Spy want to *attract* my attention?

I looked out.

There was no one down there.

Patched moonlight, that's all, in the courtyard.

Probably one of the sisters just written about. Marguerite of the remarkable clit. Greedy affectionate Gretchen. Seeing the light in my window. Annoyed that I'm not tucked up in bed with them both.

Yes, that stone certainly sounded Walloonish. Just the sort of quaint trick that they favour.

Sorry, darlings! Wagner's got to neglect you.

Press on with the story right now.

41 More Beauty

Marguerite was my first fuck. Gretchen should have been next, but she wasn't. Still, that wasn't my last fuck that night.

We were lying there in a sweet muddle of limbs, the three of us, when I heard the door open. I'd forgotten to lock it. I looked up. I saw it was Jane.

So what did Jane see?

Jane saw me stretched out on my back. I had Marguerite in the crook of one arm, Gretchen in the other. Gretchen, I remember, had just started to play with my balls. She was eager to have what her twin had had. But she wasn't too skilful a balls player. Mine were the first pair she'd handled.

Jane stood at the foot of the bed.

She was wearing a belt of black leather.

Was that *all* Jane was wearing?

It was.

She looked lovely. I must say it suited her, the belt. Dark straight hair. High firm breasts. Very English.

Jane stared at my prick.

My prick hardened.

'When you've finished your games with these kids,' Jane said, 'I'm ready.'

'Ready for what?'

'A *real* fuck!'

Jane was stroking her belt as she spoke to me.

I kissed Marguerite's ear through the warm waterfall of her hair. 'I've just had what you call a real fuck,' I said. 'With my friend here.'

Jane's eyes flashed in the torchlight. Jet-black.

'Only *one* of them?' she snapped. 'German weakling!'

There was something about Jane – something so hungry and haughty – that made my prick jerk at each word she said. Poor Gretchen! She thought it was *her* doing. She was trying to cover my prick with her two little hands, so that Jane shouldn't see it. At the same time, she couldn't stop fiddling with it. The effort proved too much for such young inexperienced fingers. My prick popped out of Gretchen's palms. It stood up for Jane, and she knew it.

I muttered:

'Well, Marguerite seemed pleased enough with me . . .'

'That peasant!' Jane sneered. 'Listen, do you think I don't know about these two? A right pair of Lesbian shepherdesses! They probably had each other coming off before you stuck that apology for a prick into either of them. They were creaming their drawers half the way from the Netherlands – coming every time the carriage hit a rut in the road – just at the *thought* of being kept in this Tower by the wicked old magician and his lusty young apprentice . . . "O Marguerite, we'll have to submit to his *will!*" "O Gretchen, will his *will* be terrible?" Are their cunts half as stupid as their faces?'

Jane had mimicked the twins' childish voices. She spoke French. This was the only bit of our conversation that Marguerite and Gretchen understood. Realising they were being mocked, they sat up angrily.

'You're a bitch,' I told Jane.

'What you mean,' she said pertly, 'is you're scared of me.'

She considered my prick, which both Marguerite and Gretchen were now striving to hide from her with their little freckled ineffectual hands.

Jane said:

'Some *will*!'

'What's the matter with it?'

'It doesn't look as much fun as my hairbrush.'

'Your hairbrush?' I said.

'My hairbrush.'

Jane sat down on the bed.

'What's your name, little German boy?'

'Christopher. Kit. And I bet I'm older than you.'

'I'm 17.'

'And I'm 21.'

'Four years bending over for Herr Faustus? You call that an advantage? Christopher! Kit! Pansy names!'

'Just fuck off,' I said.

Jane bent her wrist.

'It's like that, isn't it?' she said.

'Like what?'

'Like what!' Jane said to the ceiling. 'A pretty boy living here in the forest, in some godawful Tower, with a dirty old man . . . He's not your father, is he?'

'No. He's not my father.'

'God, he's old enough to be your *grand*father.'

'I don't think he is,' I said. 'Quite.'

'He looks it.'

'Well, he isn't.'

'My, aren't you just *devoted* to him! Him and your cuddly kids! Jane, you are wasting your time!'

She glared at my prick again.

I blushed.

'It's gone soft with arguing,' I explained.

Jane drew her legs together. She has these long legs. Aristocratic. I could just see the dark furry nest at the top, in between them. Jane was making sure I didn't see much.

'Very well,' she said briskly, 'let's see if the pansy can grow.'

She told me the story of her hairbrush.

Remember, Marguerite and Gretchen couldn't understand a word that Jane said.

I understood.

All of me.

And the twins had a hopeless task trying to conceal my understanding. But they tried. Which was pleasant. And which made matters worse.

Now, Jane was a virgin. All the 7 girls were virgins. I've not told you a single lie yet. But Jane was quite different from Marguerite and Gretchen. Marguerite and Gretchen – give or take their little games with each other – were real virginal virgins, quite innocent. There was nothing I'd call innocent about Jane.

Jane was a vicious virgin.

The reason for Jane's vicious virginity was this:

She'd been brought up in a castle, in the wild border country between England and Scotland. Her mother had died when Jane was still a child. Jane had these three brothers, all older than herself.

Jane's father didn't marry again when her mother died. Instead, he started bringing ladies to the castle. Jane's father would fuck each high-born lady, then hand her along to his sons. He said this was part of their education. The sons were as wild as the father. Sometimes they'd have orgies. They'd dance naked. The father and the sons would fuck half a dozen ladies at these times.

Jane grew up with all this going on around her. She didn't take part in it. She despised her father and her brothers for their depraved behaviour.

When they were there fucking ladies in the castle she'd go out for a ride on the moors. Jane did a lot of horse-riding. Horse-riding was a thing she really enjoyed.

Then, one hot summer's day, when she was just 15 years old, Jane had come back from the moors and was putting her horse in the stable, when her three brothers jumped her. They said it was time she gave up horse-riding and learnt a thing or two about men. They stripped off her dress and they forced her back down in the hay. One of the brothers had a pitchfork. He used the pitchfork to pin Jane down. The pitchfork prongs were either side of her neck. Jane has this long neck.

Jane kicked. Like I say, long legs also. She got one of the brothers right in the balls as he took off his trousers.

The eldest brother picked up Jane's horsewhip.

'Little sister,' he said, 'I'm going to thrash you for that. Then we're both going to fuck you.'

(The third bad brother couldn't do any fucking. His balls hurt too much.)

Jane's eldest bad brother was just raising the horsewhip to thrash her, when the father came into the stable.

The father went berserk. He snatched the whip from the bad eldest brother. Then he whipped all the bad brothers, right there in the stable, making them bend over a horse trough, while Jane still lay naked, pinned down in the hay with the pitchfork, and watching.

When the whipping was over, the father took Jane in his arms. He carried her back to the castle, and tucked her up safely in bed. The father kissed Jane on the forehead and said some prayers over her. He had just experienced a conversion, he said, and the wickedness of his past life was now very awful to him. He would put all three bad brothers into monasteries, as oblates, and reform his own life.

Well, the father did all these things, and he married again, and lived happily. That was in the future, of course. I mean, after the scene in the stable.

But that hot summer night after the scene in the stable Jane couldn't sleep. She couldn't understand it, but somehow she was very excited. She hadn't wanted her bad brothers to thrash her or fuck her, but she'd got quite worked up by the scene. Remember, all her girlhood she'd been shutting out noises from orgies. She'd gone riding out hard on the moors to escape from such things. Now she'd been brought almost face to face with them at the age of 15. It was the 'almost' that was so tantalising. As it happened, Jane hadn't actually caught sight of a prick during the whole caper. She had kicked one of the bad brothers while his legs were still tangled in his trousers. The eldest bad brother had been going to thrash Jane with his clothes still on. The father had not bothered to take down the bad brothers' breeches before giving them the whipping.

Jane lay there in her bed and she couldn't stop thinking about it.

She wept and she wailed, of course. But she couldn't stop thinking about it.

What Jane thought about most was the bulge in her father's breeches.

Had his prick got hard at the sight of her, Jane, his daughter, lying down there in the hay with her dress torn off and the pitchfork prongs on either side of her neck?

Or had it got hard at the whipping of her three bad brothers?

Jane had felt its hardness against her bottom when her father had picked her up.

It had felt harder and far more interesting than any of her saddles. And she had some nice saddles.

Jane wanted to jump out of bed and to go to her father. She wanted to climb into her father's bed and snuggle right up to him. Her brothers were odious. Beasts. She didn't want them. But her father was good. He was strong. He had saved her and loved her. And her father had had that big hard-on. Now Jane wanted him to fuck her.

However, Jane knew that if she went to her father, he'd send her away.

He'd think she was evil and wild, and as bad as her brothers.

Her father had religion now, and Jane knew that she couldn't just go creeping along the corridor and into his room and blow out the candles and jump into bed with him naked and say, *Daddy, please fuck me.* If Jane went and did that, her father would probably thrash her.

Jane got even more hot at the thought of being thrashed by her father. She tossed and she turned in her bed. She tore all the sheets off. The sheets that her father had tucked in. She was all shook up.

Then Jane got up out of bed and went over to her dressing table and she picked up her hairbrush. It was a very fine hairbrush. It had once been her mother's. The hair of the hairbrush was soft yet stiff, badger's hair, and the handle of the hairbrush was long and smooth, ivory, quite thick, with a nice little knob on the end.

Jane got back into bed.

She started rubbing herself with the hairbrush.

First she used the brush part.

She rubbed each little breast. Then her cunt.

She loved the feel of the brush on her breasts, Jane said. It did things to her nipples.

When Jane rubbed at her cunt with the hairbrush she started to feel really horny.

She went over the scene in the stable, inventing new endings. In all of the endings, her father didn't get religion.

Jane toyed with the end of the hairbrush as she rubbed at her cunt.

Then she turned it. She stuck it right in.

Jane's cunt was as wet as you like.

The handle went in with a pop.

Jane brought herself off with the nice little knob on the end of it. As she brought herself off, she imagined the brush was her father. Or, rather, the hard thing in his breeches she'd felt up against her bum when he'd carried her.

That was Jane's story.

Jane lived on in the castle for two years before Faust came.

She hated her stepmother. Her father was always in church. Their castle was crawling with priests now.

Jane tried to seduce one of the priests with a juicy confession on her 16th birthday.

The priest was a pansy, she said.

He gave her 100 Hail Marys, and said it was an insult to badgers.

Jane had no companions, no friends, and she gave up horse-riding.

She went early to bed with her hairbrush most nights, until one night she did it too hard and the handle went and broke.

That was the night before Faust came.

Jane was ripe for the plucking.

Faust plucked her.

Well, I'd listened to all this with four hands on my prick. Marguerite's and Gretchen's. They couldn't speak English. They kept slapping my prick to go down.

When Jane finished her story she pushed them aside and knelt over me.

'That's better,' she said. 'Perhaps you're not queer after all.'

She took my erection in both hands and sat down on it.

I fucked her.

Marguerite and Gretchen were jealous at first.

Then they got horny.

Those little 14-year-old twins played with each other beside us as Jane and me fucked.

Jane was better than Marguerite. And I was improving.

At first she kept shouting out *Daddy!* and *Hairbrush!* but by the time I had finished it was *Kit!*

92

42 Damnation Salvation

One o'clock by my Nuremberg Egg. I'm frazzled, pooped out. I'm exhausted. I've written enough for today.

I know that I ought to say something about this new craziness of the Herr Doktor's.

Mephistopheles sneezing fishes!

And promising Faust a reprieve if he murders the Pope!

Frankly, I've little to say on that subject.

Faust could be pretending, of course. Just making up shit to feed me some reason or excuse for this ridiculous journey.

But his insisting I mustn't tell Helen makes it rather more likely he believes in the fantasy himself.

I doubt if he'll set out for Rome if he *doesn't* believe it.

You can't wake up drunk. And, sober, would he really go all that way because Helen said she saw the Virgin Mary perched on top of a bush promising salvation as wages for his confession to the Pope?

Especially when most of the time he thinks it's damnation that's saved him . . . Snip! Snap! Freedom from what he calls God.

The fact is that drunk people see things, or think that they see things, and hear things, or think that they hear things. Hallucinations. Delusions and derangements of the senses.

They call this *delirium tremens*. The D.T.s. The hoo-hahs.

Faust's had the hoo-hahs for years.

Delirium demens, in his case.

Delirium demons as well.

I mean: Mephistopheles doesn't exist outside the Doktor's own sick head.

The way that I see it is this:

John Faust was a clever theological student who fell in love with the idea of the Devil and wanted to be a magician. Magic, of course, doesn't work, so Faust turned to drink. Drunk, you can think the world's magical. Too drunk, and you start to believe it's *your* doing, the magic. Then, eventually, you start to see things like grey friars that nobody else sees. Hear bells in your ears. All the rest of it.

OK.

This book is the facts of the case.

Let's consider the fancies.

Say Faust is *right* . . .

Say what he believes is all true. Then I could write the end of this book now, couldn't I?

The Devil will come.

And Faustus must be damned. (Saved, by his reckoning.)

Well, the Devil *won't* come.

Why not?

Because the Devil can't.

The Devil is dead and buried in Schlaraffenlande.

Or:

Say Helen is *right* . . .

Say what Helen believes is all true. Then I could still write the end of this book now, couldn't I? A different ending. But equally ordained. Predictable.

The Pope will absolve our hero.

Faustus will be saved. (Damned, by his reckoning.)

There'll be high jinks in heaven.

God will be rubbing his hands.

Well, God *won't* be rubbing his hands.

Why not?

Because he hasn't got hands to rub.

Look, God, no hands.

Look, Hans, no God.

I'm writing this book because neither Faust nor Helen *can* be right. No damnation. No salvation. People who believe in such stuff say 'It is written', don't they? Meaning there's some Great Book in which we're all characters. Meaning there's some over-all Fate which determines our lives.

Well, there is no such Fate. No Great Book. And 'it' isn't 'written'. I'm writing it . . . Just a little book.

Well, I would be. But I'm falling asleep.

43 Jumping Apple

I must set this down carefully.

After writing the last words of the last chapter, I put the cloth over Akercocke's cage. I blew out my candle. I got into my bed and I slept.

I slept for precisely 4 hours 15 minutes.

I dreamt no dreams. I don't dream.

Then, at 5.30 this morning, 1st March, Faust Year 24, I was woken.

I heard this odd bumping and thumping. It broke into my sleep.

I opened my eyes.

It was dark.

The bumping went on.

It was not at the door or the window. It was here in my room.

I thought it was Akercocke mucking about in his cage.

'Shut up, monkey!' I shouted.

The bumping went on.

I threw a book at him. It was Machiavelli's *Florentine Histories*. (I regret having thrown it. I'm fond of that book. The cage damaged the spine.)

Well, the bumping went on.

It didn't sound like Akercocke. Too regular. Too sensible.

That rat, I decided.

So I lit my candle.

I held it aloft in my left hand. I peered from my bed.

No rat. Room quite normal. Just Akercocke gibbering now under the cloth, woken up by Machiavelli. And the bumping went on.

Then I saw what it was.

I can't quite explain this. I saw what it was.

There's this apple.

It sat on my desk.

A perfectly ordinary eating apple.

A Blenheim Pippin.

I keep a small barrel of Blenheim Pippins beside my desk. I

like the smell of them. I like now and then to eat one. I must have taken one out of the barrel last night and set it there on my desk. Just touching or stroking an apple, just polishing it on your sleeve, is nice when you're writing or reading. That's what I must have done yesterday. There were certainly no tooth marks in this particular apple. I hadn't had a bite of it.

This apple was doing the bumping.

This thumping sound was the apple.

The apple was jumping up and down! Up and down there on my desk! All on its own. Up and down. Up and down. Like a ball being bounced by an unseen hand. Quite ridiculous. Each ridiculous impossible jump taking the apple 6 inches up in the air, then bringing it down with the regular thump that had woken me.

Well, I couldn't believe my own eyes.

I held up the candle. I watched it.

As I watched it, the apple jumped down from the desk.

It hopped round my room. Like a frog.

From the desk to the window, from the window to the door, from the door in a circle round Akercocke's cage, from the cage right up on to my chair, from the chair back on top of the desk again.

Bouncing.

Bumping.

Never more than 6 inches. Never less.

I couldn't believe I was seeing this.

I thought I was dreaming.

I wasn't.

I, Wagner, don't dream. I'm no dreamer.

But I *thought* I was dreaming. That's the point. I thought I was worn out with yesterday's writing, that my wits had been addled by Faust and his stories, that I was still fast asleep and just dreaming this impossible thing.

So I blew out the candle. I lay back on my pillow. I stuck both my thumbs in my ears.

OK. That was absurd.

But it was no more absurd than what happened next . . .

The apple jumped down from my desk with a terrible thump. It bounced over the room in the dark. It came nearer and nearer.

'Fuck off, apple!' I shouted.

So it hit me.

This apple went and hit me on the nose!

I got out of bed. I lit all the candles. I could only find four.

By the light of four candles, I inspected the apple.

It lay quiet and still on the floor now. No more bumping or jumping. Quite normal.

I kicked it.

It rolled.

Just an apple.

I picked it up in my hand.

Blenheim Pippin.

An ordinary apple. Red on one side. Green the other side. Quite comfortably cold to the touch. Its stalk just the same as stalks are.

So what did I do then?

I ate it.

I ate every last bit of the bastard.

Skin, pips, stalk and all. I have eaten the apple.

I have no time for rumpelgeists, thank you.

44   Pregnant Bishop

So here I sit, pen in fist, writing about a bruise on my nose the cause of which I don't believe in.

No kidding. I feel about as stupid as that Bishop of Bamberg in the story Luther tells. This bishop was always crawling on all fours at the court of Giovanni de' Medici, 2nd son of Lorenzo the so-called 'Magnificent', elected Pope Leo 10 in 1513. Which would be Faust Year Minus 3. (And at this rate I'll go mad if I don't watch it.)

Anyway, this Bishop of Bamberg went into hospital with stomach cramps on the way home to Bavaria after a particularly heavy session at the Vatican in Good Pope Leo's Golden Days. His belly swells. The doctors tell him for a joke that he is pregnant. Our Bamberger doesn't quite believe it – not until they present him with the newborn baby of a nun who dies in childbirth, informing him they delivered the boy in his sleep. Said silly bishop brings up the child as his 'nephew'.

Years later, on his deathbed, he calls the nephew to him.

'My boy,' says he, 'there's something I must tell you. You've always called me uncle, but I'm not.'

97

'I guessed,' says the lad. 'You're really my father, aren't you?'

'No,' says the Bamberg bishop, shaking his head. 'Look, I'm going to die. And it's time that you knew the truth. I'm not really your uncle or your father. I'm your mother!'

'Holy cow!' says the lad. 'So who can my father be?'

'Your father?' croaks the bishop, expiring. '*Your father was His Holiness the Pope!*'

Well, I feel as fucked-up as that.

The hell with all jumping apples.

(I've put the lid back on the barrel.)

45   The Half-God of Heidelberg

I've just been looking over what I've written, since I'm not going to get back to sleep now.

I see that I've left some facts out.

Important things, maybe. Who knows?

I must get this stuff down before dawn. Just in case, at dawn, we *do* leave for Rome. Will we? This perfectly lunatic journey? That's up to John Faust. The Tower is still. He must be sleeping.

The Tower is still . . .

But we *are* stuck on a ledge half way up the Schlossberg. Could that 'jumping' apple have been caused by some underground *subsidence*? That's it. Very likely. This Tower is a fucking romantic shambles. I shan't give a damn if it falls down completely while we're away.

First important fact I've left out, then.

There's a second *historical reference* to the Herr Doktor. (I mean, following in point of time the one made by that Abbot Trithemius, which I quoted in chapter 11.)

This 2nd historical reference occurs in another letter, again written in Latin.

I'll translate it:

'A week ago there came to Erfurt this trickster who calls himself Georgius Faustus, *Helmitheus Hedebergensis* – an incredible braggart, a fool. The things this man says! The claims that he makes! Such conceit! Common people here marvel at him, but the priests should know better. I saw him. I hearddd him. He was drunk. He was throwing his weight about, boasting about

98

the "miracles" he can do. I didn't say a word. Should I have done? Should I bother my head that others can be such great fools?'

This letter is dated 7th October, 1513. The Herr Doktor was then 33. Three years before his alleged 'pact' following the alleged events in Spisser's Wood, etc.

The interesting thing is that the letter I quote was written by Conrad Mutian, a cultured and clever man, one of the best of our German Humanists.

Conrad Mutian was born in Homberg (1471, the same year the first observatory in Europe was built at Nuremberg, designed by Regiomontanus), the intelligent son of intelligent parents. He went to school at Deventer under Alex Hegius, where he had Erasmus beside him in class. He travelled a lot. I believe he took his degree in canon law at Bologna.

At the time when this letter was written, Mutian was Canon at Gotha, in Thuringia.

They make good sausages in Gotha.

Gotha sausage was eaten by Charlemagne.

Mutian is real.

He was as real as a Gotha sausage.

I mean, Conrad Mutian existed.

He proved it by dying – he died on Good Friday, 30th March, Faust Year 10.

In the name of all that's good Gotha sausage! Why am I looking this up in my books?

Because sometimes I think I dream Faust.

I don't dream when I sleep. Do I dream when I'm waking?

I mean: Here I sit, here I am, writing these words by a windowsill, four candles for company in the before-dawn dark, in a Tower that Faust claims was built by the Devil (or the Devil's estate agent in these parts, which amounts to the same trash), and before long I shall probably be riding off to Rome with this man on some pixilated pilgrimage which will be (take your pick) either to

a) confess all his sins to the Pope and evade being claimed by the Devil in 40 days time; or

b) murder the same Pope and be rewarded with another 24 years sunburn by the same Devil . . .

! ! !

And we'll journey to Rome with this compulsive hiccuping liar he calls Helen of Troy . . .

Jesus Christ, I'm surrounded by nut cases!

99

So. Mutian's letter above. That's authentic. That's real. I cling fast to these written memorials. Other people's evidence of Faust. Do you blame me? Else I think I have dreamt him. Some nightmare!

They called Mutian, Mutianus. It was the fashion with those chaps. Everybody Latinized his name. Including John Faust = Faustus. Conrad Mutianus Rufus. The Rufus because he had red hair. Thank Christ for his carrot head, I say. It makes him a bit real, doesn't it?

Mutian. My red-headed colleague in Faust-watching. He was an influential guy in the circle that included Eoban Hess, Crotus Rubeanus, Justus Jonas and a whole heap of others who certainly weren't idiots. He was the centre, the prime mover of the Mutianscher Bund, which opposed the nit-picking metaphysical Scholastics and favoured common sense. He was behind the *Epistolae Obscurorum Virorum* – the *Letters of Obscure Men*, that satire which makes fun of Christians who strain their wits to determine such weighty matters as whether eating an egg on a Friday is a *venial* or a *mortal* sin . . . My ruddy Mutian was an early friend of Luther's, though he parted company with the Constipator when Luther started dieting on worms.

OK. So what about the letter?

It tallies at all points with Trithemius.

That's what about the letter.

It shows, Conrad Mutian's letter, that:

1) the Herr Doktor existed;

2) some other guy who met him thought he was a trickster and a fool.

I take small crumbs of comfort from this.

If I don't keep reminding myself of Faust's historical reality, I could end up in the booby hatch.

If I don't keep putting such *facts* down on paper, I begin to wonder if I'm writing about a ghost, a spook, a legend, some creature I invented.

Well, I haven't invented him. He's beyond my imaginative range.

I call Mutian Mutianus as my witness.

Always believe a witness with red hair.

One phrase in that letter used to puzzle me.

Helmitheus Hedebergensis.

What the hell does that mean?

Well, I reckon Mutian's got it just slightly wrong. I think Faust called himself *Hemitheus Hedelbergensis*.

Hemitheus. The half-god.

Hedelbergensis. Of Heidelberg.

The half-god of Heidelberg.

That sounds very like the Herr Quack.

O mute Mutian, dead red sceptic, will we really go to Rome today?

Are we really here now?

46   More Facts

*I'*m really here today. I'm writing this now. The sun's not far below the forest. It's Thursday, 1st March, 1540, and fuck Faust Years. If I put my finger in the candleflame it will hurt me. If I take a shit it will with luck turn out brown. I write words down here, black marks on white paper, to make sense of what's happened, what's happening. Someone's got to make sense of the story of John Faust. It won't be John Faust.

Next important thing I've left out, then.

A couple of months ago, at this year's turning, immediately after the 'resurrection' with the china-blue eyes at Christmas, I began to brood over the whole question of the Herr Fart's identity.

Who is Faust? And what is he?

I pursued my own investigations.

Thus, I dug up Trithemius.

Thus, I dug up Mutian.

And, thus, I've got two other bits of *hard historical fact* to give you.

1) An entry in the account book of the aforementioned Bishop of Bamberg (known to his friends and nephews as Soapy Sam). This entry was made by his chamberlain. Dated 12th February, 1520. It runs like this:

'Item: 10 silver dalers paid to Doktor Faustus *philosophus* in return for his having cast for my master a nativity or *indicium.*'

2) Something found for me at Ingolstadt. (That's right. Where we were when the boss seemed to take us flying through the air to King Henry the 8th's 3rd damned wedding.) This is sober stuff. From the Minutes of the Ingolstadt Town Council. I quote:

'Today, Wednesday after St Vitus,* 1528, the man who calls himself Dr Faustus of Heidelberg has been ordered to spend his pfennig elsewhere, and has given his word that he will.'

Something common to both these references.

Money.

Doktor Faustus *philosophus* was given 10 dalers by the Bishop of Bamberg for casting a horoscope.

If Dr Faustus had to 'spend his pfennig' elsewhere than Ingolstadt the inference to be drawn is that the Town Council of Ingolstadt had *paid* him that same 'pfennig'.

Something else.

These last two references date from 1520 and 1528.

That's after Spisser's Wood. After the 'pact'.

Faust Year 4 and Faust Year 12, respectively.

Notice another thing?

Neither of them calls Faust a fool or a charlatan. The tone has changed utterly.

Did he *really* have some powers then – post-'pact', post-'Mephistopheles' – that people would pay him good money for? A bishop? (Even a queer bishop.) A Town Council? (Even a Catholic Town Council.) The Church? The State? Forking out cash for Faust's magical services?

I can't believe it.

I don't have to believe it.

But I believe that *they* believed it – Soapy Sam, the ants of Ingolstadt – and that they paid up all right for what he kidded them were necromantic services rendered. Then, in the case of the Town Council, they wanted him out of the way.

Why should that be? Why did the Doktor's presence embarras the authorities?

Christ knows.

I must ask him.

Ask Faust, I mean.

Mem: On the road to Rome, try and get *his* side of these accounts.

Viz: Was that horoscope for the bishop or his 'son'? What great work did Faust do at Ingolstadt?

It will pass the time, won't it?

Talking of which, I don't have much.

* St Vitus Day is 15th June. His relics are at Corvey Abbey in Westphalia. His emblem is a cock.

3rd and last important thing that hasn't gone into this book yet, and should have done.

Akercocke.

47   Akercocke

Akercocke is my monkey. I hate him.

Akercocke sits in the cage in the corner of this room. He's watching me now as I write. Bright beady eyes. This cowl of hair. A Capuchin monkey.

I loathe having to include Akercocke in this book. Which is why I've resisted the subject till now. Just writing down the name of that creature upon the page gives me the shudders.

Why?

To say why is to say how I got him.

It was last Easter, the start of Faust Year 24.

The Herr Candlegrease drew up a Will.

Under the terms of this Will (drawn up before a notary from Freiburg and duly witnessed), I, Christopher Wagner, inherit the following:

Item. This Tower, this maze, this shrubbery.

Item. 1600 dalers.

Item. A dairy farm. (I've never seen this! Is the half-god a dairy farmer too?)

Item. Faust's gold chain, his much-licked bloodstone, the contents of this household.

Big deal.

Now, when Faust had made this Will, he called me to him.

'Son,' he said. 'I want to leave you something else.'

'Like what?' I said.

'Like what would you like?' he asked me.

'You mean *anything*?'

'I mean anything I have,' he said.

I thought for a bit.

Then I said the stupidest pinheaded thing I've ever said.

Not a day has gone by since, without my regretting it.

'Leave me your cunning,' I said.

What the hell did I mean by that? I don't know. I don't know why I said it. Immediately the words were out of my mouth, I tried to withdraw them.

'I just mean your books,' I explained.

'Kit,' Faust said. 'You're frightened. You *don't* mean my books. All my books are already yours, under the Will as it stands. Last item. On my death, you inherit my library under that heading "the contents of this household". I know what you meant by asking for my cunning. I know better than you know what you meant by that.'

'O God! O Christ! O fuck!' I said. 'Just forget it.'

Faust didn't forget it.

Three days passed.

On the third day's night, he said to me:

'Now, Kit, concerning this matter of the spirit you required . . .'

'What spirit?' I said.

'When you asked me to leave you my cunning,' Faust said, 'you meant that you wanted a spirit to do your bidding. Like my Mephistopheles.'

'I most certainly didn't!' I said.

'You did, Kit,' he said.

Well, I swear I never wanted any spirit. God damn it all, I don't *believe* in spirits! And even if spirits exist – which they do not – even if spirits exist, I'd very much prefer it if they just left me alone. To be excused from visions, that's my motto.

Then Faust produced this cage, with this monkey in it.

'There you go,' he said. 'I grant your request.'

'A monkey?' I said.

'Akercocke,' Faust said.

'You equate your cunning with a fucking monkey?'

Faust grinned.

'Shall I let Akercocke out of the cage?' he said.

I shook my head.

'Why not?' he said. His hand was playing with the latch.

'He looks nasty,' I said. 'He looks capable of anything. Don't let him out, please!'

Akercocke. He looked out of that cage at me just like he looks at me now. Just like he always looks. Evil and horrible. He's black and he's small and foul-smelling. He's got a tail like Faust's prick, only bigger.

Akercocke lives on eggs and young birds. Also fruit, shoots, and insects. Being his keeper, I have to feed him. I don't like doing this. Once I made a mistake. I gave him a bird not quite dead. Usually I snap their necks first. But this fledgeling was living. Akercocke played with the bird for an hour, like a cat with a mouse. There was nothing I could do. I beat on the cage with a stick, but there was no way to stop it. Akercocke picked the wings off, one at a time. Then he twisted its head off. He ate the whole lot in two handfuls, but that was much later.

I take care not to touch him, not to let my fingers into the cage when I feed him. He looks like he'd bite both my thumbs off, if he got the chance.

Twice, I've tried to poison him.

The poison didn't work.

Akercocke thrived on it.

I don't believe Akercocke's a spirit.

I do believe he's vile though.

Akercocke's evil right through.

Can a monkey be evil?

Akercocke can.

Akercocke *is*.

The Herr Fuck-up never had any intention of unlatching that cage. He was just teasing me.

He took his hand from it.

'You're wise, Kit,' Faust said. 'Wise not to want Akercocke out of the cage.'

He wiped his hand on his cloak.

'A word to the wise,' he went on. '*Never* let Akercocke out of his cage. Not until I am dead. Will you promise me that?'

'No trouble,' I said. 'It's easy to promise. I've no intention of letting that creature out of that cage *ever*, whether you're dead or alive. I want nothing to do with him. Send him back where he came from.'

'I'm afraid that isn't possible,' Faust said.

He grinned his horrible grin.

'Well, *you* keep him,' I said.

'He's all yours, son,' Faust said.

And he forced me to take the cage.

He compelled it into my hand.

I don't know how he did that, but he did.

Like I say, I've tried to get rid of Akercocke. But so far no joy.

Thank Christ, I shall be out of reach of his evil eyes on the road to Rome!

There he sits watching me.

Akercocke.

Eyes as hard and bright as the Devil's shit.

Watching me all the time.

I put the cloth on the cage every night. Black cloth, thick cloth, camlet. Akercocke's always looking at me when I put the cloth on the cage, and when I take it off there he always is, still watching. Why should he do that? Spite. His eyes are full of it. He knows I don't like him staring at me. That's why he stares at me. It's no good covering the cage with the cloth while I'm up and awake, either. I've tried that. He makes such a racket – squealing and scratching, rasping his claws in the filth in the bottom of the cage, his nails down the bars – that I have to take the cloth off eventually. Then he just sits there. Staring.

He's watching my hand as I'm writing.

Enough about Akercocke.

I shan't mention him again.

I've made a good plan for this book on the journey. I'm going to pack every page that I've written in a tin container, and wrap the tin container in waxed cloth with seals, and carry the lot with me in a well-corded box. I have this big ointment box which won't cause suspicion. I shall take plenty of fresh vellum too, and fine cotton-paper, so that when I get the chance —

Jesus Christ!

I just remembered something else.

How come I forgot this?

When Faust gave me Akercocke, he said something else (which just this minute came back into my head, and God knows I must be tired to have forgotten it).

'Kit,' he said. 'You will publish my story. All of it. All I have done and will do. You will write it in a history. And if you can't recall it all, your spirit Akercocke will help you!'

I'd clean forgotten that.

I thought I was writing this book for quite another reason.

I *am* writing this book for quite another reason, aren't I?

And Akercocke's not helping me.

Akercocke couldn't help me.

Akercocke's a monkey.

A perfectly ordinary horrible fucking lousy Capuchin monkey.

Akercocke —

They're shouting below. The sun's over the rim of the forest. It's Faust. He's shouting for me. He's shouting out:

'*Rome!*'

Part 2

The Road to Rome

1 Ta-ta, Tower

What a circus we looked! What a gang!

Like some sort of unholy family.

Two men and eight women. 20 horses. One horse to ride and one horse to rest each day. Turnabout for the horses, riding and portage. Black horses, grey horses, one sorrel, one dapple, two roans.

My own mount was a pocket stallion, Arab blood in his sticking-out veins, skinny, but as tough as a pair of old boots.

I shod him with 8 sharp nails and 3 blunt nails in each hoof. That's what they say you should do for rough roads.

I carried two pistols, as well as my sword.

The first pistol, from Pistoia in Tuscany, where these things got their name, is one of the new-fangled jobs. Short single barrel, butt lengthened out in a line with it almost. This butt has the maker's name cut in it: Caminelleo Vitelli.

My second pistol, more cumbersome, I stuck in the saddle of my pack horse. This one is an old-fashioned wheel-lock, German in origin, rather nice, ornamented, heavy, reliable enough at up to 12 paces.

My sword, which I wore at my side, is a rapier. Long tapering blade, gauntlet hilt, a point as quick, sharp and deadly as the Devil's own prick, Toledo steel.

Not exactly pilgrim equipment?

But then Faust himself came out armed to the teeth. He had two swords, one dangling from each hip, and a greater thicket of daggers and stabbers in his belt and his braces than I ever saw on one man in my life.

An enormous black hat on his head.

He also had a dab of fresh butter smeared over his boil, and may even have waxed his moustaches. They bristled in the frosty morning air like the antennae of some particularly poisonous insect.

'Ropes,' he said. 'Salt. Spoons. Wand. Ginger.'

He had this inventory in his paw.

I was supposed to check the pack horses.

'Cooking pots,' Faust said. 'Bills of credit. Oranges. Oatmeal. Tinder box. Kyphi. Beans. Biscuits.'

'Check,' I said.

'Medicines,' Faust said.

'In my ointment chest,' I said.

'Where is it?' Faust said. 'I don't see it.'

'On my horse there,' I said.

'On the horse you are *riding*?'

'That's right. You never know, do you?' I said. Then I changed the subject: 'Aren't you taking your books?'

'Are you joking?' Faust sneered. 'I know all my books off by heart.'

By this time, the 7 girls were prettily mounted, side-saddle (save Jane), and all fretting to go. Horses whinnying. Horses steaming and stamping and dunging. Girls giggling and chattering in 7 different tongues. No communication, save between each separate girl and me.

Then:

'The Eternal Feminine!' cried Faust.

'Fuck a duck,' Jane remarked.

I looked round.

This blonde wraith in the door of the Tower.

It was Helen.

She was wearing a sort of high-class nun's outfit. This luxurious grey silk habit with a golden girdle round her pinched-in waist. There was a red cross emblazoned on the habit, the arms of the cross reaching out to point scarlet fingers in the general direction of her tits. The broad-brimmed floppy blue hat with the crossed keys of St Peter on the front completed the vision. She carried a crook in her hand. The crook had sky-blue ribbons tied to it.

Fancy pilgrim gear with a touch of the Little Bo Peeps.

Ho hum.

Bad enough.

But she was lugging a great trunk behind her.

'What's that?' Faust demanded.

'Just my wardrobe,' said Helen.

She was panting. She whacked at the trunk with her crook.

'This isn't a ball,' Faust declared.

'I know very well what it is!'

'And it isn't a picnic either . . .'

Helen put on her patient face.

'I didn't say it was, my beloved. If we were going on a picnic then I'd wear just my simplest frock, of course.' She prodded the trunk with the crook. 'I shall need various changes of clothes, shan't I, John? You will want me to look my best, dearest.'

Faust bent down and lifted the trunk.

He groaned.

His knees buckled.

I helped him.

Somehow we got the thing strapped to the flanks of the stoutest pack horse.

'You must have a gown in here for every conceivable occasion,' I observed.

Helen blushed.

I gather she dislikes that word *conceivable*.

Helen's horse was a Lippizaner. A pretty grey nag. Velvet nostrils.

It didn't like the Little Bo Peep crook.

So we strapped that to the pack horse as well.

The Herr Doktor inspected his caravan.

'One missing,' he said.

I counted my girls.

Jane. Justine. Zuleika. Salome. Nadja. Marguerite and Gretchen.

All present.

All lovely.

But Faust had gone into the Tower.

When he came back, guess what?

He was carrying Akercocke in his brass cage!

'That monkey's not coming,' I said.

'Yes, he is.'

'No, he isn't!'

'Akercocke's coming,' Faust said.

'Over my dead body,' I said.

I drew my sword. (I admit I was showing off, just to impress the girls.)

'One day,' Faust observed, 'that is just what he will do.'

'Do what?' I demanded.

'Come,' Faust said, grinning.

'Over your dead body,' Faust said, crossing his eyes.

I felt sick. I could see Faust was in a foul mood. As yet, he had hardly begun his day's drinking. He had these three flasks hanging round his waist from a belt. There were another three flasks attached to the mane of his horse. His horse was a black horse, of course. Black as pitch. Dip-backed and gone in the tooth. Faust was wearing his usual black cloak.

I sheathed my bright rapier. I shrugged.

'First round to the master,' Jane said.

I ignored her.

So Akercocke, scratching, picking his teeth, was heaved up on the back of another of the pack horses. He sat there staring at me through the bars of his cage with a kind of black triumph in his shitty little eyes. He looked like some dwarfed Roman emperor setting out for the Colosseum to enjoy the latest martyrdoms.

Then Helen said:

'John . . .'

'What is it?'

Helen sniffed. She was powdering her nose and reviewing her thin pencilled eyebrows in a tiny hand mirror.

'That cloak, John.'

'Cloak?'

Faust swung into his saddle with difficulty. He loathes horse-riding. The horse always knows it. Whatever he's riding, the beast gives the old magus hell at some point on the way.

'It's disgusting,' said Helen. 'It's filthy.'

'It's my cloak,' Faust said.

Helen's face was a passion of long-suffering patience.

'Darling,' she said, 'you should have sent it to the cleaners.'

'No time,' Faust said. 'No time for the cleaners.'

'In that case,' said Helen, putting away her powder puff and favouring him with her severe smile. 'In that case, my angel, I insist that you wear something else.'

'I don't have another cloak,' Faust snapped. '*This* is my cloak, and I wear it.'

'You'll catch cold,' Helen said. 'I mean – up there in the Swiss Alps and all.' She shivered. She patted her hat.

Faust slapped with his reins.

'To Rome!' he announced.

He was standing bolt-upright in his stirrups. He dug into his horse with his spurs. The horse stood stock-still for a second, then it galloped straight into the maze.

We waited five minutes before they came out again.

Jane swore.

Helen sighed at her riding mitts.

I whistled.

Nadja was tapping a rat-a-tat-tat on her drum. She has this small drum, bound with goatskin. It was strapped to the pommel of her saddle.

When the Herr Doktor came out of the maze he was covered with cuckoo-spit. Bits of privet stuck in his white hair. His horse had a mouthful of stuff that it shouldn't have been munching.

Nadja finger-spanked a wry crescendo on her drum.

Zuleika and Salome giggled.

Helen just sat there, hands folded, smiling between the pricked ears of her horse, as though she had fixed the whole incident just to make Faust look ridiculous.

'Bugger equitation,' Faust said.

He sneezed out some privet that was protruding from his nostrils like little curly horns. He went back in the maze for his hat.

Helen called after him:

'You promise me, darling? You give me your word that you'll take that ghastly cloak to the cleaners in Rome? Before you do anything else in that Holy City?'

'Oh fuck off,' Faust said, coming back.

Helen glanced at my beauties. They were laughing. I guess they've picked up that word *fuck* from one thing and another in the three years they've been here.

'John,' Helen said firmly, lips pursed. 'I'm not setting foot from this Tower until you give me your solemn oath that you'll not disgrace me in Rome in that disgusting cloak.'

Faust spat at a wagtail hopping about on the cobbles.

He missed.

'I'll have it cleaned,' he muttered.

'First thing?' Helen said.

'I'll wash it myself in the Tiber,' Faust promised.

Helen nodded, content.

I winked at the Doktor. He glared. His eyes were deep-sunken and bloodshot, with pouchy black bags under them. He took a long pull at his flask.

Helen's never been to Rome, evidently.

Helen doesn't know the state of the Tiber.

'Very well,' Helen said. 'Let us pray.'

So she prayed at us all for ten minutes.

Nobody offered Amen.

When Helen stopped stroking her crucifix and slapping herself in the tits, Faust stood up again in the stirrups. This time he was circumspect with his spurs. But he did unsheath one of his swords. He waved it three times in the pale morning sunlight. It was nice. Really nice. I liked that.

'To Rome then!' Faust cried.

We rode forth.

2   Black Forest

We never touched Freiburg. No need. We took the road down to the Rhine, and then followed it southwards. Nine o'clock by my Nuremberg Egg when we picked up the river. Broad blue-silver surfaces glinting in bright morning sun. Through foothills, between green spring fields. Hawks and buzzards. This March tang in the air.

Just past Hartheim we met men driving cattle to market. They got into the ditch and stared at us, straws in their mouths. I guess we looked comic. Faust in his black cloak, plus brandy flasks, with a horse he could hardly control. Helen with her 'vision' face on. Me in my red cloak, tanned boots, with a new scarlet cap on my head. The girls all wearing their various national costumes. Salome looked especially delicious. Silk chemise. A ruby in the middle of her forehead. One of the cattlemen whistled. 'Get off and milk it!' he bawled. I drew my rapier, but Faust shook his head. We rode on. We followed the meandering Rhine.

I could see Jane was enjoying herself.

'Just like old times,' she said, jogging up and down there beside me, face flushed for a change, hair blown back. Like I say, Jane doesn't ride side-saddle.

About noon we came to one of those execution wheels.

It was big. It stood right by the side of the Rhine, leaning out from the bank. There was a broken-boned body pinned on it. Mostly skeleton. Some patches the crows hadn't eaten.

Faust's horse wasn't keen on the sight. It skittered about, eyeballs bulging.

'Steady on there!' the great magus said nervously.

He ended up making a detour, with copious sucks at his brandy flask, and even then the horse crab-walked fast when it got parallel with the wheel some twenty yards away in a meadow all blazing with buttercups. We're having a nice forward spring.

I trotted up alongside our Helen as we went past the wheel. She was crossing herself, eyes cast down.

'Come off it,' I said.

'Not you,' she hissed briefly. 'That *thing!*'

'Some robber,' I said. 'Just some outlaw.'

Helen didn't respond for a mile.

Then she said:

'Are there lots of them this way?'

'Pooh, only a few hundred,' I said.

We passed into the Black Forest again. The road takes that route. God knows why.

It was shadowy there in the forest. Oak. Beech. Dense dark firs. I don't like the Black Forest, but then it's got mixed up in my mind with having to find food for Akercocke. I rode all the time with at least three of the girls between my horse and that Capuchin evil clutching fast to the bars of his cage.

I must say I never heard Helen complain. She was scared, but she didn't start screeching or wailing. When she looked round, she was doing her brave face. She's not a bad actress, our Helen. She rode close by Faust all the same.

3   Holy Goat

In the middle of the way through the forest we met this old woman.

She stood at a crossroads, right under a spreading elm tree. Coarse gown and no shoes. She was holding a tray in her hands. Scraggy crocodile hands, veined and wrinkled. Her hands looked like roots of the tree.

'Going far?' she called out.

'Far enough,' Faust replied. He was drinking.

'To Rome,' Helen said, with a smirk.

Now that was a serious mistake.

Never exchange more than the time of day with a stranger. Especially not in a forest.

(And give the *wrong* time, if you can. Though agree with their view of the weather.)

Before the Herr Doktor could draw either of his two swords – while he was getting himself into a knot, in fact, going for both of them at once with conspicuous lack of accuracy – the crone had her fingers entwined in the mane of Helen's Lippizaner. Then it was the bridle she snatched.

Scarlet bridle.

Grey horse.

Ancient hand.

'Rome, is it?' she cried. 'Pilgrims, no less? You'll need these!'

She was rattling her tray with her other hand.

That tray contained trinkets. Cheap rubbish. All stolen from Freiburg, no doubt. Or fallen off the back of a waggon.

I fingered my Vitelli pistol and looked round for robbers. I reckoned this pedlar was just mouldy old bait in a trap.

'Let go there,' Faust said. He unsheathed one sword with much clumsiness, nicking the ear of his horse and dropping a half-empty flask. 'Let go, or I'll cut off your hand!'

The old woman cackled.

'Oh, sir!' she said girlishly.

Faust swiped with his sword.

Missed, of course.

'You'd better not do that,' the woman advised him.

'Why not?'

Faust was staring at his sword as if there was something wrong with it. With his free hand, he bristled one tassel of his moustaches. He looked like some ham in a miracle play. King Herod, perhaps.

'Because Rome's a long way,' the crone said. She switched her attention to Helen. 'You're a long way from Rome, pretty lady. A long wicked way. A bad world. You'll need amulets, dear. Buy my amulets?'

She jingled the junk in the tray.

'Lucky charms for your journey,' she said.

Helen petted her crucifix doubtfully.

'Each one blessed by the bishop,' the crone said.

116

I slipped out my pistol.

Faust stopped me.

'Which bishop?' he said, with a grunt.

The old woman grinned toothlessly. First she grinned at me putting the pistol away. Then she grinned as her eyes went like weasels through the leaves that half-covered her feet.

'The Bishop of Septentrio,' she said.

Faust fell from his horse.

He rolled over.

When he got up, he seized the tin tray.

'We'll have them,' he said. 'All your amulets.'

The crone backed away. This was more than she'd bargained for. 'You can't take the lot,' she was muttering. 'There's others to think about. It'll ruin my trade just to –'

'How much?' Faust demanded.

Helen frowned. 'We don't need them,' she said. 'We're protected, John. You *know* we're protected. Besides, I've never heard of the Bishop of Septentrio! He might be a heretic, or worse!'

'Fifty dalers to you,' the crone said.

The price was outrageous. Plain mad.

But the Herr Idiot undid his money bag. He poured dalers like water all round him. The old woman went down on her knees.

'Bless you, lady,' she said. 'Bless you, sir. May your pilgrimage take you to heaven!'

'You can keep the change,' Faust said.

He scrambled back on to his horse.

He gave me the tray.

It was just as I'd guessed: pinchbeck trash.

We rode on.

When we'd turned the first bend in the road, where it starts to twist out of the forest, Faust held up his arm. He was drunk as a wheelbarrow by now. Eyes pickled with tears. Eyebrows thickened with sweat like bad bladderwrack. He's got eyebrows you'd think you could pop, like those black grapes you find tangled in weed from a very high tide.

'Kit,' Faust announced, between sucks at his brandy flask. 'Kit, give us an amulet each.'

I whistled.

I handed out amulets.

Jane turned up her lah-di-dah nose.

Nadja flared her fine nostrils. She's got these superb Russian nostrils. Rather better than those on her horse.

'Fifty dalers,' I said. 'You were swindled.'

Faust shrugged.

'That woman,' he said, 'was a witch.'

'Do me a favour!'

'A witch,' Faust said, nodding and dribbling. 'I know what I talk about.'

Helen fingered her amulet as if it was hot.

'Wear it,' Faust said. 'For protection.'

He snapped his on his own filthy wrist. A shaft of sunlight through the tall trees made it shine, or tried to. The amulet was so tawdry it couldn't do much in the way of shining.

'A witch in a wood,' I said, laughing.

'Septentrio,' Faust said. 'Think about it.'

Helen powdered her nose. I could see that she didn't know what to think. A state of mind surely not foreign to her.

Then this pious light dawned in her eyes.

'A holy peasant,' she said.

'Holy goat,' I said.

I chucked my amulet into the undergrowth.

'One of the meek who shall inherit the earth,' Helen said.

'Pretty soon, too,' I said. 'At fifty dalers a time.'

Helen ignored me. She clasped on her amulet. She studied its look on her right wrist. It didn't look nice. So she put the thing onto her left wrist. It looked just as bad there, but she beamed satisfaction.

My girls were consulting me doubtfully, a babble of tongues. Sweet babble. I often enjoy it. Not this time.

The Herr Doktor drew one of his swords. He held it to my throat, hand trembling.

'You will retrieve,' he said thickly.

'Do what?'

'Retrieve what you so ignorantly flung from you,' snarled Faust.

Helen liked this high-falutin crap.

I didn't. I didn't like it at all.

Besides, the sword was tickling my throat.

'Get stuffed,' I said.

'Dismount, sir,' Faust said.

The point of his sword was biting my Adam's apple.

I glanced down. There was a trickle of blood on my best shirt. Faust stared at me crazily.

'Septentrio, my son, Septentrio!'

His breath would have turned a skunk pale.

I made an issue of opening my jampot, and sticking more jam up my nose.

Then I went and found the wretched amulet where it had fallen among brambles.

I swung into the saddle again. I sought to make my swing look insouciant, for the girls' sake, especially Jane.

'On your wrist, Kit,' Faust said.

'Second round to the master,' Jane said.

4   Something to Do with an Amulet

So I wear this plated bangle on my wrist as I write these words concerning our first day on the road to Rome.

I write them at Mullheim, where we rest for tonight at the inn. Having covered a measly 20 miles since we started. But then our Helen gave up being brave soon after we emerged from the Black Forest and continued our way down the banks of the Rhine. Rather, her backside was aching.

As for Faust, he was so pissed by this afternoon that a decent long ride this first day was never really on the cards. He was trotting up and down in the saddle, clanking his brandy flasks, when his horse was just ambling, half-asleep in the spring sunshine. Poor horse. I could see it had got the bad news.

Never mind.

A bangle has its uses.

Tonight Nadja came to me in my bed at this inn.

Nadja's thing is wanking.

She won't let me touch her. She's as cold as an icicle. She detests it if I lay a hand on her. She likes to lay her hands on me.

Nadja loves to sit astride me, stark naked, her hair round her shoulders like a harvest, and to play with my cock till I come.

Nadja's got these strong hands, long fingers.

The hands of a Russian princess.

Nadja likes nothing better in this god-forsaken abortion of a world than to sit on a man and to wank him.

She wanks like a queen, not a milkmaid.

In Russia, she told me, she once wanked the Tsar's army. They stood to attention before her in the Winter Palace, and she went down the line of stiff pricks.

She's imaginative, Nadja.

Well, tonight she had this really imaginative notion. She shut the bedroom door behind her. She locked it. Then she slipped off her dress and her knickers.

I was lying on my back in the moonlight.

Nadja climbed on. She straddled my loins.

She played with me idly for a bit, a faraway look in her eyes.

Then she snapped with her fingers.

'The amulet!'

She never says very much, Nadja.

But I know her ways well. I don't argue.

I took off the ridiculous bangle.

Nadja fitted it right round my prick.

It was a loose fit at first, naturally. She could cram my balls into its circle. The metal was cold.

Then Nadja started to fiddle and massage and rub me in earnest. Up and down, round and round, tossing me off in the end without touching my cock with her hands, making me come with the amulet.

That was pleasant.

My amulet's christened.

5   When the Spanking Had to Stop

We rode only another miserable 20 miles today, 2nd March, from Mullheim to Basel, via Welmlingen and Haltingen, into Switzerland, the road unremarkable, the weather raining. We passed a leper with his clack-dish at the border. Bowl with a clapper for alms. Faust cursed him. Helen blessed him. When nobody was looking, I gave him a pfennig or three.

I'll give you the order of our riding:

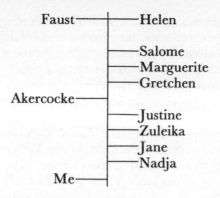

```
Faust————————Helen

                ——Salome
                ——Marguerite
                ——Gretchen
    Akercocke——

                ——Justine
                ——Zuleika
                ——Jane
                ——Nadja
        Me——
```

The reason for this order is the ages of my 7 girls. The eldest is Nadja, now 21, so she rides at the back. Salome is the youngest. She's barely 16 yet, so she comes * at the front behind Helen. The idea of me riding at the rear is to protect our troupe from attack. Hum. Well. I have the two pistols, and that reasonable Toledo sword.

Of course, in some places the order does vary a bit. Faust falls off. Marguerite and Gretchen like to ride slipper to slipper, playing footsie. Justine is a law to herself. But that's the main programme. The pack horses amble alongside the girls. The one with the burden of Helen's wardrobe slogs along next to Jane. I guess that the thinking behind this is that Jane's good with horses, so she can look after the wretched beast. It occurs to me also that Jane has her eye on Helen's great trunk for possible hairbrushes. She knows that I'm watching her. I don't imagine for a minute that my watching would stop strong-willed Jane, though. As for Nadja, she's a useful person to have at the back there. She carries this drum she keeps banging.

Like I say, it was raining all day.

We all got soaked through.

Salome looked nicest, soaked through.

Salome wears this silk chemise called a pirahan. It reaches just to the middle of her thighs, when she's riding side-saddle. It's embroidered with gold thread and pearls. Her glossy black hair she has covered with gem-spangled gauze – this weird Persian head-dress, a charhadd. The charhadd was dripping by the time we passed into the cobbled streets of Basel. The pirahan was clinging to her.

* *Came?* I'll explain in a minute.

121

Basel has always been a hang-out for Humanists. For seven years to 1529 it was the city of old ear-muffed Erasmus. Then the Mass was abolished, and the place taken over by the reformer Oecolampadius and his gang. Nice irony: both Erasmus and Oecolampadius are now feeding the worms here. Prudent worms breed in Basel, and some liberal maggots as well. Hans Denck the Anabaptist found refuge in Basel. Even the freethinker Sebastian Franck, after he'd been hounded out of Strassburg and forced to earn his living boiling soap. All the same, just as the city is divided into two halves by the Rhine that runs through it, so its spirit is divided too. Maybe that great earthquake that all but destroyed Basel a couple of centuries back went deeper than earth. Calvin published his *Institutes* here only four years ago. The *Christianae Religionis Institutio*, that is, first edition, six chapters, with the creepy crawly prefatory letter to Frank 1, King of France. French Johnny brought out an enlarged edition, 17 chapters, last autumn. I'll bet that's not the end of the story. It's the sort of book you could go on expanding for ever. Theological elastic.

I took Salome straight to a tavern and ordered hot grog. Then I made her strip off and gave her a rub with a towel.

'I'm still cold,' she complained, standing shivering.

This is no place for a young Persian maiden.

Blue eyes.

Full-moon face.

Dimply smile.

She's tiny in stature, Salome. You could clasp her two feet in one hand.

She was born in Isfahan. She's a Zoroastrian.

O the sweet musky scent of her cunt!

Salome's sexual interests.

She's the opposite of Nadja, in that.

Salome likes me to spank her and wank her.

She can't get enough in that line.

I set this fact down just to make it clear how the rest of this evening's events came about.

I took her upstairs in the tavern. I got a servant to light a big fire in the grate.

'I'm still freezing,' said Salome. 'Warm me!'

'How does Salome want warming?'

'You know how!'

Well, we started having a nice time by the fire.

We were just in the middle when there's a knock at the door. The Herr Nuisance. I'd know his knock anywhere. Old hairy knuckles.

'What is it?' I called.

He said: 'Calvin!'

I was rubbing grog into Salome's buttocks.

When I heard the name Calvin, I stopped.

'Go on, Kit,' begged Salome.

I said: *'Calvin?'*

'Calvin,' Faust said.

'Oh, Kit!' Salome murmured. 'Kit! *Please* . . .'

I gave her a half-hearted smack.

'. . . Umm! Lovely!' she said. '. . . Umm! Some more!'

Faust was rattling the handle.

'Leave whatever you're doing. Calvin's preaching!'

'I can't wait to miss it,' I said.

I spanked on.

But too lightly.

I don't like it when that fart is listening.

Salome doesn't like it when I do it too lightly.

'This is serious,' Faust roared. 'Calvin preaching!'

He kicked open the door.

He came in.

(Fuck these lousy Swiss locks! Switzer locksmiths!)

'Some other time,' I told Faust.

'Right now!' he ordered. 'She can wait . . .'

He was drunk, of course. He also had Akercocke.

It was Akercocke's presence that decided me.

Bad enough, the Herr Voyeur leering at my love games. But that monkey . . .

'Get your clothes on,' I told Salome. 'I'm sorry.'

She was kicking her legs with frustration.

Nice little legs. Slightly bandy.

'Not in front of the monkey,' I said.

So Salome got dressed again.

Faust turned his back, the old hypocrite.

Akercocke didn't.

I threw a sheet over his cage.

'You round up the others,' Faust said.

'They don't want to hear Calvin!'

'Neither do you,' Faust said. 'But we're going to.'

So we troop from the tavern, back out into the rain, and Faust leads us through the streets of Basel to this dump called the Münster. Sandstone building, deep red, built on a terrace high above the Rhine. It looked like a seedy sort of wedding cake, set out to rot in the weather. I detest modern architecture.

A Switzer church à la John Calvin.

In these places, servants and others just sit as they come, and there's no distinction of rank or pew.

We sat down in a row at the front.

Faust always goes right to the front. That's his style.

Helen's too. Helen walks into a church like she owns it.

Not that Helen would go into the Münster.

'This is a *Protestant* church,' she said, crossing herself.

Nothing would budge her.

So we left her outside in the rain, with her powder and paint peeling off.

I felt a bit sorry for Helen. She'd got all dressed up in her best blue Mass-going gown, and now she had nowhere to go. Faust should have explained about Calvin. As it was, she was left standing in the dripping porch of that Protestant wedding cake like a jilted dwarf bride. I don't know what Helen did with herself for the two hours we spent in there.

6   Calvin's Sermon

Two hours, yes! No wonder I'm whacked.

Two hours of pure Calvin?

Not quite.

There we sat, though, in French Johnny's Münster. Herr Doktor Damnation and party.

Right in the front pew.

What a sight!

And – in Faust's case, of course – what a pong!

Calvin came in wearing this gown like a nightshirt. Head like a Bavarian sugar loaf turned upside-down. Wide cold eyes just the colour of snot.

I noted the buckles on his boots as he hauled himself into the pulpit. High-heeled boots. True height: 5 foot five.

Now, John Calvin's asthmatic. He's got this voice which seems to come out down his nose. He wheezed some long prayers. Then he started. He shuts his eyes tight and he started.

'Satan!' he shouted out. 'Satan!'

Faust drank a toast. He was slurping. But Calvin doesn't open his eyes. Calvin's away. Calvin's running.

'What does Scripture teach?' Calvin demanded. 'Brothers and sisters, I'll tell you. Scripture calls Satan the god (II *Corinthians* 4, 4) and prince (*John* 12, 31) of this world. Scripture speaks of Satan as a mighty armed man (*Luke* 11, 21), the spirit who holds power over the air (*Ephesians* 2, 2), a roaring lion (I *Peter* 5, 8). And what does this mean, my friends? *Watch it!* That's what Scripture tells us. To watch it! Watch out for the Devil. He's after you!'

Well, Calvin wasn't watching it himself. Eyes still shut, he was wiping his nose on what looked like a yard of hair shirt.

He continued:

'Life is military service, my friends. This military service against the Evil One ends only at death. We are God's soldiers. Stand fast in the face of the Enemy! God is our captain. God alone can supply us with the armour we need. Yes, and the armaments. Scripture! Our cannonballs!

'Scripture, brethren, Scripture tells us that there are not one, not two, not a few scattered foes, which wage war eternal against us. It is great armies we are up against! We have to battle against an infinite number of enemies, never yielding an inch to their strength or our weakness.

'Yet Scripture speaks of Satan in the singular. What can this mean? It means, I say, that there is an empire of wickedness which is opposed to the Kingdom of Righteousness. Empires have emperors. Satan is the emperor of unrighteousness itself. Just as the church has Christ as its only Head, so the army of the unrighteous has this supreme evil, our Adversary, as its commander. For this reason, it was said: *Depart you cursed, into the eternal fire, prepared for the Devil and his angels* (*Matthew* 25, 41).

'War, brethren, war! No surrender! We must wage total and irreconcilable war with those who at this very minute and at every minute are laying traps to overturn God's Kingdom and plunge man himself into eternal death. The Devil and his angels! Our opponents!'

Calvin blew his nose. It was like a trumpet. A sort of squashed trumpet. A trumpet that has seen better days. But still a trumpet.

He went on in a somewhat quiet tone. A bad flute. He had been the general haranguing his troops on the parade ground. Now it was like the chief of an espionage service. He still didn't open his eyes.

'Brothers and sisters,' he hissed. 'I have heard some people grumble that Scripture does not tell us much about the matter of the Fall of the devils, what made it happen, when it was, and why. I say that this has nothing to do with us. We had better mind our business. We should acknowledge meekly that the Lord's purpose was to teach nothing in his sacred texts except what we need to know for our edification. Be content, fellow soldiers, with this brief summary of the nature of the enemy. That they were first created angels of God. That by degeneration they ruined themselves. That they were made the instrument of ruin for men. That is all we need to know. Paul, by the way, in speaking of the *elect angels* (I *Timothy* 5, 21), is referring to us.

'I turn now to our glorious prospect — our victory —'

7 Black Dog

But I can't carry on with this stuff. I didn't really hear the rest of French John's sermon.

To tell you the truth, from about when he got to the bit about the *elect angels* my mind and other parts weren't concentrating at all on that skinny snot-nosed figure bowing and mowing and wheezing up there in the carved Noah's Ark of the pulpit.

It wasn't just Faust on the end of our pew, sneaking a swig at his brandy flask to toast every mention of the Devil and his boys.

It wasn't just that five of my 7 girls had dropped off to sleep, unable or unwilling to follow Calvin's argument, and were snoring away prettily.

The trouble was Nadja and Salome. Nadja and Salome weren't sleeping.

Far from it.

From the start of the sermon, Nadja had been flexing her

fingers in her fur muff. I know all the signs. She was wanting some action.

So was my dear little Salome.

Salome's too young for abstinence. Too young and too warm and too tender to appreciate the dubious delights, the adult pleasures, of *having to wait*.

Her silk chemise was half ridden up round her thighs. She'd had to slip it back on while it was still damp. She had this cloak over it, but she was letting the cloak fall apart. I could see her plump thighs, sweetly pale in the gloom of the church. Salome was wriggling about right next to me, shifting her behind, teasing herself this way and that on the rough wooden kiss of the pew.

I'd left her half-spanked, please remember.

Never leave a girl not-quite-16 half-spanked.

It only makes them itchy.

Salome was there on my left. Nadja was there on my right. The rest of our pew, as I've said, was asleep. All except Faust, who was drunk, sitting sucking his moustaches, luxuriating intellectually in Calvin's spiel. Or thinking, maybe, his own thoughts. Running over in his mind (or what's left of that valuable particle) just how he will kill Pope Paul 3.

Well, God knows what John Faust was thinking.

Christ knows what John Faust was experiencing, there in French Johnny's great kirk.

I can record my own experience, that's all.

Nadja slipped her left hand out of her muff. Her fingers crept under my cloak. She groped for my prick and she found it. She started to tug it and rub it, slowly and gently at first, through the stuff of my doublet. Then she moved a bit closer. I felt her furs tickle my cheek. Hand still concealed under the cloak, she unpicked my doublet. She fumbled, but not very much. Nadja's expert. She knows what men like, and she loves it.

Well, Nadja slips out my prick and starts stroking it.

Up above us, Calvin snorting on through his asthma about the Devil and his cohorts being not thoughts but actualities.

Down here, Nadja with a handful.

I'll say this for Protestant churches. The pews are ideal for your balls when you've got a girl sitting wanking you under your cloak. I suppose it's the very long sermons and the absence of kneeling. All those Protestant bums make the wood smooth.

Another advantage of a Protestant church is the forbidding of candles. No statues, no votive candles, so not so much light. French Johnny's place had just the two windows, high up, and he was determined to go on until dark by the look of it. Like I said, our pew was in front, but there was this wall of wood between us and the pulpit, and the back of the pew was high, and the pew was deep. So: it was getting nice and gloomy in there. I doubt if Calvin would have seen us, even if he hadn't been preaching with his eyes shut, and even if Nadja had popped my now well-throbbing organ right out of my cloak to say boo to him.

What about Salome?

I'll tell you what about Salome.

Salome's a Zoroastrian. That makes Salome intuitive, so she says. Well, it doesn't take the intuition of a sybil for a girl on one side of you to realise if the girl on the other side is tossing you off. Salome looked down. She saw the bulge of Nadja's hand going to and fro and up and down under my cloak. She knew what was happening. She drew her breath in a bit sharpish.

I knew then I'd made a mistake.

I shouldn't have let the Herr Sermon-fancier stop me in the middle of my romp with that little Persian.

Salome needed it now.

Salome was determined to get it.

So she wriggles right down in the pew.

I glanced round. The church was half empty.

There was no one at all in the six pews behind us. Faust's stink helped our privacy.

Now you're not supposed to kneel in John Calvin's church. They stand up to say their prayers, facing him. Kneeling is Papist, they reckon. Still, nobody noticed my Salome. She's so tiny, and when her head disappeared from the tall back of our pew no doubt people thought she'd just lent forwards considering Scripture. In fact, though, Salome slid down to the floor. Then she moved right along there in front of me, her face still upturned to the preacher. If Calvin had opened his eyes he might well have supposed that a moon-faced Persian teenager was crouching down there to adore him.

The truth is less idolatrous.

Nadja likes situations like this. They appeal to her sense of humour. *Piquant*, she'd say.

128

So when Salome backs up in between my legs, and hitches up her silk chemise (still damp), and presents the cheeks of her knickerless backside, Nadja really gets to work with my hard tool. She's spanking the little Persian number on her bottom with it. A readymade rod of correction. The best that there is.

Nadja urges me forward in the pew, so that I look like I'm rapt with attention, straining to catch Calvin's least word. In fact, I'm letting Nadja smack my erection this way and that against Salome's bare butt. And Salome's wriggling on it. And I couldn't have stopped what then happened even if I'd wanted to. By that stage, I can tell you, I didn't.

So Nadja brought me off smartly by slapping my prick against Salome's buttocks. And Salome came (I could tell) when she felt my seed spurting all over her cheeks. And Nadja –?

God knows if Nadja ever comes. Nadja gets her kicks making others come. She's a real Russian iceberg, my Nadja. But she seems to enjoy what she does.

Just then Calvin opens his eyes!

He considers us.

For a moment I thought that we'd had it. That Calvin would bawl. Point the finger. We'd be seized. We'd be burned in the square before the entire population of Switzerland (750,000). Immorality. Blasphemy. Perversions.

Does he know about that Gnostic sect which used to do just this? I mean: the one that made a sacrament out of it. The Catharistae. Whose doctrines were similar to the Bogomiles of Bulgaria. There were Catharists in Germany less than two centuries ago. I'm not a Catharist. I just enjoy free will.

He's shortsighted, French John.

He blinked just the once.

His nose sniffed the air.

A faint fog of spicy steam rising like incense from my sperm on Salome's chemise.

Calvin sneezed.

He went on.

Asthmatically.

Dogmatically.

On.

About soldiers and devils.

Eyes shut fast again.

Rocking this way and that on his high-heeled boots.

129

Nadja squeezed every last drop from my balls.

Salome gets up demurely, and goes out.

I don't know why she did that. She went out.

Nadja, matter-of-factly, pushed my prick back into my doublet. Did it up. Slid her hand out from under my cloak. Replaced her hand in her muff. And stared into space for the rest of the sermon. Cold eyes, full of steppes, wolves, and snow.

Whew.

I've forgotten the rest of what Calvin said.

When he'd finished we all sang a hymn.

Except Faust, we all sang a hymn. (The girls just made sounds in their various languages, but they do like to sing when they can.)

I wondered where Salome had gone.

Faust was too drunk to sing. He stood up and went through the motions. His lips moved, but he didn't sing. Good job too. He's got a singing voice like a raven with rust in its throat. He was belching a bit between verses. That sounded religious enough.

Where's Salome?

Did Faust realise what we'd been up to?

I don't think so. He made no such reference.

Where's Salome?

I don't know. She walked out of that Münster in her pirahan. She went down a side aisle. She's gone . . .

I mean: I expected to find her back here at the tavern. Helen was here, looking sulky. I asked her if she'd seen Salome coming out the church. She said no. Helen must have stalked off from the porch and come back here through the rain before Salome walked out.

But where did Salome *go*? Where's she *gone*? At the moment of writing – midnight, 2nd March – there's no sign of her.

My little Zoroastrian has disappeared! I suspect she's been kidnapped, poor thing.

It's quite nice, this tavern. But Swiss food! Toasted cheese is about all that they eat.

Helen wouldn't touch it.

She made out it was annoyance with Faust that kept her from eating.

'Going into a Protestant church,' she said. 'What a waste of time! They're not *real*, you know . . .'

'Reality?' Faust said.

'They just preach there and pray,' explained Helen. 'God doesn't listen, of course. Because that's all that they do in those places. Just preaching and praying. No action.'

I smiled across the toasted cheese at Nadja. But Nadja speaks only Russian. She didn't understand my smile at all.

Faust went out for a walk later on.

I didn't follow him. I thought he was out on the prowl for a brothel. Helen, in that mood, would be having one of her 'headaches'. He'd be looking for solace elsewhere.

I'll say this for the magus secundus. He never interferes with my girls. He got those 7 * beauties for me, and he leaves them to me. It's an unspoken rule. They don't break it either. Who could fancy him anyway? That polecat!

I didn't bother to follow him. I should have. But I was waiting for Salome to come back, and enjoying a quiet game of cards with Jane and Zuleika and Justine while I waited. Justine cheated, but I didn't mind. I don't cheat at cards. I don't mind when other people do.

When Faust came back the others had gone up to bed.

I sat by the fire playing patience.

'Any sign of Salome?' I said.

Faust just shook his head drunkenly.

He had this black dog at his heels.

He sat down. He started to groom it.

'Here, Satan,' he said.

The dog licked his hand.

It's a mangy thing. I don't know where he got it.

Faust looked at me, expecting that I'd ask him.

I didn't.

'She's been kidnapped,' I said. 'We should tell the authorities.'

'Good boy, Satan,' Faust said.

I sat there wondering what to do. I couldn't think of anything suitable. How do you tell the authorities that you've lost a 15-year-old Zoroastrian with a jewel in the middle of her forehead and your sperm up her pirahan?

Besides, maybe she'll come back tomorrow. Maybe she's just out on the tiles.

Faust was too drunk to talk to about it.

* 6 now?

131

I left.

I came up here to write down the facts.

I patted the dog as I left. That amazed the Herr Doktor. I think it surprised the dog too.

8 Gone Home

This morning I rode up beside Faust for a bit. It was safe enough. We left Basel by the wooden bridge over the river, then took the main road across the Rhine plain. Quite a lot of traffic on that road. Just beyond Münchenstein we met this army on the march. They were coming the other way, towards us. (To join Calvin's army for Christ?) Pikes, guns, arquebuses, swords, bills, and bows. We had to pull off the road to let them go past.

Helen was still sulking. She wore a green riding habit. It suited her complexion. Green around the gills, she was, and popping little pills into her mouth when she thinks no one's looking.

Our stop for the army gave me the chance I'd been waiting for. To get to Faust early. Before the daily flood of brandy makes him sour.

'Hey, Faust,' I said. 'Salome's gone.'

He crossed his eyes coyly.

'I know,' he said.

'Well, *where* has she gone?

'Home,' he said.

He stared into the distance.

That mangy black dog was crouched at the heels of his horse. The horse doesn't like it. But it seems that we're stuck with the creature. Satan! An accomplice in his plot to kill Pope Paul 3?'

'Home to Persia?' I said. 'Back to Isfahan? You've got to be joking!'

'Then you should be laughing,' Faust said.

Helen sniffed, sitting stiffly in her saddle, her green face matching the foothills of the Jura Mountains.

A soldier with purple trousers and an arquebus winked at her.

'Come off it,' I said. 'Salome can't just have set off for Persia on her own.'

The army finished passing. They all turned eyes right for my girls. Zuleika waved when the final soldier made an obviously obscene suggestion with his carbine. Zuleika's getting a bit above herself. I can see that I'll have to teach her some seriousness before we reach Rome.

Faust sucked at his flask.

'She's gone home,' he said. 'Your Salome.'

'There must be some other explanation.'

'No, there mustn't,' he said.

Helen popped a pill. God knows what quack in Basel she got them from.

Faust wiped his mouth.

We rode on.

9 Two Rivers, One Red

No rain today. The air warm and bright. Young shoots on the trees. I plucked out a few to feed Akercocke. He can do without birds and the rest of his ghoulish diet for a bit. Let him suffer for Lent, I say. Let him starve on sap. Let him pine for blood. Let him die.

We passed over a bridge. The river beneath it ran red.

'Hey, Faust,' I said. 'Those soldiers must have been in a battle.'

'No, they mustn't,' Faust said.

'There's blood in that river,' I said.

Helen crossed herself, banging her tits.

'Tell Wagner to ride at the back, John. It's not safe this way.'

'The battle is over,' I said, inspecting the water meadows. Those meadows were empty and peaceful. Not a sign of grass trampled. Not a single dead body in sight. But that river ran red. It was curious.

'We'll be ambushed,' Helen said. 'We'll be robbed. We'll be raped. We'll be hacked in a thousand pieces.'

A black-robed Dominican trotted by on a small shaggy donkey.

'Good morning. God bless you,' he said.

'This is the main road to Moutier,' I told Helen. 'We're perfectly safe here. Herr Doktor, there must —'

'You're all *musts*,' Faust said. 'Back to the back with you.'

But he winked, with his head turned from Helen.

I returned to my place at the rear.

The girls were singing. Six different languages. One song. I wish I knew the name of that song.

We rode over another bridge coming to Moutier.

This second river was crystal clear, not a trace of red in it. It flowed through the meadows, a sweet stream bending the long grass on the bank to the left with its ripples. Crisp ripples. Clear water. I liked it.

I reined my horse. He stood in the stream to his hocks.

I let the others ride on for a bit before I bothered to gallop after them. The gallop was nice. I enjoyed that.

When we rode into Moutier, Faust said we'd stay for the night. We'd done 25 miles. OK. But that's little enough. Why we couldn't press on and reach Solothurn I'll never know. Maybe Helen was tired. Or that mangy old gristly dog. It just loped there behind Faust all day long.

I haven't heard Helen refer to it yet.

I shouldn't imagine a black dog called Satan can hold much appeal for her.

The inns here are crowded. Faust found one room for Helen and him at a good place. I have to make do with a flea-pit. So of course do the girls. They don't like it. None of them has complained, but Jane went round the room with her perfume. I've thrown incense to burn on the fire. It doesn't help much. The wind's in the wrong direction, and I write with my eyes full of smoke.

We're in Catholic country now.

O Switzers! O Switzerland! Land of toasted cheese and other extremes. French Johnny's Basel is as Protestant (half of it) as any modernist could wish. But the Pope rules down here in Moutier, and no mistake. Why, on Ascension Day they get a statue of Christ to pop up through a hole in the floor of the local church and then hoist it with ropes and pulleys through another trapdoor in the roof.

One token of Moutier's religion.

And another.

There's this Iron Maiden.

She stands in the square just outside the big church, on a bridge. There's a mill under the bridge.

This Iron Maiden is made to do executions of disobedient children. If there are children so wild that their parents can't bridle them, and the children commit some offence, and the parents want rid of them, then the poor kids are brought to kiss this Virgin.

The Virgin opens her metal arms. The child has to kiss her.

The machine is constructed so that when her lips are kissed, the arms close together so hard that they crush all the life from the child.

Then the arms open again, and let the crushed body fall into the mill. The mill grinds it to morsels, which the water carries away.

Does the blood from that Iron Maiden flow down to the river we crossed earlier on? If it does, how come it fails to pollute the other river, the one nearer Moutier?

I've looked at my maps. But the rivers aren't marked on them. Swiss cartography also leaves much to be desired.

10   A Relic for Madam

I was waiting with the girls outside the posh inn where Faust and Helen spent the night when this guy rides into the court-yard.

He's wearing a hat like a pirate's, only instead of a skull and crossbones there's a full-fledged crucifixion on it.

Expensive horse.

Fur slippers.

Saddle bags absolutely plastered with papal seals.

A pardoner.

The minute I clapped eyes on him I knew that we'd had it. So far as getting a good start goes, I mean.

No sooner does his bell begin than the window of an upper room bangs open. It's Helen.

'My prayers have been answered!' she cries, looking down, feasting her eyes on this priestly crook with his bag of tricks. 'As usual!' she adds.

The pardoner sweeps off his hat.

'What do you have?' cries Helen.

'Indulgences, madam. Enough to see madam safe through Purgatory.'

Helen pointed her nose at the sky.

'I'm going straight to Heaven,' she announced. 'Heaven is my destination. I've been promised that by Very High Authority.'

The pardoner bowed. He had a fancy way of bowing. He must have been out East.

'Madam,' he bawled, 'then it is I who must crave indulgence of you.'

'Granted,' Helen said graciously.

'But I have other items,' the pardoner said, indicating his papal saddle bags. 'More important things.'

'Ooh! *Relics!*' screeched Helen. 'Don't go away! Don't part with anything! Don't cast your pearls before that infidel and his swine! I'll be down directly. Just let me fix my face.'

The pardoner meditated upon his fur slippers until Helen appeared in the courtyard. He was a fat freak. He looked like an egg.

Helen started skipping round his bags.

'Would a square inch of the sail of St Peter's fishing boat be of interest to madam?'

I sat down on the trough. I could see business was going to be good. I told Jane and the others that they might just as well take a stroll.

The pardoner was showing Helen a bloody cap which had belonged to one of the Holy Innocents slaughtered by Herod, when Faust reels out. Faust's face was white with lather. He had his razor in his hand. He also had the shakes. The inn-keeper comes behind him, carrying a high-backed chair.

'Set it down in the sun,' Faust says. 'I like the sun.'

Hey ho.

So the chair is set down in the early morning sun and Faust sprawls on it, tilting back his head and handing me the razor.

I had to shave him.

While Helen goes on pestering the pardoner, and the pardoner is only too glad to be pestered.

'A nail from the True Cross?'

'No, something less yukky!'

'Just you watch it with the symmetry of my moustaches . . .'

I watched it with the symmetry of his absurd moustaches, and I watched it as Helen persuaded Faust to part with a plump sack of dalers in exchange for the pardoner's prize piece.

'A unique relic, madam. Very clean. Very nice. A feather from the wing of the Archangel Gabriel, dropped at the time of the Annunciation!'

I managed to nick Faust's Adam's apple.

Helen treasured and adored her angel feather. She skipped back into the inn. I expected her to emerge with the feather in her hat. She didn't. It was concealed somewhere about her person, beneath a scarlet riding habit. I don't care to think about where.

Before she came out, the pardoner disappeared as these fellows do. He couldn't believe his luck. He was blessing himself and his horse with an aspersorium filled with holy water.

Faust just sat there grunting. He scrubbed at his cheeks with his fingernails, examining my shave. Then he started playing with a hand mirror, catching the sun in it, making a dot of light dart around the courtyard, flashing it into my eyes.

The dog loped out.

To stop the mirror caper, I asked Faust the question about the dog that I knew that he wanted me to ask.

'I got him from Calvin,' Faust said.

'Do me a favour!' I said. 'It's just a stray.'

'Bet your life he's no stray,' Faust said. 'He was Calvin's dog. Here, Satan! Here, boy!'

'Don't you mean *heel*?' I said.

Faust grinned at the cur.

He fondled its ears, which looked as if they would fall off if you fondled them much.

'Strictly speaking,' I said, 'I believe that the correct mode of address in this case is neither *here* nor *heel*. You should say *Get thee behind me, Satan!*'

The creature sidled up puppyishly. It tried to lick my hand. I took a running kick at it.

Then I turned on Faust.

'The pfennig's dropped,' I said. 'Septentrio!'

'I wondered how long it would take you,' Faust said.

'That's one of your grey friar's phoney words,' I recalled. 'He told you he was boss of the world from Septentrio to the Meridian.'

'Under the Devil,' Faust said.

'Under my arse,' I told him.

Faust leered, licking his lips.

'Well, Kit, it's been a long while since you let me . . .'

'Bugger off,' I said.

'To Septentrio,' I added.

11 Little Kisser, Hard Slog

I went to keep the girls company where they sat making daisy
chains and watching the Iron Maiden claiming her first kisser of
the morning. It was a lad of about eleven. He reminded me of
me. Long ago. The old days of my childhood in the Wartburg.

Faust and Helen joined us eventually. The bells of Moutier
were ringing for noon when we passed beyond its walls and hit the
road.

The road!

It was steep, it was long, flanking two mountains, the Has-
enmatt and the Weissenstein, all shagged with hanging woods
then lost in clouds.

What a slog!

I dawdled at the rear of our slow column.

I kept fiddling with my amulet. It was something to do. As I
expected, the cheap gilt is flaking off. It looks as black as iron
underneath.

The road went on and on. And up and up.

We were a shambles by the time we rode through the pass
into Solothurn and found this hospice for pilgrims.

My chop had maggots.

We covered a mere 10 miles or so today, but it seemed like 50.

There's worse to come.

The Alps lie before us now.

I can smell their cold.

12 Satan's Dinners

'In what sense,' I said, 'was this John Calvin's dog?'

'In the best sense,' Faust said. 'He gave Satan biscuits.'

'Calvin?'

'Yes.'

'Calvin gave this dog biscuits?'

'And bones when he could, no doubt. Cow's cheeks. That
type of stuff.'

'Not very many, by the look of it,' I said.

'You criticise Calvin?'

'It's a fucking disgrace,' I said. 'Look, you can see its rib cage, can't you? Some dog lover, French Johnny!'

'I expect the dog had to live on much the same diet as Calvin,' Faust explained. 'Satan would be an ascetic dog.'

'And you're proposing to make it run to Rome?'

'I'm not making Satan do anything,' Faust said, grinning. 'He followed me when I left Calvin, that's all.'

'What did you see Calvin about?'

'The obvious,' said Faust.

'Why bother?' I demanded. 'You're home and dry. You only have to knock off His Holiness, don't you?'

Faust shrugged.

'I remain technically interested.'

'In damnation?'

'You might call it that.'

'So what did Monsieur Calvin have to say on the technicalities of damnation?'

'Nothing new.'

'Pull the other one.'

'You won't let me pull *anything*, will you, Kit?'

'Stick to the subject.'

'I'd love to.'

'Damn you! What did Calvin *say*?'

Faust sucked at his Saracen bottle. He keeps that for indoors. Then:

'Have you started my story?' he said.

I stared out the window. Two days to the feast day of St Thomas Aquinas, doctor of angels. Would an angel travelling from (say) Staufen in the Breisgau to Rome be able to waste a whole day talking about dog's dinners in some God-forsaken Swiss dump in the middle of Swiss nowhere? I saw the sun setting. The misshapen mess of the Alps to the south. We're still here at Solothurn.

'One day down the drain,' I remarked.

'Helen's sick,' Faust said.

'I told you not to bring her.'

'Ah, yes. You said our great work was no job for a woman. Then you went on to say that you wanted to bring your *seven* women along.'

139

I whistled.

'Six now,' I said. 'What happened to Salome?'

'She went home,' Faust said.

'You mean back to the Tower?'

'I mean home,' Faust said. 'How much have you written?'

'Not much. About Salome –'

'So you *have* started . . .'

'You know that,' I said. 'You broke into my room and looked for it, didn't you?'

Faust was buttering his boil.

'Ash Wednesday,' I said. 'Remember? Herr Spy?'

Faust poured me a drink.

In a cracked pilgrim cup.

I ignored it.

'Own up,' I said.

'I believe our little trip is getting to you already,' he murmured.

'You mean you didn't?'

'Didn't what?'

'Spy on me? Try and read my papers?'

Faust poured himself a pilgrim cup as well. His was in better condition.

'I don't need to do that,' he said.

It was maddening.

The saphead started fondling the dog's ears. One ear sticks up, the other ear flops down. It's a crazy-looking lopsided creature. As black as pitch, except for the red running sores.

'Lie, Satan!' he said. 'Good boy, Satan.'

'Is that what Calvin called it?' I demanded. '*Satan?* You really expect me to believe that John Calvin had a dog he called Satan! And he gave it to you!'

'He didn't give the dog to me,' Faust said. 'I told you. Satan followed me.'

'OK. What did Calvin call it when it belonged to him? When he was its master?'

'I don't know what Calvin called the dog,' Faust said. 'The dog came when he called, I daresay. But since I didn't hear Calvin call, I don't know the name that he called. The dog comes to me when I call *Satan*. That's what he answers to now.'

He drank all his brandy in the pilgrim cup. Then he reached out for my cup. He drank my lot too.

'You went to see a man about a dog,' I said. 'Ha ha.'

'I went to see Calvin about Satan.'

'This Satan? Or the commander-in-chief of hell's army?'

'Ah! You heard that bit . . .'

Faust raised his seaweedy eyebrows. He looked at me mischievously.

I felt like I'd been caught.

Yet I'm sure he was too drunk to realise what happened that evening in John Calvin's kirk. And the pew was so nice and dark too. He couldn't have noticed. Even though he's got eyes like a hawk. Pissed hawks don't see much.

'Calvin is nothing,' Faust said.

He dismissed the theologian with a flick of brandy.

'But his dog's something else,' I said.

Faust was splashing brandy into his palm. He held out his hand to the dog. The dog licked it and lapped it.

'About Salome,' I said.

'Easy come, easy go,' Faust said. 'Never mind about Salome. The Devil, you know, is my brother-in-law.'

'Your brother-in-law?'

'The Devil.'

'Making Helen his sister?'

'I'm not married to Helen.'

'You're not married to anyone. So how can the Devil be your brother-in-law?'

'That's a fact,' Faust said. 'Put it down in your book. The Devil's my brother-in-law.'

He's a screwball. He's gone right round the twist.

'Do we press on tomorrow?' I said.

'That's up to Helen,' Faust said.

'Which way through the Alps? The St Gotthard?'

'Straight to Rome,' Faust said. 'Quickest way.'

He shut his eyes.

He started to snore.

The dog snored as well on his boots.

I sat there. I thought to myself. Wagner, I thought, maybe you should get drunk so that you could understand him. How can anyone follow a drunkard unless they are drunk? But then I don't want to follow him. Only make sense of him. The distinction seemed important at the time. Ho hum. Now I'm not sure what the hell I meant by it.

I looked out across the plain of the River Aar at the white threshold of the Alps.

It was pissing with rain. Some of the rain fell as snowflakes.

'Calvin said one thing that was interesting.'

Faust's eyes were still shut.

He was talking in his sleep.

'Calvin told me why the sun is red at evening,' Faust said.

'Why is the sun red at evening?' I asked.

'Because it goes towards hell,' Faust said.

I got up to come to my room.

There are limits to the shit that I will eat.

At the door, Faust called after me:

'Don't forget, son,' he said. 'Anything you can't remember, Akercocke will help you.'

13 Doom

So today I tried to murder Akercocke.

Murder?

I mean kill.

Murder implies the presence of a soul.

Akercocke has no soul.

Akercocke's only a monkey.

So today I did my best to get rid of the fucker.

Jeez. Have you ever tried killing a creature you can't bear to touch? It's not easy. Poison's no good, like I said. Akercocke thrives on it. I didn't dare open his cage either. I couldn't get at him. I had to kill that monkey without any direct contact.

How?

Two methods occurred to me.

First, acting on the principle that your monkey is an imitative ape, I tried shaving in front of his cage and pretending to cut my own throat.

I made my face frothy with soap. Then I kept slashing at my neck with this big razor.

Akercocke watched all the time. He seemed quite interested.

But when I shoved shaving soap and razor into his cage, what did the bastard go and do?

He ate the soap.

He spurned the razor.

Then he gave me a V sign.

(He must have seen me doing that often behind Faust's back.)

I was hopping mad. I seized the cage and thrust it in a bag. Plan number 2.

I ran down to the river.

The River Aar is broad and strong at Solothurn.

I went to the middle of the bridge. There was no one about.

I put the bag up on the parapet.

I could hear Akercocke thumping and scratching about in his cage inside. I turned my back. Not a soul in sight.

I shoved backwards with my shoulders, knocking bag, cage, and Akercocke off the bridge and down into the river.

I heard the big plop but I didn't look.

'Bugger off, Akercocke,' I said. 'Good riddance!'

And then:

'Amen.'

But it wasn't *amen* at all, God damn it.

I walked back slowly to the hospice, enjoying the sense of freedom and the morning air. No guilt. Not a scrap. I felt like a man reborn. I even stopped to give a pfennig to a blind beggar. (He chucked the coin in the gutter when he saw it was German.)

I came in by the stables, giving my horse a pat.

There, on the doorstep, was this ancient, a fisherman. Long white hair, eyes bright with the most disgusting and absurd honesty, a net in his left hand.

And in his right, of course, my wet bag held aloft!

'Sir, you dropped this.'

There was no denying the wretched saint. I had to pretend I was grateful. I offered him cash.

Somehow it made matters worse that the man shook his head.

'The Lord will reward me,' he said.

Better not comment.

Since there was no sound of life from inside the bag, I came indoors with it still not without some small hope in my heart.

I should've known better.

I undid the bag – which was dripping with Solothurn's sewage.

There was Akercocke, grinning, horrible, crouched in the cage, his hands over his ears, none the worse for his dip in the

Aar, looking for all the world like one of those emblems of monkeys that will hear no evil.

Then he opened his mouth and spat a great gout of vile water straight in my face!

Am I doomed to go to my grave with this creature astraddle the coffin?

We shall see. Doom I do not believe in. I leave doom for Faust.

I shall have the last word yet, Herr Akercocke.

14 The Predestination Shuffle

This is the second whole day we've wasted at Solothurn. It wouldn't be so bad if the hospice wasn't a rat-hole. The mattresses are sour with the piss of previous pilgrims, bed-wetters to a man. They're hopping with virulent Swiss fleas too. I put mulberry twigs under my bed to divert the fleas. There's nothing I can do about the regiments of beetles.

The walls are like paper.

I slept with Justine last night. We didn't do anything, just held hands when we weren't busy cracking fleas or flicking beetles. You might as well try to sleep in a market-place on market-day as in this bloody hospice.

Helen seemed fit enough, to me. Fit enough to prance off to Mass in a gown of red velvet. Had her Gabriel feather blessed, she said. A trifle redundant?

It was Faust who was incapable of travelling.

He's got to keep moving, or be kept moving, or he's a paralysed man. It's tragic. It's comic. One day off the road, like yesterday, and he drinks so much alcohol that it's impossible to get him to stay on his horse. You push him up one side – he falls off the other. You jam his boots in the stirrups – he goes arse-over-tit down the horse's neck.

I spent the afternoon and evening with him, not letting him out of my sight. Jane helped, and Nadja. Idea being to sober him up. Not that we succeeded in that – despite keeping him walking and talking.

As to walking: He walks this lopsided walk, like a bat that's not used to the ground.

As to talking: I got him going with the sort of patter he can never resist.

Predestination!

We had this long hassle about Predestination.

Whether it's adumbrated in the Old Testament (*Exodus* 32, 32).*

And presupposed in the Gospels by for instance St Paul (*Romans* 8, 28–30).†

Then we ran through St Augustine on the subject, and the Pelagian heresy.

From there to St Prosper of Aquitaine and the Council of Orange.

Interestingly (?), the old clown reminded me that the brains behind that Council was St Caesarius of Arles whose opponent was the semi-Pelagian *Faustus* of Riez! And that Augustine had had an opponent called Faustus too! Faustus of Milevis, late 4th century, a Manichee, whose basic ideas can be made out from Augustine's *Contra Faustum Manichaeum*.

Some more bad apples on the family tree?

Or should it be other incarnations?

Like Simon Magus.

I only wonder the Herr Nutcase didn't claim a post-dated sex-change and drag in the Roman Empress *Faustina*, wicked wife of Marcus Aurelius, while he was at it . . .

Consider:

An old German and a young German processing about a Switzer town locked in debate as to whether there is any divine decree according to which some guys are infallibly guided to eternal damnation and other guys to its opposite.

The old German held up by an English girl on one side and a Russian girl on the other.

The young German having no interest in the subject save to keep the boss talking.

Too much!

* *Yet now, if thou wilt forgive their sin —; and if not, blot me, I pray thee, out of thy book which thou hast written.*

† *And we know that all things work together for good to them that love God, to them who are the called according to his purpose. For whom he did foreknow, he also did predestinate to be conformed to the image of his Son, that he might be the firstborn among many brethren. Moreover whom he did predestinate, them he also called: and whom he called, them he also justified: and whom he justified, them he also glorified.*

145

But at least it restricted Faust's intake of brandy and foul Swiss white wine.

Incidentally, he didn't say a word all day about his chances in Rome, either on the score of

(a) confession and blunting the Devil's scissors, or

(b) assassination and getting a fresh 24-year contract from Mephistopheles.

Maybe he was inhibited by the girls? But Nadja couldn't understand a word of our talk, and if Jane picked up the odd phrase it plainly bored the pants off her. I've noticed that he never speaks his mind about his maggots in front of my girls. That honour is reserved for me and Helen.

Helen.

Our Lady of Hiccups.

When Jane and Nadja and me got the Herr Debater off early and (for him) not-too-drunk to bed, I took the chance to ask Helen what she thought of our 4-legged friend Satan.

(Which followed us around town all through the great Pre-destination Shuffle, do I need to add? Tongue hanging out. Picking fights with the odd St Bernard.)

'It is a Christian's duty to tend for stray creatures,' Helen decided.

'Even a Protestant dog?' I said.

'Dogs are not Protestants.'

'It was Calvin's dog. That makes it a pedigree Protestant, I should say.'

Helen frowned.

Then she favoured me with her 'enlightened' smile.

'We must love our separated brethren,' she said. 'And their dogs. Besides, it has seen the error of its ways. The dog *left* Calvin! It followed John!'

'But a dog called *Satan*,' I said.

Helen shuddered.

She crossed herself.

'Who says that's the dog's name? Calvin?'

'Faust.'

'No, he doesn't.'

'I heard him.'

'You must have heard it wrong,' Helen said smugly. 'Trust you to hear it wrong!'

'Well, what do you think he calls it?' I demanded.

'Samson,' she said.

'It's not Samson! It's *Satan!*'

'You have a funny sense of humour,' Helen said.

'I need it round here,' I said.

'And your ears could do with a wash,' Helen said.

'*Samson?*' I said.

'That's right,' Helen said.

'You really think he's calling Samson at that creature when what he's saying is Satan?'

'Samson,' Helen said. 'Fine name for a dog.'

'After the blind guy?' I said. 'The Old Testament character with the hair and Delilah and no eyes?'

'I shouldn't think so,' Helen said. 'St Samson, more likely.'

'*Saint* Samson?'

'A very holy saint. He was Cornish. When I was a girl in Cornwall –'

'Welsh,' I said. 'Feast day 28th July.'

15 Bumbach

Lost? I wish that we were. We're worse than lost.

March 7th. Our 5th day on the road (following two whole days wasted kicking our heels in damned Solothurn).

We got Faust on his horse at dawn, Jane and me, with Justine and Nadja helping. Crammed him into his saddle, half-asleep, with brandy for ballast.

In one sense: a good day. We did maybe 30 miles.

But what a 30 miles! What a route! What a rout! I can't make head or tail of it.

There isn't head or tail.

There isn't anything.

It's just a game of Follow my Leader, the leader being drunk to start and getting drunker and drunker as the game goes on.

I kept looking at my maps. I kept spurring up to the head of the crazy column. I kept telling him we should be making for Burgdorf, then Brunig. From there, we'd be in striking distance of the St Gotthard Pass. That's the sensible way – if anything is sensible in such country!

Here. I'll draw it.

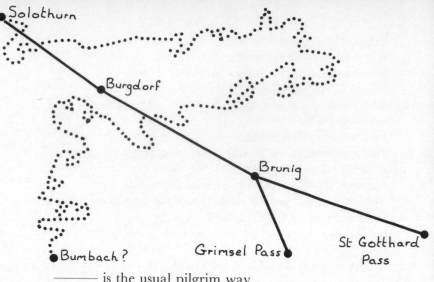

——— is the usual pilgrim way.
········· is my stab at the way that I reckon we took.

Faust won't listen, won't heed, won't even look at my maps.
You know how he navigates?
He follows that fucking black dog!
I watched him. Each crossroads, he stopped. Then the dog
takes a road, and Faust follows it. I say 'road', but some of the
places we've been through today had no road. Just tracks
through the bleeding Swiss wilderness. Up and down. Through
a wasteland of crags, snags, and gulleys.
Following a dog!
The wonder is we're not back where we started.
We're at somewhere called Bumbach.
No comment.
So far as I can make out, it would be possible to get from here
to Brunig. If Satan or Samson has a bone buried there.
A long day.
A hard day.
I'm knackered.
We didn't get to Bumbach till dark.
Up and down and round and round on those incredible
'roads', in pursuit of a dog. Faust falling off. Helen popping
pills. All my girls frightened, even Jane, even Nadja. Marguerite
and Gretchen wailing in duet. The horizon always mountains,
mountains, mountains.

Only Akercocke seemed to enjoy it. He crouched there in his cage, grinning at snowflakes, catching them, licking his claws and his chops.

I've given up hope that the Alps might be the death of him. Christ, but it's cold!

And Bumbach doesn't even have a hospice.

2 old men, 3 old women, a billygoat.

That's Bumbach.

We're spending the night in the church.

I shall kip on a pew, with Zuleika.

Faust and Helen? In the pulpit, no less.

16   Trout Tickling

We've lit this big fire in the church. Faust smashed up a pew, and I chopped it. It will keep us from freezing, though of course we must sleep in our clothes.

I write in the fire's glow.

Justine and Nadja are cooking our meat on a spit.

The horses are in the chapel beside us. Faust gave silver to the two men of Bumbach. They went off, leaping from rock to rock. They came back with a bundle of grass. I can hear the horses munching it, making those peculiar snorts which horses make when they sniff too much cold.

Marguerite and Gretchen are heaping saddles and sheepskins on the pews. Sheepskins for warmth, the saddles to do duty as our pillows.

I shall sleep with Zuleika, to comfort her. She feels the cold terribly, poor thing.

Zuleika loves being tickled. I tickle her.

She has a very sensitive skin.

My Turkish delight!

My sweet trout!

When I was a boy in the Wartburg I used sometimes to tickle trout with my fingers, dipping my hand in the stream on a warm summer evening.

Zuleika's nicer to tickle than trout.

She wriggles and begs for the tickling to stop. But you know that Zuleika doesn't really want it to stop. Not till you've tickled her cunt till she pees herself.

Zuleika always pees herself when well-tickled.

O, she always says. *O*.

Allah! Was there ever a pilgrimage like it?

17 Up the Crystal Mountain

O.

Zuleika's favourite word.

O.

We should never have gone.

We should never have left this church. We could have stayed here, safe if not smug, just burning a few more pews. I should have prevented it. I should have sidetracked the old fart with more Predestination. Peter Lombard, Bonaventure on divine predilection, even French John and his squabbling disciples, etc. 'Herr Doktor,' I should have enquired, 'are you a Supralapsarian or a Sublapsarian?'

Instead of which . . .

Instead of which, there I was at dawn, helping Jane saddle our horses. I was wearing a greatcoat with fox-fur collar and cuffs, buckskin breeches under the coat, but I could still feel the frost forming on my balls. I must have looked like Erasmus, with earflaps.

Saddling the horses was no easy job. My fingers were ten frozen turnips. To tighten the girths I had to tug them with my teeth.

Jane showed me a good trick. She smeared goosegrease into the horses' hooves, packing it tight. Prevents snow getting stuck there.

I was reeking with goosegrease by the time Faust came out. Brandy under one arm. Helen on the other. Helen swathed in bearskins, with a beaver bonnet, beaver gloves, beaver stockings, and what looked like a whole beaver in the way of a muff.

'To Rome,' Faust announced.

We all mounted.

'Which way?' I asked.

'All roads lead to Rome,' Faust declared.

He clapped spurs to his nag.

The usual result.

When we'd pulled Faust out of the village dunghill, and got him back (more or less) in the saddle, he trots off straight up this mountain.

The Crystal Mountain, he called it.

The road was incredible.

Road?

It was more like the edge of my sword.

That dog he calls Satan was woofing and wagging its tail.

It ran through the snow.

Straight as an arrow today. An arrow loosed into the Crystal Mountain.

So that was the way that Faust went, and the way that we followed.

Predestination my arse!

18 Several Million Snowflakes

It took us an hour to struggle just half a mile up that snow-covered razor-sharp track. Hailstones in our faces. The sky getting darker and darker.

Then Helen had vertigo. Bending, clutching her horse round the neck, scared silly that she would fall off.

'John! Listen! This *can't* be the way!'

'To Rome!' Faust cried, his cloak streaming back from his shoulders like big black wings.

'To hell!' I called out.

I'd had to dismount, tying my horse to Nadja's. I scrambled up, dodging the slipping hooves of the other horses, to try and talk sense into him.

As well try and talk to the wind.

'This is suicide,' I said.

'Rome,' Faust said.

He was sucking at one of his oranges. There were icicles there on his chin.

'I'll strangle your mongrel,' I promised.

The black dog stood in the driving snow about 50 paces above us. It was howling its head off.

'To kill Satan,' Faust said, 'you first have to catch him.'

'You hear that?' I shouted at Helen. 'You hear what he calls it?'

'Good boy, Samson,' screeched Helen. '*Ave* – hic – *Maria!*'

'It's not Samson! It's Satan! We're following a dog he calls Satan . . .'

Helen went bright green with the hiccups.

She clutched at Faust's hand.

'Plea – hic – se, dearest . . . We can't . . .'

We couldn't.

But we did.

Faust kissed her hand.

We went on.

The wind rising every minute, the snow getting thicker. I couldn't see where I was going. I could scarcely stand up.

And, all the time, that abominable dog looming up out of the snow, barking, wagging its tail, then dashing off ahead again, showing our column the way to ridiculous death.

I'd had enough.

I struggled up in front of Faust, on foot. I turned round.

'We go back,' I shouted. 'I'm taking the girls back. Back down where we've come. If you must, you go on – on your own.'

Helen was hiccuping now to St Jude.

St Jude: the patron saint of hopeless causes.

I felt in my pocket. I had a raw onion.

'Good for vertigo,' I told Helen.

Then I saw Faust draw one of his swords.

He used it to slice at me.

He aimed at my neck.

He missed. But he cut off an earflap. So much for Erasmus. Still, better the flap than an ear.

Faust was getting himself together for another go at me, when Helen cried out:

'Wagner's – haec – right! I want to go back down with – hic!'

Faust stared at her.

The sword fell from his hand.

He sat hunched in his cloak on his horse. He couldn't believe it. That Helen had sided with me.

Well, I was surprised too.

You could have knocked me down with a snowflake.

Instead, Zuleika was knocked down. Not by one, but by several millions.

19 Confirmation

Who can say what Faust would have done, if what happened next hadn't happened?

Followed his dog, I guess.

Followed that Satan.

But just as we stood there, glaring at each other, me with one earflap missing, Faust maybe considering drawing his second sword and having another swipe at me, Helen hiccuping over the onion, the wind whirling snow all about us, there was this horrible dull boom.

Then I saw it.

Snow pouring, a great snake of snow, a white serpent coiling and falling down the Crystal Mountain.

An avalanche!

The boom of its coming made the horses go wild. They were neighing and prancing, kicking out with their hind legs, swishing their tails round like windmills.

A pair of spare horses, two beasts unburdened with luggage, began dancing backwards. Red eyes. Flakes of foam from their mouths.

They snapped their long reins. Then they bolted.

Zuleika's horse went after them. And Zuleika's hands were wound fast in its reins.

The three bolting horses plunged through a bank of loose stones, right into the path of the avalanche.

It was all over before you could shout.

My poor little Turk who just lived to be warm, wet, and tickled – buried alive under depth upon depth of cold snow.

The last thing I saw were her arms.

Arms smooth and rounded.

Two amulets, one of them mine, gobbled down in the great suck of snow.

I gave her my amulet last night.

Christened by Nadja, but confirmed on Zuleika.

20 Down the Crystal Mountain

I was wading through white filth. I was shouting her name. O Zuleika.

Faust caught me. His claw at my neck.

'It's no use,' he bawled out. 'She's gone.'

Zuleika!

I couldn't stop shouting her name.

I bit at Faust's hand. His wrist was like stone in my teeth.

We stood, eyeball to eyeball, both up to our thighs in the snow. The brim of his black hat was white with it.

Then he hit me.

He must have had his second sword in his other hand.

He zonked me with the hilt. He zonked me hard.

When I came round, I found myself strapped to the side of Akercocke's cage. That vile ape was grinning. Then he threw a snowball at me. We were back here at Bumbach. Limping back into Bumbach, where tonight we sit again in the church, huddled around a fire of burning pews.

No one says anything.

I could almost wish Allah existed, for your sake, Zuleika.

Satan's howling. I don't know why. He's had his dinner.

Faust's lit a black candle.

Helen's hiccups have stopped.

21 Ice Cream

Faust says he's seen his friar again. Here. In Milan. Outside the cathedral, he says, on the Piazza del Duomo. Broad daylight. The Herr Doktor was taking his ease, eating an ice cream. That's a Milanese delicacy, a compound of sickly sweet custards congealed into ice.

Mephistopheles wasn't eating ice cream. He came out of the cathedral. It was half past three.

No doubt he'd been hearing confessions.

22 In the Funhouse

We're still in the funhouse. Here, in Milan, Tuesday 20th March, nearly three weeks since leaving the Tower. To make matters worse, I have to report that the funhouse is the Castel Sforzesco. Yup, we're staying overnight in the best castle in Milan, as guests of the Spanish Viceroy! It seems he's a chum of the Doktor's. He greeted him like one, no kidding, and didn't so much as raise the old viceregal eyebrows when Faust introduced Helen and me and the rest of our Rome-going gang. So, tonight, oh such bliss, feather beds!

I've just taken a bath. I've washed the Alps out of my hair. I've my own room to write in. (Well, with Akercocke.)

We had truffles for dinner.

23 Helioeccentrics

From Bumbach to Milan is 100 miles as the crow flies. We're not crows, and we follow a dog Faust calls Satan. (It's still around, cocking its leg on the Viceroy's throne last time I saw the creature.) A crow, like I say, might think it a mere 100 miles. The way we came, nearer 200.

A hard coming we had of it.

As Martin Luther said to the actress.

We went over the Furka and through the St Gotthard Pass. That took us four days. On the trail up the Furka, we had to walk *behind* the horses, holding on to their tails and letting them pull us. You can guide a horse by the tail. Which is more than you can say for a Faust.

The road was really slippy coming down. We soon found we couldn't manage it mounted, so we walked in front, the horses following us like dogs. Like every dog in the world, except John Calvin's. Satan, that mangy agent of Predestination, he loped in front.

We met quite a lot of traffic once we got back on the main pilgrim roads. People. Laden mules. Hordes of dun kine when we hit the Ticino.

Coming through the St Gotthard, we saw this eclipse of the sun.

Faust said it was like the fall of Lucifer out of heaven. He got really worked up. He stood on a crag just to toast it.

Helen said it was an emblem of salvation. God's hand in the sky, she said, blotting out the sins of mankind. She went on moralising and allegorising that eclipse for about 7 miles. It was like the glory depicted by old painters around the head of a saint, she said, etc, etc.

I put my hands over my ears. I thought of Copernicus. I should have been apprentice to him.

It was the first time I'd seen an eclipse of the sun.

I was fool enough to say so out loud.

So Faust says:

'I once saw a better one.'

'Where?'

'In Gitta in Samaria.'

'When?'

'Oh, during the reign of Claudius.'

He'd have been wearing his Simon Magus suit then.

'If you're that clever,' I said, 'could I have Salome and Zuleika back, please?'

Faust shut up.

24   A Diet of Worms

Bellinzona's built on hills, on the left bank of the Ticino. It's a town with three castles. We put up at none of them. We stayed in the brothel.

I'm not bitching.

Our rooms were clean enough. Nice high beds. And they'd just changed the paper in the window panes.

Brothels are OK with me. Erasmus had the pox. Also Pope Julius 2. Then there was Ulrich von Huten. Who was Ulrich von Huten? A clever man, Ulrich. He wrote a bestseller, *How to Cure Your Own Pox*, and then died of it.

You know the one about Luther and the pox?

When he was a young spark, Justification by Faith Alone

156

already hot in him, the Constipator goes down to the whore-house in Erfurt and asks for something special: 'A diet of worms.'

'What you mean?' says the madam.

'I mean, madam,' says Luther, 'I require a young lady with syphilis.'

'You're sick!' says the madam. 'I keep a clean house. Not one of the girls here has syphilis.'

'In that case,' says Luther, 'goodbye and God bless you.'

'Wait a tick,' says the madam. 'I could always oblige you myself . . . But *why* does it have to be someone with syphilis?'

'I want to catch it,' says Luther. 'So I can give it to the housemaid.'

The madam thinks that this isn't nice. 'Sweet Mary Mag-dalene!' she cries. 'What kind of monster are you? Just what you got against the poor girl?'

'Not a thing,' answers Luther. 'But she'll give it to Dad.'

'So you hate your dad, do you?'

'No, I don't,' explains Luther. 'It's just that he'll give it to Mother, that's all.'

The madam is shocked. 'You want to kill your poor mother?'

Luther's shocked too. 'No, of course not,' he explains. 'It's just that Mum will give it to the priest.'

'The priest!' shrieks the madam.

'You're an understanding woman,' says Luther. 'Yup! You've got it! That priest is the son-of-a-bitch I'm after!'

25   And Cream

I shared a room in the brothel with Justine. It was right next to Faust and Helen's room.

There was this spy-hole in the wall between the rooms.

I didn't sit there all night watching them.

I had better things to do.

Like Justine.

Justine's dad was a usurer in Venice. Justine was bought by one of the Medici family, she says, when she was only 12 years old. The Medicis are great patrons of the arts. Justine was introduced to Michelangelo. She was also introduced to the

Medici bed. When I first met her, she was still a virgin, but a virgin brought up on the cream of Italy's most noble family. Justine at 15 had sucked more Medici pricks than she'd had hot dinners. Not that I libel the Medicis. They're generous with food, you understand.

Anyhow, that's Justine's excuse.

The girl can't help it. She just likes sucking prick.

She's got a mouth made for it.

Red as two rowanberries.

Lips always cool.

Thin hard tongue.

She likes me to stand while she sucks me.

High arched eyebrows.

Deep throat.

A really nice person, Justine.

26   An Inspiring Message

Well, at midnight Justine wakes me up. She points to the spy-hole. I peep.

There's Faust, sprawled flat out with his boots on. God knows how he did it. He must have taken his boots off to get his breeches down. Then he must have put his boots back on. His boots were *all* that he was wearing, you understand.

Helen's kneeling beside him.

She's wearing her 'Anne Boleyn' nightie. The one with the scarlet ruff.

'John! Angel! It's happened again!'

(The wall was that thin. I could hear every word that they said. Not that Faust got too many in.)

She was holding him hard by the boots.

She shook him like mad.

Faust opens one eye, then the other.

'To Rome!' he yells out.

'Yes, of course. We are well on the way, dearest heart. But just listen! I've seen Her again!'

Faust fell back asleep with a crash.

'My poor darling!' says Helen, stroking his boots. 'Have faith, John. Have faith, sweet. Have faith!'

She emptied the chamber pot over him.

I think it must have been the chamber pot.

There weren't any flowers in it, and it was brimming.

Faust struggles up, like he's swallowed a newt.

'She was there in the street,' Helen said, for all the world as if he's asked her a question. 'Don't spit, dear. It's common.'

She cradled his boots in her arms. Which made Faust lie still.

Scraggy wrists. Show her age. She's no chicken.

'I was *drawn* to the window,' Helen said. 'I'd just finished my prayers for you, darling. Something told me to look out the window.'

I wonder, did the same something tell her to punch a hole in it? Like I said, those Bellinzona windows were paper.

'She was *hovering*, John. Oh, so pretty! She was wearing this dinkiest dress of sky blue, of blue sky, with just a hint of pale mauve at the cuffs. She called up to me, darling.'

Surely 'She' must have called *down*?

'She gave me a Message,' Helen said. 'She gave it, and then She was gone. There was that *melodious twang* again as She went back to Heaven. Our Lady, dear. You know what She said?'

Faust showed no signs that I could see of either knowing or caring what the Virgin Mary had said up or down to Helen from her hovering position just outside the whorehouse.

He'd plugged his brandy back into his mouth. He was guzzling, and staring at the ceiling. Pornographic cartoons all over the ceilings in both rooms, incidentally. Did Michelangelo ever not sleep here?

'*Helen*, she said,' said Helen. '*Just you tell him to buck up and not to worry! It's going to be All Right!* Then she evaporated. Well, isn't that an Inspiring Message, John? Straight from Our Lady's mouth. Delivered to me. *Buck up! Don't worry! It's going to be All Right!* Of course, it doesn't mean you can skip the little problems in our path. You still have to make your Confession to the Pope. But he'd bound to forgive you your sins. And then you'll be happy. That's what the Message means, dear. The Blessed Virgin has given Her word to your Helen. We're going to beat that old Devil! We're going to win!'

Faust was snoring. He'd fallen asleep in the middle.

Helen took his bottle away.

So Faust kicked her.

He can do things like that in his sleep.

159

Helen planted a kiss on his forehead.

'I'm so glad it's soothed you,' she said. 'Such lovely words. Like ointment. I thought so myself.'

All the same, her face seemed to be thinking some different stuff as she squatted alongside that snoring tormented nude figure.

Faust's chest looks like a harp, he's so gaunt. His loins grind into his paunch like broken levers.

I shook my head at Justine. I went back to sleep. But that wasn't the end of the night's visions.

27   An Awful Warning

Justine must have stayed wide awake. She'd be wanting more sucks. It was just before dawn when she woke me.

'Madonna,' she whispers.

I looked sleepily through the small spy-hole, half-expecting a gown of the dinkiest blue. Instead, there was Helen, dressed to kill in a black riding habit, a little box of a hat on her head, helping Faust to get into his breeches. A task made more complicated by the fact that she was clutching the feather from the wing of the Archangel Gabriel in her right fist.

'A fly in a jamjar?' Faust said.

'Buzzing,' said Helen. 'A whizzing and whooshing sound. I was dozing. I opened my eyes. She was standing right here where I'm standing now. I smiled at Her, darling. After all, I'm getting quite used to her company. But she didn't smile back. She looked terribly stern. *Tell him*, she said, *tell him not to mess around with Other Ideas.* What can she mean, John?'

Faust patted his codpiece.

Then:

'Wagner,' he says.

The old sod! I nearly hammered the wall.

'I suspected as much,' Helen says. 'We should never have let him come with us. Him and his whores. A Bad Influence!'

Me.

His disciple. His pal.

'Then she opened her hands,' Helen said. 'Her hands are so pretty, beloved, but the light shining out of her fingernails went right down through the floorboards and into the earth. I saw a great sea of fire. There were demons and souls in the fire down there in the earth, and the souls were like red-hot coals, and the demons were shovelling them.'

Helen was shaking her archangel feather.

'O my love!' she exclaimed. 'It was *Hell!*'

'Sounds like it,' Faust said.

'Don't go there!' Helen cried. 'Don't go there with Wagner! Go to Rome, to the Pope, to Confession. It's your only hope, precious!'

Faust was having trouble pulling on his boots.

'I *am* going to Rome,' he said, panting. 'What else does it look like I'm doing?'

'No Other Ideas?' Helen said.

'Of course not,' lied Faust.

Helen blessed him with her feather.

'I knew you'd heed Our Lady's Warning,' she said. 'But why do we have to take that boy and his whores and his monkey? Let's run away now! Leave them here!'

Faust stood up uncertainly. For a moment I thought he was going to agree with this monstrous suggestion. Then he shook his head.

'I can't do that, Helen.'

'Why not?'

'Wagner's writing my history.'

'A book? What nonsense! I'm talking about your immortal soul, John!'

'So's Kit,' Faust said.

Helen stamped. First one foot, then the other.

'I don't understand you,' she said.

This was the only sensible remark I heard through that wall in the brothel.

Faust strapped on his swords. He went out then, whistling for Satan.

'Kit needs me,' he called back from the door.

Oh yeah?

Like a hole in the head!

28 How Tall is the Virgin Mary?

Faust rode on alone on the way to Lugano.

I chatted up Helen.

'How tall would you say the Virgin Mary was?'

She sniffed at me angrily.

'That's a very odd question,' she said.

'I'm just curious,' I said. 'Six feet eight?'

'Why are you always so *rude*?' Helen said.

'I read somewhere that Mary was really tall,' I said.

'Has anyone ever told you you're a jerk?' Helen said.

'The Virgin Mary,' I said.

'Our Lady wouldn't *lower* herself to speak to you!'

'So she's taller than me?'

'You're a spy!' Helen said. 'You're a creepy eavesdropper. I'll tell John.'

'She must have been taller than Jesus,' I said.

'Blasphemer!' Helen said.

'I'm just curious,' I said. 'I believe –'

'No, you don't,' Helen said. 'You don't believe in anything.'

'I was just going to say that I believe in free will and that I'm interested in people's heights.'

Helen rode on in silence for a bit.

Then she said:

'I don't know what you're talking about. But you're barking up the wrong tree if you think that Our Lady is tall.'

'I see,' I said. 'So she's small then?'

'Oh, yes,' Helen said.

'Small and indescribably lovely?'

'That's right,' Helen said.

'About your own height?' I said.

I daresay Helen would have had hiccups, but at this point we caught up with Faust. He had fallen from his horse. He was rolling in the dirt of the road. He was chewing it.

I went to retrieve the stray animal.

29   Customs

We crossed the Swiss border at a place called Chiasso next day.
At this frontier certain Spanish sex-maniacs calling themselves
Customs Men detained us. They fingered the girls in the name
of the Holy Roman Emperor Charles 5.

I protected my ointment box, by treating it as of no import-
ance. It was overlooked, with these papers safely inside it.

However, they relieved me of my Caminelleo Vitelli.
Foreigners aren't permitted to bear modern weapons in Spanish
dominions, these Customs Men claimed. More likely that one
of them fancied it. There was nothing I could do. I suppose I
was lucky to hang on to my old German wheel-lock. They
treated that just as a joke.

Helen was having puppies that the Customs Men would take
away her Gabriel feather. She'd secreted it down in her drawers
– which was, of course, the very first place that they looked. But
its discovery just led to a lot of eye-rolling and moustache-
twisting plus what I took to be lewd Spanish speculation concerning what turns German women on.

Faust sobered up sufficiently to bribe the Customs Men with
silver. This was what he should have done before we were
pestered at all. They saluted quite smartly for Spaniards. We
passed into Inquisition Land.

30   Romance

Como squats at the end of its lake. A nasty spot. Crawling with
silk merchants, red snails, and flagellants. We found shelter in a
ruined Roman villa outside the town walls. Satan dug up a
sepulchral urn and ate the contents.

We stayed there three days, Faust drinking, Helen complain-
ing, and Justine with toothache. I got so depressed that I even
fed Akercocke. The third night, for something to do, I took
Marguerite and Gretchen for a sail in a boat on the lake. It was
really romantic. The wind got up. Gretchen was sick. The stars

looked just the same as the ones I used to see back at the Tower. But I'm not an astronomer.

Still, tonight it's Milan and the viceregal palace and Faust telling me he saw Mephistopheles among a pack of Franciscans (no better than tramps) coming out of the cathedral.

Over ice cream.

'Bugger Mephistopheles!' I said.

'I couldn't,' Faust said. 'Not in broad daylight on the Piazza del Duomo. What do you take me for?'

31 A Chainmail Freak

We'd not gone far out of Milan when we met this old-fashioned knight.

He was guarding a crossroads on the Piacenzan Way.

Helmed, armoured, encased in plate inches-thick. A dirty great lance under his oxter, couched at the ready. Huge horse, armoured also.

A chainmail freak.

We could have left the road and gone round him, but Satan went running straight past the spot where the knight stood guard, so of course Faust insists that we follow the dog.

When we're not far off, the knight snaps shut his visor and shouts. It was impossible to hear what he shouted, because of the visor. But the meaning was plain.

'Dr Faustus,' the boss roars out. 'V.V.V.V.V.'

'We're pilgrims,' cries Helen. 'Simple travellers to Rome, to the Holy Father, in the Name of the Virgin – O crumpets!'

The knight had clapped spurs to his steed, finding a couple of areas uncovered by armour, and knight and horse bore down on Faust like a rusty metal mountain with four legs and a prong stuck out the front.

Luckily for the Herr Vs, his own horse took fright at the prospect. It threw him, then bolted. Faust face down in the mud. His hat rolling.

It's a difficult job stopping one of those war-machines once they're wound up. The knight and his horse went straight over Faust and came thundering on towards my girls.

Much shrieking and jumping. But nobody struck save the

knight, Nadja getting in a good sharp crack with her long-handled whip as he trundled past her.

Faust scrambles to his feet, unhurt, spitting out a mouthful of Lombardy. He draws his sword and takes several swipes at the morning. His cloak's swirling about him. His sword catches in the cloak, makes a trap of it, and he's down in the mud once again.

'Ride on!' I called to the girls, once all were remounted and the pack horses back in a line.

Then I drew my wheel-lock pistol from its saddle-holster. I fired a ball over the knight's helmet just in case he had plans of attempting a U-turn when his horse lost momentum. I needn't have bothered. Satan's come bowling through the lot of us and pelted off in full cry after the cranking lunatic. The armoured horse veers from the road, jumps a ditch, and deposits the knight in a bush.

Faust's upright. He puts on his hat like a crown.

'You see that? The coward! I killed him!'

'He's just stuck in the holly,' I said.

I pulled up a spare horse alongside the mud-plastered magus where he was now attempting to sheathe his sword and swig brandy at the same time. Jane and me hoisted him over the horse. We forced him off Romewards in pursuit of the others.

When Satan came back he was wearing a beard.

It was half of the knight's horse's tail.

Faust went on insisting for the rest of that day that he'd 'slain' the knight in 'mortal combat'. I got tired of repeating the truth. Especially when Helen said: 'Why don't you shut up? You're always determined to *spoil* everything! You and your scoffing!'

32 Trithemius Revised

We slept that night in a barn. I can't remember where it was. I can remember only the smell of olives, and the fact that at dawn the trees on the slopes round about us changed colour from green to white as the wind got up. Our breakfast was wine and stale cake.

The Herr Doktor appeared in uncommonly talkative form, inspired no doubt by his slaying of the chainmail freak. Whether for this reason or some other, he dropped back from the head of the column and we rode for a while spur-to-spur.

'How's my history going?' he asked.

'Truthfully,' I said.

Faust laughed.

I was startled. He doesn't often laugh these days, despite his alleged subscription to that theology of Aristotle's – that laughter is what distinguishes man from the other animals. Grinning, yes. He does a lot of his horrible grinning, his lips pressed together, the corners of his mouth curling into those clotted moustaches. He crosses his eyes when he grins. When he crosses his eyes it's like two fish – blue, freezing – coming swimming together in the long sunless pool of his face.

I expected him to make some Pontius Pilate crack about *What is truth?* Instead, he said:

'Have you got to Trithemius yet?'

'Long ago.'

'What he wrote about me?'

'Yes.'

I was wondering how Faust could possibly know about that letter from the Abbot Trithemius to the court mathematician Virdung (concerning 'the so-called Sabellicus'), unless he had indeed spied upon these papers back at the Tower, when he cancelled my train of thought with a curse.

'Fuck Trithemius!'

'Because he saw through you?'

'Saw? The bastard was blind!'

'Just because he disliked you then?'

'Trithemius didn't dislike me. He liked me too much.'

'I see. There's another version of what happened at Kreuznach is there?'

'There's always another version,' Faust said. 'I don't mean just a second version, either. I mean after you've told everything you think you know in as many different ways as you can, there will still always be something that you've not told, and another way of telling it which is better than all the ways you've tried. Take Trithemius. You're inclined to accept his version of me at its face value. But what if I told you that he was a magician himself? Wouldn't that fact alter every tone in the picture?'

'Was he?' I said.

'He tried to raise the dead in front of the Emperor Maximilian,' Faust said. 'And failed.'

'I didn't know that,' I admitted. 'I do know he wrote several books on occult subjects. Books I've never been able to get hold of.'

'Not several,' Faust said. 'One. *Steganographia*.'

'That's its title?'

'Yes.'

'What's it like?'

'Pure shit!'

'Shit?'

'Pure shit!'

I had heard that critical judgement before. When I first met him. His opinion of Aquinas on angels.

Does the Herr Sage have such an extremely excremental view of all literature?

I rode along thinking of turds and angels.

Faust, meanwhile, gave me *his* version of what happened at Kreuznach. He was working in that town, he said, as a school-master, pursuing magical and alchemical experiments at night. One evening he went to the churchyard to try and raise the Devil. He was drunk. He fell into a freshly dug grave. It was comfortable, he said, so he just lay there dozing on his back. Round about midnight, he began incantating, more to pass the time than anything else. Immediately, lights appeared around the edge of the grave, torches burning, and other voices joined his incantations. Faust sees these figures in long black robes in the moonlight. He leaps from the grave! He's convinced he's succeeded in summoning the dead!

The guys in black robes treat Faust with great fear and deference for a brief while. Then they slug him. He's carted off to Sponheim Abbey, Trithemius's place.

What has happened, of course, is that Trithemius's monks went to the graveyard to do a spot of Devil-raising on their master's behalf. They half-believe that Faust came in answer to their prayers, just as he half-believes that they came in answer to his.

This state of affairs is soon altered, on Faust's side at least. He finds that Trithemius is as queer as a coot, a very kinky devil indeed. Sponheim Abbey's a nest of ninnies, a paradise for brown hatters, a home from home for every anal passive in the Palatinate. Trithemius is King Bugger in this hive. For his part,

he more than half-believes Faust is the Devil's dear brother-in-
law.

Until Faust says no.

Until Faust refuses to be buggered by Trithemius.

Faust fled.

The abbot, piqued, wrote as he did.

Attributing his own sins to his new enemy, he cooked up that
story of Faust sacked from his job as a teacher on account of
buggering the schoolboys. The truth was, Faust said, that he
fled because he didn't feel like bending for Trithemius.

'But what of those boys of Kreuznach?' I asked him.

Faust stroked his boil.

'I didn't touch them,' he said.

'Are you telling the truth now?'

Faust pulled a sour face.

'Never mind big words like *truth*,' he said. 'They were all far
too ugly.'

33   Dot Dot Dot

This was the day that Jane began getting restive.

The horse riding was giving her the hots.

'Kit,' she said. 'I've an itch in my knickers.'

'Well, scratch it,' I said.

'I'd rather you scratched it,' Jane said.

Faust had ridden up to the head of the column again. A sultry
spring day, most unseasonable, the Lombardy landscape very
boring and the sky like a lake of burnt yellow.

Jane was bored.

I was bored.

So we fucked.

Dot dot dot, I would say. That fucking in the middle of our
day's journey being in itself a natural and private matter, nothing to do with Faust's story. But three others came * into the
fuck, so I can't leave it there.

We had retired from the road to this field that was bounded
by a low stone wall. The field was full of beginning spring corn.
My knuckles got green where they pressed down into the earth

* And went! You'll see.

under Jane's behind. I had to perform this small service of cushion for her, since the corn was so prickly. What with the thrust of the spring corn up and my thrust down, Jane came really quickly. I was taking longer when I heard giggles. Two heads peeping through a hole in the wall. It was Marguerite and Gretchen. They'd sneaked back to watch.

'Clear off!' I shouted.

They wouldn't. And I was in no position to make them do anything. Jane wouldn't let me out. 'Ignore them,' she said.

That I could hardly do either. Marguerite and Gretchen were only a few yards away, squatting level with my head. They looked so young and innocent you'd have thought butter wouldn't melt in their cunts. But the sight of me fucking Jane was too much for the pair of them. First, Marguerite stroked Gretchen's breasts, then Gretchen started kissing Marguerite on the mouth. They soon had their fingers in each other's knickers. The twins wanked each other in time to my fucking of Jane.

I came.

So did Nadja.

That's to say — Just as I reached my orgasm, Nadja appeared behind the twins in the hole in the wall. She was cracking her horsewhip. Marguerite and Gretchen screamed. They leapt the wall and scuttled away across the cornfield, trying to pull up their knickers as they went. Nadja went after them, cutting at their bottoms with her whip.

This made Jane the more horny.

She grabbed me by the prick and tugged me across the field in another direction. We went into this coppice and fucked again. Twice. Really nice.

Afterwards, we had to gallop our horses to catch up with the others.

No Nadja!

No Marguerite and Gretchen!

I kept looking round for them.

The road was empty.

They didn't come back.

. . .

34 Monkey Talk

I had no peace to think about it. All that afternoon, as we rode down the Emilian Way towards Piacenza, Akercocke kept up a steady stream of chattering. Gibberish, it sounded. He was leaping about in his cage. Eyes bright. Baring his choppers. Then, gradually, it seemed to my ears that his noises had turned into one noise, and that what had been a meaningless torrent of sound was now the soft utterance of a single word.

'Hell,' Akercocke said.

Over and over.

Hell. Hell. Hell. Hell.

Grinning at me.

Rubbing his cowl.

Hell!

'Can monkeys learn to speak?' I asked Faust. 'Do they imitate their human masters, ever?'

'Akercocke isn't a monkey,' Faust said. 'He's a spirit.'

'He's a Capuchin monkey,' I said.

'I see you've lost three more,' Faust said. 'You'll be celibate soon, at this rate.'

I clenched my fists. Walked away. Calmed myself down by watching our horses roll and graze to their hearts' content in sweet spring grass. We spent that night in a cave near a village called Medesano in the Apennines.

35 Perfection

Next morning I woke feeling jangled. My nerves were like guts on a gamba.

Akercocke started chattering as soon as we hit the road. The same word. *Hell, hell, hell, hell.* His voice high-pitched and hoarse. His tone mocking.

'OK,' I said. 'OK, Akercocke. If it's hell you want, it's hell you're going to get . . .'

We were riding through an eerie volcanic landscape dotted

with hot springs and craters. The springs were sulphurous. Tall scalding plumes of steamy yellow filth. There are one or two patches like this on the fair face of Italy. Notably the Phlegrean Fields, at Pozzuoli, near Naples, so I've heard. But if the Phlegrean Fields are more hellish than that pock-marked country in the first tract of the Apennines then I'll be an enema for Luther.

I made up my mind to drop Akercocke down one of the holes.

I took Jane into my confidence. I reckoned I'd need help, and Jane was strong.

We lagged further and further behind, pretending with our spurs.

Jane held the reins of the horse that bore Akercocke in his brass cage.

The monkey fell silent. Almost as if he guessed what I planned to do. But of course he couldn't have.

We turned aside, into the Solfatara . . .

We rode for about a mile, following a deep crack in the earth. At the end of this crack was perfection: a scalding hot fountain screaming up out of the ground through a hole like the grin in a skull.

'Hell,' Akercocke said.

'Too right, monkey,' I told him.

I tied one end of a rope to Akercocke's cage. I threw the rope up over a blasted tree. I took the dangling end and walked around the hole. The idea was simple. I'd pull on the rope. Then I'd drop cage and Akercocke, when they were hanging in the middle of the steam. If the scalding didn't kill him, the fall would. Jane's job was to make sure the cage swung the right way.

I hold Akercocke responsible for Jane's death.

While I was still walking, before I'd even tugged on the rope, the monkey must have thrown himself against the side of his cage with such force that it swung free from the rock where it rested.

The cage hit Jane in the back.

She fell forwards down the spurting sulphur fountain.

The cage swung against the tree.

I heaved and pulled.

It wouldn't budge.

Akercocke had grabbed hold of the tree trunk.

171

36 Credo

Look here.

These things really happened.

Marguerite and Gretchen disappearing across a green field, pulling up their knickers as they ran. Nadja going after them, and brandishing a whip.

Jane head-first down a hell-hole.

These things *happened*.

But I can't believe they happened either!

So just what do you do when you can't believe that what happened *did* happen?

You can write it down carefully, factually, leaving nothing out, and concentrating on externals, that's all you can do. Who knows? You might make sense of it.

I tried to do that in Part One, with the Rat and the Spy and the Jumping Apple. Suppose now, just for a moment, that I witnessed the phenomena as described, but that there was no Rat, there was no Spy, and the Apple really did jump on its own ... Where would that leave us? In the angelic shit, I guess. Looking for some supernatural explanation.

Believe me, I'd much rather write about angels.

Or, if not angels, sausages.

I'm here in Siena where the beds are soft and the chimneys are like flower pots, and I'd rather not believe in the twins disappearing, and Nadja disappearing, and in particular poor Jane disappearing down that boiling fountain.

I'd rather not believe in Faust, if it comes to that.

All belief is essentially an act of the will.

My first lesson at Wittenberg.

Well, I am *un*willing. Unwilling to believe that these things that happened round me *could* have happened.

I'd prefer not to believe them possible.

I'm writing them down against my will. I have to.

I'd rather be thinking of angels or sausages right now.

Angels are works of pure fiction.

Sausages are works of pure fact.

They make very nice sausages here in Siena. All the streets smell of sausages.

Angels are zero.

Sausages you can count.

(I ate 3 while I wrote the last chapter.)

Hey ho.

There we go.

I can't write about angels or sausages because angels and sausages didn't happen to me on the road from Milan to Siena and the things that I'm telling you did.

37   Legless Bees

'Hell,' Akercocke said.

And we rode.

(Why didn't I leave him? I don't know. Maybe because it seemed too inconclusive. I was stunned by what happened to Jane. I hardly knew what I was doing. I just rode after Faust, taking Akercocke, still in his cage.)

I caught up with the others as they forded the River Taro. Faust was pissed. He fell in the river. When I pulled him out he just grinned.

He said nothing about Jane not being with me. So I didn't explain. We rode on, behind Satan. We rode on all night.

At dawn we came into the valley of the River Serchio, which is called Garfagnana.

Our horses were exhausted.

Faust curled asleep under a tree. Justine slept too. Helen crept off to pray at a shrine by the wayside. She fell asleep praying.

I sat and watched Satan. It was using its right hind leg to scratch fleas from what's left of its coat.

Then the dog fell asleep. So did Akercocke.

I couldn't sleep.

As the sun got up, that valley turned into an oven.

The others slept on.

I walked into the shade of some cypresses. There I found this dead calf.

It was crawling with bees. Black and yellow bees, hairy, long-tongued. They swarmed up and buzzed round my face. They appeared to be stingless. Lots of them settled on my hands and my neck, and I had to brush them away, but I wasn't stung.

I saw that the swarm of bees had hatched out in the carcass itself.

There was one other peculiar thing. These bees had no legs. I can't figure out if this had something to do with their lack of the usual poison glands.

Virgil once saw bees like that.

Legless.

A swarm of them.

Hatched in the carcass of a calf.

It's somewhere in his *Georgics*.

The world doesn't change much. I saw no more than a poet saw, all those centuries ago. (Poets in general I dislike. They are liars. But Virgil is different. An *observer*.)

Well, then, as I crouched there, under the cypresses, beside the carcass, the significance of seeing this sight, then, that morning, came home to me. I remembered that when I was at Wittenberg there was this French priest, Guillaume Michel, a translator of Virgil, who insisted on moralising every image the poet drew from his plain observations. This particular image – legless bees hatched in a dead calf – excited Michel to one of his wackiest flights. It must represent something, he said, and that something would be Virgil's unconscious meaning. Since Virgil lived and wrote without the benefits of Christianity, his priestly interpreter waxed hot and ingenious under the surplice. According to Michel, the image must stand for 'the new man regenerated in the blood of Jesus Christ, with no power of his own to walk and make progress along the path of virtue.'

I ask you!

I say I saw a swarm of legless bees in a dead calf.

I say Virgil did too.

Bees mean bees. Legless means legless. Calf means calf. Dead means dead.

Here ends the first lesson.

And I was glad I had jam up my nose.

38 Manners

At sunset we limped into Lucca.

White oxen. Cool streams. A gibbet where 10 bodies swung.

We put up at a reasonable hostelry. Good stables for our poor tired horses.

But the manners of Lucca . . .

Manners?

Pigs play pianners!

'Where's the privy?' I asked the potboy.

'Out the back in the courtyard,' he said.

I went out into the courtyard. A bright moonlit night. But I could find no doors at all.

I came back to the potboy.

'Where *exactly* in the courtyard?' I enquired.

'Oh, wherever you like, sir,' he said.

39 'God'

Akercocke started saying a new word that night.

'God,' he said.

Over and over.

Just the single word: *God.*

Like water dripping in an empty cave, it was.

God. God. God. God.

I got out. I met Helen. That wasn't much better. She was kneeling in her nightie on the stairs, telling her beads.

'Don't you need your beauty sleep?' I said.

'God's Mother has preserved us this far,' she replied. 'You should join me in thanking Her.'

I went for a walk instead.

In the Piazza del Mercato, carved out of the ruins of the ancient amphitheatre, I met Satan and Faust.

The dog seemed as drunk as the doctor.

They were sprawled there in the shadow of an arch, both scratching, both staring at the moon.

'Akercocke's saying *God* now,' I said.

'He'll get over it,' Faust said.

I was in a foul mood.

'Why don't you keep Mephistopheles in a cage?' I demanded. 'They could talk to each other, him and Akercocke. Between them, they might know enough words for a spell to bring my girls back, even . . .'

Faust was rubbing his boil against Satan's muzzle.

'The Devil looks after his own,' he said.

I whistled.

'I see,' I said. 'According to Helen, I'm supposed to believe that we journey to Rome under the skirts of the Virgin Mary. According to you, that the Devil has his pitchfork in us all. Well, I think you're both bananas. And that's that.'

I came back to my room. Akercocke had fallen asleep at last. I took the opportunity to check over the contents of my box. These papers were safe inside. I started to read them by candlelight, needing the comfort of some contact with reality, with sanity, with the order that my mind alone seems able to bring to this whirlwind of crazy adventures that goes with John Faust.

But my own words danced in front of my eyes. I couldn't follow them. I was shagged out. I must have fallen asleep with my arms crossed on the pages, making a pillow.

40 Bald Conrad

When I woke it was morning.

Faust was sitting on the windowseat of my room. He had a small heap of coins in the lap of his cloak. He was counting them. It was the noise that the coins made that woke me.

'Conrad was bald,' Faust remarked.

I rubbed at my eyes.

'What?' I said.

'Conrad Mutianus,' he said. 'He was bald as an egg.'

I stuffed my papers back in the ointment box.

'Get lost,' I said.

Faust grinned.

He crossed his eyes, holding up some Tuscan coin between thumb and forefinger. A livre, I think it was. Perhaps a paul.

'It's a fact,' Faust said. The bright coin winked in his grasp. 'Facts,' he went on. 'That's what you're after, isn't it? Well, I'm telling you, son. Friend Conrad didn't have a hair on his head.'

'You're just trying to throw me,' I muttered. 'If Conrad Mutian was bald how come he ever got a nickname like Rufus? Red-haired. I wasn't born yesterday, clown!'

Faust tossed the Tuscan coin and caught it deftly. Then he bit it between his teeth, and pulled a face.

'Toothache?' I said.

'My gall stones,' Faust said. 'Bit of gravel in the old kidney. Another nice fact for you. Hope you're putting it in?'

'Get Helen to bleed you,' I said.

Our voices woke Akercocke.

'God,' he announced, from under the cloth that still shrouded his cage.

'You hear that?' I said.

Faust shrugged. The shrug rucked up his cloak. That cloak's unbelievably crusted now, quite stiff with the accumulated dirt he's picked up from the roads.

'Just thought you ought to know, Kit,' he said, pouring the coins into a green velvet bag and drawing a cord tight round its neck. 'That red hair wasn't real hair at all. A wig, boy, a wig! Herr Mutian was a vain little prick. When I met him at Erfurt I remarked how the wig didn't suit him. *Your head lies*, I said. He never forgave me.'

I was resealing my ointment box while I thought this one over. The implication was obvious. Faust had looked at my book. He was poking sly fun at the way I'd clung to Conrad Mutian as a reliable witness concerning Faust's folly back there three years before the alleged events in Spisser's Wood.*

'Hey, half-god,' I said. 'Hey, half-god of Heidelberg, if you're really so devilish smart, how come you got chucked out of Ingolstadt?'

Faust frowned at me.

'Eck,' he said.

'Eck?'

'Eck. I did a little job for him. Then he wanted rid of me. But what's all this about half-gods? I don't understand.'

I let *Eck* go.

Eck, Johann Maier of Eck, chief opponent of the Constipator.

* See Part One, Chapter 45.

Eck, bright light of Ingolstadt, theologian, fornicator, drunk, defender of interest up to a return on capital of 5 per cent. Did Faust really want me to credit that he could have helped Eck against Luther? Eck, who got the Pope to excommunicate his enemy by that bull *Exsurge Domine*. (The Constipator wiped his arse on it, and then burned the proceeds in public.)

'Helmitheus Hedebergensis,' I said. 'Mutian said that's what you called yourself. It used to puzzle me. Then I worked it out. He got it wrong. Hemitheus Hedelbergensis, wasn't it? Half-god of Heidelberg. One of your fancy titles?'

Faust shook his head.

'Facts,' he said sarcastically. 'You won't get far with your sticking to facts if you get them as wrong as you've got that one. Listen, I'll tell you. Your Conrad was deaf in one ear as well as quite bald. He must have misheard me.'

'So what *did* you call yourself?'

'Hermes Trismegistus,' said Faust.

I groaned.

We were back to another bad apple on the Herr Phoney's Reincarnation Tree. Hermes Trismegistus ('Hermes the Thrice-Greatest') was some Gnostic, 2nd century, who wrote all this starry-souled cosmological crud about man ascending to God through the 7 spheres of the planets. *Poimandres*, his treatise was called. First published in Latin by the Platonist Marsilio Ficini about 80 years back.

'Let's drop it,' I said.

'Bald Conrad,' Faust said, tossing his bag of coins from one hand to the other. 'Mutian mouldy ear.'

'OK,' I said. 'Thanks a lot.'

'Just thought you'd like the facts,' Faust said.

He was taking the piss out of me.

41 Joking Jesus

Faust's mockery continued, off and on, all the slow way to Siena. It took us 6 days, so we averaged not much more than 10 miles a day. Hard-baked landscape, big hills, and the weather unnaturally warm.

Nothing much to report as to incidents along that road.

On the 26th we were passed by a Papal messenger travelling north. Helen asked for his blessing. 'Mad Germans!' he cried, without stopping.

On the 28th, a Wednesday, we encountered a caravan of gipsies. Glittering teeth, greasy ringlets, eyes like sloeberries. Faust purchased a Tarot pack from them, saying that by an oversight he'd left his own behind at the Tower. Helen wouldn't speak to him all afternoon. 'The Devil's Bible,' she said.

There was one small adventure on the night of the 29th, yesterday. We'd put up at a hospice in a dump called Poggibonsi. In the middle of the night, Helen comes screeching into my room (I was busy with Justine, which embarrassed her). 'John's gone!' she informed me. I buttoned, and ran. I found that Faust had sleepwalked, mounting his horse without saddling it, and ridden through the town shouting *To Rome! To Rome!* before toppling into a trough. The experience sobered him a bit. But today he was back on the bottle.

The reason for our snail's pace was exhaustion plus Satan.

Every time the dog stopped, Faust stopped. If it crapped, if it went after rabbits, if it got a thorn in its foot, the Herr Doktor used this as an excuse to dismount and plug in with his brandy. Helen and Justine being saddle-sore, they didn't mind. They just waited, fans busy in the unconscionable sun. Helen prayed. I stared back down the road.

'They aren't coming back,' Faust remarked.

I'm grateful these last days have been quiet.

Quiet, that is, in events.

Not quiet in voices.

I could have done without Akercocke chanting his *God*.

I could have done without Faust altogether.

'Talking of facts,' he said, as we were riding across the plain of the River Arno. 'Some say that Christ wasn't crucified.'

'What on earth does that mean?' I demanded.

'There's a gospel,' Faust said, 'which teaches that Matthew, Mark, Luke, and John got it all wrong about the crucifixion. It was Simon of Cyrene who died on the cross.'

'Where was Jesus then?'

'Laughing.'

'*Laughing? Where?*'

'In the crowd,' Faust said.

I was speechless.

'Seth,' Faust said, patting his hat.

'What?'

'*The Second Treatise of the Great Seth*,' Faust said. 'A lost gospel.'

'If it's lost,' I said, 'how come you know it?'

Faust didn't answer.

'Jesus laughing while someone else was crucified,' I said. 'It doesn't make sense. Anyway, what's that got to do with me?'

'Facts,' Faust said. 'Facts are various. Matthew, Mark, Luke, and John all thought they were telling the truth.'

'But they weren't? And your lost gospel was?'

'I didn't say that. I just said it was *different*. Facts are ghosts. People see what their eyes can see.'

Drunken, inconsequent, he went on with some rigmarole about how he would have got married, only Mephistopheles advised him against it, apparently.

Helen perked up.

'We'll marry in Rome,' she said. 'The Holy Father will marry us, angel! After your Confession, of course.'

Faust shut up pretty fast then.

Was it Luther or Calvin who once said that hell is other people?

42   A Kick in the Balls

Before dawn, Saturday, March 31st. In 13 days' time, the sun will come up for Good Friday. Riding as pilgrims are supposed to ride (i.e. not stopping every time a dog called Satan takes a shit or sniffs a bitch on heat) we could cover the remaining 100 + miles between Siena and Rome in three or four days. It's a safe bet, we won't.

I've roused myself early to jot down a savage nonsense of last night.

I spent a long evening in the privacy of my room, writing those chapters which saw us here from Milan. When I finished I was thirsty. I'd been eating the local sausages, as I think I said, and while tasty they leave you feeling that you need a drink. It was midnight. I thought I'd broach a wine barrel in the parlour.

My room at this inn is at the top of a flight of stairs which come down in the hall near the main door. Bleary from too much writing about things which no sane man should ever have to write about, I wasn't looking where I was going. Also, that hall was ill-lit.

A figure ran into me as I stepped from the bottom stair. It was taller and heavier than me. I was knocked over.

I got to my feet with a curse. Made a grab at my assailant. His cloak came away in my hand.

He was shrieking:

'His leg! Christ! *His leg!*'

Then he made a swift exit, leaving me with the cloak.

(Quite a nice cloak. Ermine lining.)

I walked into the parlour. Faust was there on a couch by the fire. He had this black bag, silver clasps on its sides. He was emptying it out. Tuscan coinage ran everywhere, little rivers of sequins and scudi, livres and pauls.

'Kit, dear boy. I just got a good rate of exchange . . .'

'What's that?' I said idly, drawing my wine.

'All this,' Faust said, waving. 'In return for a leg.'

'I don't know what you're blethering about. As usual.'

'Then I'll tell you,' Faust said. 'While you sat up there scribbling, I was busy. I went down to that fountain in the Piazza del Campo. The Fonte Gaia, they call it. It's *the* spot for after-hours business. Well, I chatted up this merchant. I told him I'd good German dalers I wanted to change. He quoted some rate that would've beggared the Emperor. I said that was fine.'

'What you need so much money for?'

Faust ignored my question.

'I told the fat crook to call on me here, bringing the Tuscan loot with him, and I'd give him the dalers. The number of dalers he wanted! All our horses couldn't carry them!'

'And you tricked him,' I said.

'Listen, will you?' Faust said. 'When the gangster turned up with his money I was lying right here on this couch. Snoring my head off. Dead to the world.'

'That shouldn't have taken much effort. So what did he do?'

Faust grinned as he counted the scudi.

'What would you have done, Kit?'

'Shaken you. Woken you up.'

'That's just what he tried,' Faust went on. 'He put down his bag on the table. Then he seizes my arm and starts shaking me. He got annoyed when I didn't wake up. So he grabs hold of my

181

leg, and he starts to shake that. You know what I did then? I farted. But I didn't wake up. I just farted. So the bastard gets more and more violent. Both hands pulling hard at my leg. And what happens next? Why, *my leg comes right off in his hands!* That's what happens next.'

I gazed stupidly down at Faust's legs.

Both there, of course.

'He left in a hurry,' Faust said. 'Overlooking his bag.'

'That figures,' I said. 'How'd you do it? You have a false leg somewhere here?'

'I do not.'

The wine made me bold.

'I'm fed up with your boasting,' I said. 'Let *me* pull your leg off!'

Faust winked.

'You'd believe me then, would you?'

'I'd have to.'

Faust stretched out his leg.

I hesitated.

Then I reached for the grimy black boot . . .

Faust kicked me.

Hard.

Right in the balls.

'You're not ready for that yet,' he said.

I rolled on the floor in the firelight.

'Leg pulling?' I gasped.

It was nasty.

'No, son,' Faust announced. 'I mean wisdom.'

43   Sanctuary

The Abbey of Monte Oliveto Maggiore lies about 25 miles to the south east of Siena, in mountain country broken by ravines.

To this abbey we came in a thunderstorm at the end of our 33rd day. It stood like a castle on a long spur of rock under a jet-black sky being riven apart by fingers of lightning. The horses were scared. I had to hold Justine's by the head.

'You know this place?' I shouted to Faust, as we clattered up the rocky path to a battlemented gatehouse.

'The Mother House of the Olivetans.'

'Never heard of them.'

'A congregation of the Benedictine Order,' Faust said.

'*Ave Maria!*' cried Helen. 'We shall seek sanctuary here for the night.'

Faust reached up in his stirrups. He tugged at the bell-rope. I wondered if they'd hear the bell for thunder. The noise was deafening, the thunder echoing in those deep ravines.

A many-coloured Madonna stood guard above the portal.

'Bit tall wouldn't you say?' I asked Helen.

A grille in the door slid open.

I couldn't see any face behind the grille.

'Dr Sabellicus,' Faust shouted. '*Vi Veri Universum Vivus Vici.*'

The door swung open as the rain pitched down. We rode into the abbey. Monks took our horses. The monks all wore corpse-white habits.

Satan was wagging its tail.

One monk, taller than the others, patted the dog. His face was hard to make out in the cave of his cowl.

'Father Abbot is in the refectory,' he said in High German to Faust. 'Will you come this way?'

We started to follow him. He stopped then, and held up his hand.

'The ladies, I think, should go straight to their dormitory. I will have food sent up to them from the kitchens.'

Helen clawed at Faust's sleeve.

'He cannot mean *me*, John? I'll not sleep with Wagner's creature, and that's an end of it!'

Faust grinned.

He took the guestmaster to one side. I heard him mutter in Latin. I couldn't make out what was said.

When the guestmaster turned back to us, his palms were pressed together in a gesture like prayer.

'Dear sister,' he said to Helen, 'you shall have your own room, in the circumstances.'

Helen simpered.

I explained the arrangements to Justine. She didn't seem worried.

The guestmaster bowed his head. He beckoned.

Faust loped and lurched behind him, Satan at his heels. I watched Justine turn one way up a stair of ugly red brick, and

Helen the other. Each of them was escorted by a silent white-robed monk. I ran across the cobbles to catch up with Faust.

'You have been here before?'

'In a manner of speaking.'

'What the hell does that mean?'

'Ask Akercocke.'

I glared at the monkey. He was swinging in the brass cage on my arm.

'You're a devil,' I told Faust.

'Devil,' says Akercocke, as clear as you like.

'Ah! Another new word?' Faust observed.

We passed into the cloisters.

44   Il Sodoma

Stabbings of lightning lit the cloisters like day. I saw these weird frescoes adorning the walls. Their foregrounds showed monks in the corpse-white habits that seemed common to this Olivetan Order. The figures were slapdash and epicene. The back-grounds looked unusually lovely. Not Italian at all, to my eye. There was one with a delicate bridge like an eyebrow across a blue stream. The small boats in the water beneath the bridge looked so real that you got the impression they would rock up and down if you touched them. I saw a plate like that once in the Wartburg. Willow-pattern. A gift to the Elector from Japan.

'Scenes from the life of St Benedict of Norcia*,' Faust murmured. 'The third one's the artist's self-portrait.'

This third scene, showing one of St Benedict's early miracles, when he was still learning the trade, had a swarthy confident lout in the foreground, a far more striking figure than the saint himself. At the lout's feet I made out the shapes of two badgers and a raven.

'Il Sodoma,' Faust said.

'You're joking me!'

'Giovanni Antonio Bazzi,' Faust said. 'Nicknamed the Sodomite.'

'And was he?' I said.

* 6th-century wonderworker. Severe and solitary. Died standing up. Emblem: a broken cup.

'Have a look for yourself,' Faust replied. 'End corner. South wall.'

The lightning obliged us.

In the far corner of the south wall, just as we reached it, I saw this fresco that seemed hardly religious.

'Tell my friend here the story,' Faust said.

The guestmaster spoke with his back to us.

'The subject,' he said, 'is the wicked Florentius who, foiled in an attempt to poison Benedict our founder, sought instead to poison the souls of his monks by bringing females into the abbey.'

'They don't look like females,' I said.

'Let him finish,' Faust said.

The guestmaster went on:

'Il Sodoma let no one see this fresco while he was working. He hung a linen cloth across it, and fastened the cloth to the wall with nails. When the cloth was removed, the females were seen to be not only naked but voluptuous.'

The monk shivered.

The wall went black.

'The abbot of that day was outraged by the artist's impertinence. He ordered the work to be destroyed. But it wasn't destroyed. Il Sodoma was a joker, a prankster, a trickster. He sang obscene songs while he painted. His house was like a Noah's Ark, besides, and even when working here he brought his pets along. Tame badgers. A raven that talked. Anyway, he agreed to compromise.'

The lightning lit the cloisters once again.

I observed the exact nature of the artist's 'compromise'.

He had put dresses on the females and hardened up their figures. They looked like boys in drag.

The guestmaster hurried on.

He may have been chuckling.

45   The Abbot

We went up a flight of stone steps and came into the refectory, where the guestmaster bowed and then left us.

'My Lord Abbot,' Faust said.

The Abbot of Monte Oliveto Maggiore stood framed in an alcove. He wore pink satin robes and a little black cap on his head. He was tiny – not an inch more than five feet tall, I'd say. When he spread out his thin hands to welcome us it was like a moth or a butterfly drying its wings in the sun. I made out a regular pharmacy in the alcove behind him. Shelf after shelf of majolica jars with big stoppers.

'Dr Sabellicus,' the abbot said pleasantly. 'It is an honour to have such a distinguished guest.'

His voice was like honey poured from a great height.

He held out his hand.

Faust knelt. He sweeps off his hat.

Yup. The old creep.

He was kneeling and kissing the ring on the abbot's left hand.

I sat down, nursing Akercocke's cage. That was something to do. The chair was well-cushioned. A huge fire of cedarwood blazed in the grate to my right. I watched Satan stretch out on the hearth.

'This is Christopher Wagner,' Faust said.

'My child,' said the abbot. 'Most welcome. May I wash your feet?'

I blinked at him.

Pink cheeks.

Wispy eyebrows.

Eyes like cold buttermilk.

'You are a pilgrim,' the abbot went on. 'You have come far, and the way has been difficult, yes? Permit me then to have water brought here for your comfort . . .'

'Wash *his* feet!' I said, pointing at Faust. 'His need is much greater than mine. It won't do much good though!'

'*Good*,' the abbot murmured, reaching for a silver bell with the Magi hammered into it in ornamental relief. 'How refreshing it is to hear the word *good* on the lips of one so young.' He tinkled the bell. 'The good is the proper object of the will,' he said, smiling.

When this abbot smiled the buttermilk went sour.

Another monk in corpse-white came in. He carried a bowl in his hands. There was a towel folded over his shoulder.

'I don't want my feet washed,' I said.

The monk set the bowl down beside me.

'Your boots, Kit,' Faust said.

'Get knotted!'

The abbot had tinkled his bell again. The refectory was suddenly filled with his monks. I fought, but there were too many. Brawny arms grabbed me and forced me back down in the cushions. A cowl fell back. I saw a face as soft and featureless as a peeled egg. The monks wrestled my boots off.

The abbot rolled up his sleeves.

He washed my feet.

The abbot's hands were soft. They felt like fur. The water was warm. I kept flicking my toes. It was all I could do to protest.

The abbot said:

'Water disgusts you?'

'No. You do!' I said.

He dabbed my feet dry with the towel.

'*Pax vobis*,' he said.

The monks went out, sandals slapping.

I tugged on my boots.

The abbot was kissing his fingers dry.

'Everything here is designed for your comfort,' he said. 'First, for the comfort of the body. Then, for the comfort of the soul.' He turned aside to where Faust was helping himself to a goblet of wine. 'We should eat now. I trust you will sup with me? You and your charming disciple?'

'I'd rather starve, thank you,' I said.

'My child! Such banality!'

Faust belched.

'A decent vintage,' he said. 'Kit will eat. Kit likes his grub. You have another bottle of this stuff?'

'As many as you need,' the abbot said. 'I think you will find that particular year goes down agreeably with a little *porchetta*. Cold roast suckling pig well-stuffed with herbs. A favourite here in Umbria, you know, as in Latium and the Marches –'

'Devil,' Akercocke said.

He'd been squatting there quite quiet in his cage, bemused by the heat of the fire. Now he spoke his new word. For once, I was glad.

The abbot smiled at me.

Vile buttermilk.

'So your spirit has started,' he said.

'Jesus Christ!' I said. 'Akercocke isn't a spirit! He's just a monkey. A fucking horrible talking monkey, that's all.'

187

'*Fucking*,' the abbot said, putting pincers around the word as if to hold it up for examination and then remove it from his scrutiny. 'This *fucking* is a word I do not relish. An old-fashioned word, my child.'

His belly rumbled. He reached for his bell again.

'Lent,' he apologised. 'I permit my flesh just the one meal a day.'

46   The Gospel According to Judas

So it went on. The abbot chattering. Faust drinking. Me sitting silently by the fire, hugging my boots. Monks coming in and out, setting food and drink on the refectory table in silver platters and goblets. Not one of the monks said a word.

'Your disciple has just noticed our strict vow of silence,' said the abbot to Faust.

'And that you don't observe it,' I said.

'Myself and the guestmaster,' said the abbot. 'It would be tedious otherwise. The rest keep their tongues for more important things.'

'Like what?' I asked.

'Why, the recitation of the Divine Office, of course. And for readings when I am at table. Let us eat now. Sabellicus, you are my guest. What shall it be?'

Faust sat down at the table.

'*The Gospel According to Judas*,' he said.

'Amen,' said the abbot.

The abbot blessed their food. They began to eat. Faust looked at me enquiringly. I stayed where I was.

A monk entered, his cowl pulled close across his cheekbones, his eyes downcast. He looked like a gorilla.

'Brother Bridget,' the abbot murmured, wiping his lips with a sponge. 'Read to us from the Iscariot if you please.'

The monk bowed. Then he crossed to a lectern.

I watched as he picked thongs from a leather-bound codex encrusted with jewels. The codex was evidently ancient, a set of waxed wooden tablets bound together. He opened the tablets and kissed the first of them.

Then, as Faust drank and the abbot forked meat in his

mouth, the gorilla read aloud from the codex. The language was
Coptic, I think. I couldn't understand a bloody word of it.

The monk who had been addressed as Brother Bridget by the
abbot read this gibberish aloud for about five minutes. Then he
pressed his thick lips again to the tablets. He closed the codex
with a snap, and bound it again with the thongs. He glided from
the refectory as smoothly as he had come into it.

I was starving.

I crossed to the table.

I sat down and started to eat. The stuffed suckling pig tasted
good.

Faust drank and the abbot said nothing.

I ate like a maniac. I bit my own tongue.

'My child,' the abbot remarked. 'Try not to choke on your
tongue-meat.'

Faust grinned at me, crossing his eyes.

No more was said until I had pushed my platter aside, and
another monk had brought in a large dish that was loaded with
apples, pears, cherries, and sweet-water grapes.

Then:

'Where did you get it?' I said.

'The Iscariot codex?'

'Well, I didn't mean the fruit out of season . . .'

The abbot scooped up a handful of grapes and cherries and
toddled across to Akercocke in his cage.

'He'll eat your fingers,' I said hopefully.

The abbot ignored me.

He pushed the grapes and cherries through the bars. Akercocke ate them with incredible daintiness.

'I have a way with spirits,' the abbot remarked.

'You're dodging my question.'

'Devil,' said Akercocke, spitting a cherry stone at me.

The abbot raised one wispy eyebrow, glancing at Faust.

I looked at Faust too.

He was dribbling. He was shaking his head.

The abbot crossed himself.

'Amen,' he said.

He picked up the bell again.

'My child, you are worn out with travelling. Brother Barbara
will show you now to your room. Perhaps we will speak more
tomorrow.'

189

47 Pink

My room was about what I'd expected. There were flowers in china vases everywhere. No chairs, no table. A carpet of some deep fluffy white stuff. Walls painted pink with a series of pictures hung round them. I noted the Stations of the Cross on one level, with coloured copies of the Il Sodoma frescoes just below. Statues of saints. Ornaments of pink terra cotta. A cartoon version of the martyrdom of St Sebastian, with real miniature arrows stuck into it. Over the bed, a Madonna with Sacred Heart instead of breasts.

The bed itself was deep and broad. Pink curtains about it. Pink coverlet over pink sheets. The pillows were pink as well, with lacy edges. A single pink rose by the bedside. Pink ceiling where pink cherubs sported on pink clouds and plucked at pink harps.

I turned to my escort. His face was lost in his cowl, but I knew he was watching my reactions.

'Brother Barbara,' I said.

He didn't answer me.

'Brother Barbara, Brother Bridget,' I went on. 'Do all you monks have the names of female saints?'

He drew back the sheet without speaking.

I saw a pink nightdress beneath it, neatly folded, newly laundered.

'Gee, thanks,' I said.

If he thought I was going to strip for him, and put that thing on, he'd another think coming.

I sat on the floor on my ointment box.

The monk stood a moment in what may have been silent prayer.

Then he pinched out the pink candle that was the room's sole illumination, and went. He locked the door softly behind him.

'Night, Babs,' I said.

I sat on the box all night. I had no wish to sleep.

48   The Chosen One

In the morning, Faust came.

He looked weary.

'Shall we walk in the garden?' he said.

'And talk about Judas?'

Faust shrugged.

I was glad to see he'd a flask of the abbot's Montepulciano wine in his paw. Anything's better than that brandy which pickles his wits.

The gardens of Monte Oliveto Maggiore were curious. No flowers grew there. The pond was scummy, overgrown with weeds. Most of the trees seemed blasted by some disease. Their most unaccountable feature was these mirrors. They hung from the withered branches everywhere. The mirrors caught the sun. They shivered and danced in the breeze that blew over the mountains.

Looking down from the terrace, I saw vineyards and olive groves. The storm had rolled away south in the night. There were puddles upon the cracked paving stones. The light from the mirrors made the water look stretched out and torn.

'Why have we come here?' I asked.

'It is on the way.'

Faust jabbed at a mirror with his forefinger, making it dazzle. 'Sleep well?'

'Not a wink.'

'You don't trust the abbot?'

'Never trust a man who washes your feet.'

'Forgive him,' Faust said. 'He doesn't have many young visitors.'

I picked up a pebble.

I chucked it hard into the pond.

'Judas Iscariot,' I said. 'What did all that stuff mean?'

Faust was angling the mirror so that it shone in my eyes. A fool trick of his. I remembered him doing it that day I had to shave him while Helen went buying her Gabriel feather.

'Will you please just stop blinding me?'

Faust made the mirror spin.

The withered trees looked on fire with the flashing of it.

'Facts,' he said, grinning. 'I'm glad you like facts. I got beyond mere speculation a long while ago myself.'

'In Spisser's Wood,' I said.

'If you like. The location is merely amusing.'

Helen appeared at the end of the garden. She had bread-crumbs. She was feeding the birds.

I sat down by this gargoyle.

The lip of the gargoyle was cracked. Green water came from it like spittle.

'OK,' I said. 'Let's have facts then.'

'Jesus laughed,' Faust said.

'When they crucified Simon?'

'When he took bread and broke it, and dipped the bread in the sauce and gave it to Judas.'

'Is that what the codex said?'

'Jesus laughed,' Faust said. 'Judas was the chosen one.'

'I don't get it,' I said.

Satan appeared from behind a sundial. I suppose the black tyke had been dozing there. He sat down on Faust's feet.

Faust spoke in a whisper:

'Judas, the son of Simon Iscariot, of the tribe of Reuben, the man of Kerioth, the only disciple who wasn't from Galilee.'

'What about him?'

Faust let Satan lick his hand.

'My name shall be reviled till the end of the world,' he said. 'I shall be cursed even unto the last generation of the sons of women.'

'You're quoting that gospel?'

'Judas,' Faust said. 'The beloved disciple.'

'But Judas betrayed Christ!'

'You think so? Christ *gave* him the bread . . .'

'You mean you think Judas was *chosen* to do what he did?'

'That's a fact,' Faust said.

He shut up. He had seen Helen coming.

'I don't get it,' I said. 'But then I'm not ready for wisdom. All I get is a kick in the balls.'

'Next time,' Faust muttered.

'Ah, next time! A kick in the head?'

'Yes, it might feel like that,' Faust replied.

49   A Sweetie

Helen was wearing this billowing gown of Madonna blue. She
came straight to the point:

'John, this is a *lovely* place! I just met the abbot. He's a
sweetie. You know what he told me? There's a church in a
meadow near here, called San Biagio, all honey-coloured stone,
and Our Lady appeared there last June. There were cows in the
meadow, my angel, and the cows *all knelt down*. It makes you
think, doesn't it?'

I don't know what this 'fact' made the Herr Judasite think.
It made me think it was high time I looked for Justine.
I couldn't find her. I searched all over the abbey.
Justine now.
Gone.

50   Soup

That night we dined once more with the abbot. Faust and me,
waited on by white monks. The soup was delicious: *cacciucco*.
Faust complained that it had too much pepper in it, but in my
opinion the pepper was in exactly the correct proportion to the
garlic. I could have done with more onion, perhaps. I said so,
and Faust said: 'Tomatoes.' Causing the abbot to remark: 'Not
at all, my dear Sabellicus. As well require more red wine as an
additive! The effect would be crude, that I promise you.'

Trivialities. I record them just to show that my wits are in fair
working order.
Justine.
Gone.
All my 7 girls.
Gone.
Akercocke, very much, not gone. He was crouched in his cage
beside us on the well-waxed oak of the table. I hadn't seen him
till that evening. He had spent the day, so it seemed, in the
abbot's company. When I clapped eyes on him – and it was the

first thing I noticed on entering the refectory – I was astounded to see that the monkey now sported a neat red jacket studded with amethysts. There was also a golden collar about his neck, with a small silver bell attached. I remembered the abbot saying that he had a way with 'spirits'. Hadn't he pushed his fingers between the bars of the cage and fed Akercocke cherries? All right. But how he contrived to dress Akercocke up in this garb without getting his eyes torn out I cannot begin to imagine.

All my 7 girls.

Gone.

They came and they went.

It was nice while it lasted.

'Devil,' Akercocke said.

'Tomatoes,' said Faust, before shutting his mouth around more of the abbot's good wine.

51 Bell Ringing

Next morning I was woken by the angelus.

I counted the strokes, half-asleep. Then I realised they were all wrong. The angelus consists of 3 strokes followed by a pause 3 times, and then 9 strokes. The bell in the tower of the abbey rang out that lot all right, but then it went on. There was no proper rhythm to its pealing. I went to investigate.

I found Faust in the bell tower.

Wine bottle in one hand, he was tugging the rope with the other. The effort seemed great. I looked up into the belfry and saw why.

Two monks were up there. It could have been Barbara and Bridget.

They were playing a dangerous game.

The bell was enormous. The monks sat astride it. They were straddling the top of the bell.

Sweat poured from Faust's face.

'You could kill them!' I said.

'But I won't,' he said, grunting.

The bell rocked and boomed.

'Why not?' I demanded.

I sat down on the ladder.

I was having to shout at him. The noise of the bell was so loud.

'They deserve it! They've murdered Justine!'

Faust stopped working the bell rope.

He pushed back his hat. He grinned broadly.

'Kit,' he said. 'You're a simple little soul when it comes to it.'

'Just fuck off,' I muttered. 'Justine's gone.'

'And you blame the monks?'

'Wouldn't you?'

Faust drank. Then he tugged on the rope.

'Why *Sabellicus* here?' I demanded.

'Different places, different names,' grunted Faust. 'It's all one. You know that.'

'And why *Judas*?' I said.

'That's a fact.'

'What's a fact? Some cult of Judas Iscariot?'

'You're learning.'

'Like hell I am! I thought we were going to Rome. But here we are, wasting time, more mumbo jumbo . . .'

Faust paused. He shook sweat from his eyebrows.

'Why not go and have a think about Judas?'

'I'd rather we left here,' I said.

'Well, we shall.'

'When?'

'Soon enough. Want a go with this rope?'

'You play your own games,' I said.

Faust drank. He went back to his ringing.

The scene for some reason disgusted me.

'One thing about Judas,' I shouted. 'One thing that almost makes sense.'

Faust stopped swinging the rope.

'Come on,' he said. 'Say it!'

'I can't find the right words. But – well, not that I believe it – but if you take Judas seriously, and Jesus, you end up with damnation and salvation being almost the same thing . . .'

'Not almost,' Faust said. 'That's a *fact*!'

He danced on his rope like a puppet.

I cleared off.

Some music's too much.

52 More Angels

That bell went on ringing for ages.

I walked in the garden where the withered trees had no leaves, only mirrors. I watched the fish circle in the pool. Green scummy water. Gold fish, metallic-looking, like mechanical toys invented for the delight of some Byzantine emperor. My thoughts went round and round with those fish. I wasn't thinking really. Such musings as I had were like a roundabout of images:

Zuleika's arms as she drowned in that snow.

Jane disappearing head-first down the hell-hole.

That jewel-encrusted codex.

Akercocke.

And, most of all, a dozen crazy images of Faust. Faust on the table with napkins. Faust falling from his horse. Faust eating the dirt in the road. Faust grinning while the abbot washed my feet. Faust stretched out snoring with just his boots on. Faust's hand on my wrist when I flew my kite from the Tower. Faust lighting the black candle at Bumbach. Faust flicking at Aquinas when he met me. Faust sitting in the chair to get his shave. Faust with the pigeon on his head. Faust asking Will Somers for water. Faust dancing on that bellrope. A hanged man.

As I watched the bright fish, I began to think of angels.

Not in any worked-out way. Just names.

I found myself reciting angels' names out loud:

'Abdiel. Gabriel. Michael. Raguel. Raphael. Simiel. Uriel. Abaddon. Apollyon. Satan . . .'

I chucked a big stone at the fish.

53 Flirt in the Cloisters

When the bell ceased its ringing, I wandered off into the cloisters.

Might have guessed it.

Our Helen was there.

Dressed in pink. Little artificial flowers in the assisted yellow locks of her hair. The Gabriel feather in her hand. She was using the feather as a fan.

Brothers Barbara and Bridget were with her.

They looked sweaty. I'm sure they were the ones who rode Faust's bell.

Those two brawny monks said nothing to Helen. Their vow of silence must have forbad it.

However, it didn't stop them flirting with her. They kept rolling their eyes, gesturing with their fingers, and stroking her angel feather.

Helen did nothing to discourage them. On the contrary, she was simpering and curtseying and giggling. With every now and then – but not often enough – a skip back and an *Ave Maria*.

The three of them were playing this game in front of Il Sodoma's Florentius fresco. The one with the girls like boys in drag.

She was asking for trouble, I thought.

54   The Sophia

I dodged dinner with Faust and the abbot. I went early to my room. (This was last night.) I shut Judas right out of my mind. I was glad of the absence of Akercocke.

I fell asleep thinking of angels. Not their travelling problems and pinhead capacities. Just their names. *Abdiel . . . Raguel . . . Abaddon . . .*

When I woke, it was dawn. I'd slept deeply. I lay on my back, eyes half-closed, looking up at those nasty pink hangings. I had fallen asleep in my clothes. As usual, I'd dreamed no dreams.

Then I heard it.

That bell.

Tolling crazily.

Faust back playing his game with the monks?

Then screaming . . .

Such screams!

It was Helen.

197

I burst out of my room. I started running as I strapped on my sword.

The pale light of dawn gave me scarcely a shadow on the walls or the floors as I raced through dim corridors, down flights of stone stairs. The cloisters were empty. Il Sodoma leered down at me. His badgers. His raven. I ran.

I shouted for Faust as I ran.

Christ knows why. A man has to shout something.

'*Faust!*'

Bell still tolling. The bell in the tower of the chapel. And the screaming was coming from there.

Monks appeared, barring my way. Monks garbed in the usual shroud-habits. They had staves. A wall of corpse-white between me and the screams and the bell.

The monks didn't move.

I went at them.

I slashed with my sword. I'm no swordsman, but these were nice burly targets.

I got one monk. I chopped off his ear.

The others closed on me, staves whirling. Going down, I cut another monk clean through the knees. His praying would be easier now.

But there were too many. Blows rained on my skull and my shoulders. Then a stave knocked the sword from my fist.

Silently, slowly, they circled me.

Cadaverous faces, cowls back.

I heard footfalls.

Lurching footfalls. Lopsided. Familiar.

Dirty cloak. Dirty hat.

Brandy bottle.

No sword.

'Faust!'

He ignored me. Burning eyes that saw nothing. Blind drunk.

'Faust! For Christ's sake! Hey, Faust!'

'*Pax vobiscum!*'

The door of the chapel swung open.

The abbot. His fingers raised in blessing.

He extended his left hand.

Faust knelt.

Creak of bones. The great magus. He knelt.

Faust kissed the abbot's ring.

When he got up, he had trouble standing. His whole body was racked with the shakes. He grabbed hold of my shoulder and lent on me. Blood streamed from my head down his chest.

'*Pax Domini sit semper vobiscum.*'

'*Et cum spiritu tuo,*' said Faust.

'*Kyrie eleison,*' the abbot said.

'*Judas eleison,*' said Faust.

The abbot turned, a delicate pink-winged moth, black-capped. He led us into the chapel.

A forest of tall candles flickering. Seven lamps above the altar all ablaze.

A thick fog of incense. I was glad. Faust leaning on my arm smelt worse than Lazarus just before the main event.

The bell still tolling.

No more screams.

We moved slowly down the aisle, the abbot leading.

The incense stung my eyes.

Then I saw the figures at the altar.

Brother Barbara.

Brother Bridget.

And Helen.

All three wearing white.

The monks their shroud-like habits.

(One to the right hand of Helen, one to the left.)

And Helen herself in a long white bridal gown. Very rich. Very sumptuous. Brocaded.

The monks were holding Helen by the arms. And Helen *was* screaming. Her face was contorted, her mouth twisted open, but there was no sound coming out.

Either the boom of that bell was drowning her cries, or – more likely – poor Helen had screamed herself hoarse.

Head thrown back, lips agape, her veins making knots in her neck, she gazed wild and wide-eyed at the three of us coming towards her through that forest of candles and that twilight of incense.

I saw her mouth make the word *John*. But no cry came from her.

John.

No.

John.

Shapes of cries. But no crying.

The abbot removed his black skull-cap. He mounted the steps to the sanctuary.

He threw himself down at her feet.

That wizened pink figure, prostrated at our Helen's feet! His face buried into the ground, his body full-length, like a fallen-down statue.

Faust staggered. He snatched off his hat.

Then he went up those sanctuary steps.

I stood rooted. My feet couldn't follow. I was sweating. My eyes felt like cinders.

The two monks stepped aside in a single movement, like making a turn in a dance. They didn't let go of their victim. They were facing the altar, broad backs turned to us, holding Helen's wrists and pulling her arms so that she stood there outstretched, staring over the abbot at Faust.

She looked like a crucifix.

Helen!

Faust walked over the abbot. He trod on him.

He went up to Helen.

He bowed. Then he kissed her.

Full on the lips.

Faust kissed Helen.

The bell stopped.

This must have been some kind of signal. Or a part of the rite. For the monks facing altarwards immediately released Helen's wrists. They fell down on their knees. I heard it. The smack of monks' bones on bare stone.

Helen just stood there, arms outstretched.

No more screaming.

She was smiling at Faust.

Not the shadowy smile I knew well. Not that 'Mona Lisa' enigma designed to conceal her bad teeth. Helen's smiling was radiant, queenly. Those red lips apart in pure pleasure. Yellow teeth, some quite black, several missing. I'd have laughed if I hadn't been crying.

My tears are no easier to explain than anything else in that scene. There was blood in my eyes. Also incense. Blood and incense distorting my vision. Maybe incense and blood made me cry.

Faust kissed Helen again, with much passion.

Then:

'*Behold the Sophia!*' he cried.

Behold?

I could hardly see anything.

Just a blur.

Just my tears.

Just a dream.

I think incense and blood made me see things.

Because, as I rubbed at my eyes, I imagined I saw Faust plunging his hands into Helen's hair and he was tearing her hair from her head, and he was casting it down like a crown, only it wasn't a crown, it was a wig, and Helen was hairless without it, bald, bare, and white, a pure skull.

And I thought I saw Faust put his hands to the neck of Helen's white bridal gown, and he ripped it from top to bottom, and Helen was naked beneath it.

Faust knelt, hat in hand. Faust adored her.

Her?

Helen?

I saw it. Or I dreamt that I saw it.

It wasn't a woman.

Female breasts.

But the balls and the prick of a man.

55 More Trouble with a Nuremberg Egg

My Nuremberg Egg has gone mad.

I just took it to pieces.

Examined it.

Everything just as it should be.

Everything just as it always was.

But the fucker's gone out of its mind . . .

A small enough item.

But it fits.

Fits, like hell, with the facts I've just written. With a world with no clockwork of sense.

I ran from that chapel. I ran through the gardens where the trees have no fruit except mirrors. I ran to my room. Locked the door.

Just locking the door was some comfort.

Lock out Faust.

Lock out Helen.

Lock out madness.

I turned the key on every crazy event of the last three days. Only to lock myself in with the need to make sense of them.

I went to the window and stood looking out, the glass cold against my hot forehead. It took me a while to start seeing things. To exorcise images that had nothing to do with those long sloping limestone terraces, those outcrops of travertine rock. It was sun shining harsh on the ilex that finally did it. Far below, deep dark cracks in chalk landscape. *I like the sun.* I remembered Faust's bathos. Well, Herr Doktor, I like the sun too, but not for your reasons. It shows us what stands in our way.

Faust's world is all shadows. His own.

I must write with a pen dipped in sun.

I washed incense and blood from my eyes. I washed away dreams and absurdities.

I got out my box and my papers.

As I did this, I said it out loud:

'Don't explain. Just describe.'

And:

'*Amen!*' says this voice right behind me.

It was Akercocke.

There in his cage.

Red jacket. Gold collar. Silver bell.

He was grinning. He was eating an olive.

I said: 'So the abbot got sick of you, did he?

Akercocke flicked at his bell with his claw.

I threw the cloth over his cage.

He shut up. Just scratching.

Amen.

I sat down. I started to write.

57   No Time at All

When I started my watch stood at noon. Was that the right time? I don't know. Christ knows how long I stood staring out of that window before I saw anything outside the images in my own head. Then the washing. I washed my eyes thoroughly.

Still, my watch has been perfectly reliable. It could well have been noon when I started that Chapter 43 – the beginning of my record of our three days spent here in this abbey. Anyway, like I say, both hands of my watch were pointing to twelve.

I wrote slowly. I'd a lot to get down, but I needed to re-member it right. When I got to the flirt in the cloisters my watch told me 6 hours had passed. That seemed credible. I believed it. Took a piss. Ate a fig. Heard this barking and laughing from the garden. When I looked, I saw Faust out there playing with Satan. The great magus was throwing sticks for the black dog to fetch. An innocent scene. Some relief from the stuff I'd been scribbling.

I sat down.

I wrote Chapter 54.

Those were difficult pages, and by the time that I finished it was dark. I got up and lit my one candle. I had cramp in my fingers. My head ached.

I just sat for a bit in the candlelight.

Then I looked at my watch.

The two hands were pointing to twelve.

Well, at first I supposed that meant midnight. Supposed I had dozed, or got lost here just chewing my pen in the trance of my struggle to set it down true.

Not at all.

It's not midnight.

Christ only knows what the time is.

Because as I stared at my watch I saw the two hands move together.

And the two hands went *backwards*.

Backwards. Then forwards. Then around and around like mad things.

So I took it to bits, like I said.

Now the trouble with these watches used to be the main-spring. The mainspring got erratic as the watch ran down. They tried to put this right with a part called a stack-freed, a sort of second spring. Crude. No improvement. But then someone came up with the fusée. The invention of the fusée was genius. The mainspring turns on a barrel with catgut wound round it. The other end of the catgut is wound round a spiral drum, so the watch still keeps time even when the spring runs down, because as fast as the spring loses its tension the drum winds it tight again.

I found nothing wrong with the fusée.

The catgut's intact and untwisted.

The drum moves OK.

I made sure the hands weren't loose either.

So what it comes down to is this:

I've a watch in which each *part* is perfect, but the *whole* makes no sense.

I've set it at this time and that time. The same result always. The hands go round just as they please. One goes forwards even while the other goes backwards.

Both hands coming back without fail to the twelve!

My watch has gone crazy. That's all.

Should I be so surprised or upset? Isn't everything crazy round here? What's the madness of a Nuremberg Egg compared to the madness of Faust?

It's *my* watch. That's what I don't like.

Watches and clocks are modernity. They're emblems of man being free. Before watches, a man's daily life was measured out for him by liturgical hours. In those old days a man only knew the time by courtesy of the church telling it to him with its bells. With a watch at his waist a man has his own time, the world's time, the real time.

Now my watch tells me no time at all.

I shall take it to be mended in Rome.

58 Venus

Faust and me left the abbey this morning.

Just the two of us.

Nobody else.

(Well, Akercocke . . . But I mean: *no Helen*. Helen's gone. And I'm past asking questions.)

Skylarks throbbing.

Not a cloud in the sky.

The abbot and his monks made a formal farewell of it. Bells pealing. Aspersions. A blessing. In fact, all as it should be for pilgrims. I could almost believe it made sense. (Except one of the monks had the hiccups.)

Faust was shaven. He'd groomed his moustaches. He even rode right. Didn't drink!

A brilliant day's ride, the best yet. Our horses refreshed by their rest, no doubt. The roads good. The way straight. No encumbrances.

We galloped.

The two of us.

Galloping.

San Quirico.

Acquapendente.

San Lorenzo.

Like I say, we rode fast.

Never faster.

Faust was riding in front of the dog. Faust leading Satan! Incredible. I had quite a job keeping up with him.

Pienza.

Chiusi.

Orvieto.

I can jot down names only, and some of them just glimpsed from milestones. For the most part Faust went round the towns. Sun and dust. Dust and sun. Lathered horses. Galloping on. Swift and south towards Rome.

Somewhere north of Bolsena we crossed over the border and into the Papal State.

I began to smell Rome in the distance.

Not a word out of Faust the whole day.

I kept riding.

Which kept me from thinking.

The moon was up by the time Faust's horse went lame. Without that small mercy, I believe we'd never have stopped till our horses dropped dead under us.

Where are we?

On this heath. By this lake. And under this great breast-shaped hill.

My maps say this must be the Hill of Venus, so we're now on the edge of the Campagna. A mere 20 miles more and it's Rome!

Hill of Venus.

Lake of Venus.

We're camped by the side of the lake.

I write by the fire we have lit.

I'm shagged out. One word more then I sleep.

Fuck Venus!

I just dived in her lake.

The night being warm, and me filthy with grime from our riding, I stripped off my clothes and dived into the stars in her lake.

I came out all plastered with leeches.

59   Across the Campagna

Our horses were stolen in the night!

When I woke it was the first thing I noticed.

I roused Faust. He shrugged. He didn't seem worried.

'We walk then,' he said.

So we walked.

We walked down from where we'd slept under the Hill of Venus and out into the great heath which they call the Campagna.

No sun in the sky.

Low clouds the colour of ink.

Thick fog rising out of the swamps.

We walked through a landscape that was scarcely a landscape at all.

Swamps, sedge, and mud.

Vapours and vagueness.

Twisted spirals of foul-smelling smoke.

I carried Akercocke in his cage. It was strapped to my back. I carried my ointment box also. Thank God, I'd used it as a pillow, or the horse-thieves would have had it, and this book. Those robbers took everything else.

A dull, dark day. Desolate.

A tract of country like a mind that can't sleep.

Faust drinking again. He must have slept on his brandy flasks. He walked with them looped round his neck. He'd his Saracen bottle as well.

We walked down the Cassian Way.

An old shambling man in a black cloak. A young marching man in a red cloak. Striding on down the Cassian Way.

We walked steadily. In silence. Faust in front.

He set the pace, long head bowed, and his chin buried deep in his chest.

As the fogs became thicker, Faust was soon just a shape in a cloak and a hat.

We met nobody at all. Not a soul.

It was nasty.

Even Akercocke was subdued. Every now and then, when Faust stopped to drink, I set the cage down and I rested. The monkey crouched low on the floor of his cage. Not scratching. Not chattering. His eyes looked quite dead when I glanced at them.

As for Satan – that dog's scraggy tail hung down between its legs. It was shivering. It looked feverish. It never once barked. It walked at Faust's heels, not in front of him.

When Faust had drunk enough, he just started walking again.

He didn't say a word. He didn't look back. He seemed not to care if I was following him.

I saw no village, no house, no sign at all of any human habitation or presence anywhere on that great blasted heath. To each side of the road the little I could see of the countryside consisted of nothing but miles and miles of swamp.

I heard no bird cries.

I saw no birds.

My watch being useless, I can only guess how long it was that we walked before we encountered the locusts.

Maybe it was round about noon.

With the sun shrouded above us, I'd no means of telling.

It might have been evening.

It all seemed like evening out there.

But the locusts . . .

Quite without warning. The locusts.

That road all encrusted, all covered.

A vile carpet of locusts.

Dark.

Horrible.

Crawling.

Like some evil black sand.

Then there were shrubs looming low in the fog to the left of the road, and I saw that each one of these shrubs – they weren't green, they weren't growing, they were the shade and the substance of the fog itself – that each one of these shrubs bore a rich fruit of locusts as well.

Locusts hung from them, dripping, in bunches.

Like bunches of grapes.

Grey grapes and black grapes and the worst like a colourless poison.

And there was this stench that came off them.

A stench like the grave.

I used jam.

Faust strode on.

I followed him.

We walked through the stench and the vapours, our boots treading softly through locusts. Every step left a patch of mashed bodies.

Squatting, squinting, I saw the crushed locusts were quickly devoured by the living ones.

I was glad when that ended.

The death-smell lingered on. Rising up from my boots, I suppose. But we passed through the locusts at last.

60 Bog

We walked on.

The further we walked, the more fog.

It got down in my lungs. I kept coughing.

Faust didn't cough. He must have lungs like old leather. Akercocke didn't cough either. Nor did Satan.

Christ knows how long it was after the locusts that Faust led me away from the road.

A long time, I guess. I was tired. I was limping. But then time had no meaning out there in that murky Campagna. Time and space seemed wiped out by its vapours. My mind was clogged up with the fog.

I knew things had gone wrong when my feet sank down fast into – *what?*

I groped round my boots with my hand. I held my hand up to my eyes.

It was now dark as night. I saw nothing.

I licked at my fingers.

No taste.

Not water. Not mud.

Just no taste.

A bog like fog under my feet.

'Hey, Faust!' I shouted.

No answer.

'Faust! I'm lost, Faust! Where are you?'

No answer.

I cursed his perverted sense of humour.

He'd played this cruel trick on me. He'd misled me out into some swamp that seemed bottomless. Black vapours and silence and my legs sinking fast into something like nothing at all.

'Help me, Faust!' I cried out. 'What's the game?'

Not a sound.

Not even the squelch of a boot.

And I was fast sinking.

I was up to my thighs in it now.

'Hey, Faust! Shit, man! Save me!'

I was up to my waist.

Akercocke's cage didn't help. That weight on my back dragged me down.

I was up to my neck.

I was drowning.

'Faust!' I cried. 'If I go, your story goes with me!'

Then his hand gripped my hand.

As usual, it hurt.

Those long fingernails.

61   A Kick in the Head

'My story,' he said. 'That's the thing.'

He was grinning, the fuck-up. He was pulling my ointment box out of the bog with his free hand.

Then the sun started shining.

No fog.

That fog went.

It didn't disperse. One moment it was there. Then it wasn't. Wop weather!

One moment I couldn't see anything. Then I saw Faust. He was pulling me up. He was hauling me out of that bog with one hand, and retrieving my box with the other. He was wiping the box on his cloak.

'You're hurting my hand,' I complained.

Faust didn't let go of me.

There was good ground there under his boots. Not the Cassian Way. Some black track.

'It's bleeding,' I said.

This was true. Those fingernails of his were clawing so hard into the palm of my hand that blood dripped from the wound.

Faust put the box down on the track.

Then he dragged me out. Akercocke too.

I sat down. The good ground felt great.

The sun on my shoulders was nice.

'Amen,' said Akercocke.

The Campagna.

The same endless plain. Same bare landscape.

Only now there was no fog and the sun shining on those leagues of heath made them beautiful. The Campagna glowed with a wealth of soft colours. Rich, delicate grasses. I saw light on bright streams in the distance. I smelt rosemary.

'What the hell's going on here?' I asked.

'You're crying,' Faust said.

Then he started to laugh.

His face flashed in the sunlight. He was rocking to and fro on his heels, black cloak swirling about him, and there were these birds that flew all about us, blue birds and gold birds and birds like strange jewels. Yet they were real birds, I swear it. And the tears were real that ran down Faust's face as he laughed. And the blood on my boots was for real.

'For Christ's sake!' I cried. 'What's so funny?'

Faust didn't answer. He pointed, still laughing.

I turned.

I saw Rome right behind me.

'I warned you,' Faust said. 'It might feel like a kick in the head.'

Part 3

Holy Week

1 Transfusion

Luther nearly died in the Wartburg. It's a little-known fact. The Holy Roman Emperor Charles 5 was determined to get rid of him. When his spies found out where the Constipator was hiding, they had a nun smuggled into the castle, in the guise of a nurse, and this nun was sticking all kinds of poison up the great man's arse, telling him that it's enemas.

So there's Luther, dying, because the poison made him bleed something terrible, and nobody knew what was causing it. The Elector, his protector, was doing his nut. Fred 3 was no Luther-lover, you understand, but he *had* been responsible for the guy's kidnap, and now he was scared that if the Constipator went and died on him then he'd have a thousand rabid Lutherans at his neck, saying that their leader had been murdered by his own prince.

However, Luther survived.

How did Luther survive?

Through nice human weakness, that's how.

Through *two* nice human weaknesses, male need and female.

The point of this story.

You see, in the middle of what looks like Luther's last night, when he's lying there on his back, as white as the bed sheets themselves, and with only the wicked nun for company, he suddenly starts up and stares at her.

His eyes have a fire in them, which the poisoner takes for contrition.

'Brother Martin,' she says. 'You are dying! Will you make your peace now with God?'

It isn't contrition.

She's a really sexy nun. Luther's noticed.

'Nurse,' he says. '*Am* I dying?'

'You are.'

'Then there's something you can do for me. I beg you! A dying man's last request . . .'

'Go on.'

Luther takes the nun's hand in his own.

'I've never been down on a woman,' he whispers. 'This is my last chance. *What about it?*'

The nun is both horrified and excited. Mostly excited. Who will know, after all? The man's dying. And having to play-act as a nurse among Protestants for months, she hasn't been enjoying her regular sex-life with her father confessor.

All the same, she blushes.

She looks quite embarrassed.

'Look,' she says. 'Let *me* go down on *you*. Wouldn't that be as good?'

Luther shakes his head angrily.

'Not at all. I've had plenty of that. This is the *one* thing I've *never* done. *Please!*'

So the nun comes right out with it:

'The truth is – I'm having my periods!'

Luther shrugs.

'What the hell? I don't care! I'll be dead by the morning. I don't want to die without this last experience.'

The nun says a dozen Hail Marys under her breath at top speed. But there's good in the worst of us. So she hoists up her habit . . .

And how come I can tell you this story?

How come I know it?

Well, next morning I went into Luther's room. They sent me. They thought he'd be dead. I guess that they reckoned it would look more innocent if a little boy found him.

Luther wasn't in bed.

The nurse/nun? No sign of her. She'd scarpered.

Then I heard lusty hymn-singing from the bathroom.

I knocked. I went in.

There's Luther, ruddy-cheeked, in high spirits, standing in front of the mirror and shaving himself.

'Excuse me,' I said. 'I thought you'd be dead.'

'Dead?' roars Luther, eyes sparkling, and dancing a jig. 'One more transfusion like that, lad, and I reckon I might live forever!'

2 Washing

All the bells of Rome started ringing as we came to the city, but I don't think they were ringing them for us. It was just after dawn of Palm Sunday.

I had sore feet, and Akercocke's cage bent my back. I wouldn't have minded a kip in some nice quiet graveyard. A bite of cheese, say, and some *pasta*, and then a snooze under the cypresses. Faust, though, had other ideas.

It strikes me that we must have looked absurdly conspicuous even in that huge motley crowd of pilgrims already thronging the dirty narrow streets of Rome for the first day of Holy Week.

A gangling drunk German.

A black dog.

A boy with a monkey.

It was plain we were up to no good.

So why weren't we arrested immediately and thrown into jail?

I don't know.

Maybe *because* we looked mad, bad, and dangerous to cross.

Maybe because we were lucky.

Maybe because Faust certainly made his way into Rome with a kind of authority. Head thrown back, eyes staring straight ahead, the Saracen bottle of brandy clasped tight in his fist like some emblem of power, he went through that crowd like a black knife through butter.

People got out of our path.

'Where we going?' I gasped. I was having to trot to keep pace with him.

'First things first,' was all Faust would say.

I must say the old maniac knows Rome like the back of his hand. Down alleys, through a tangle of side streets, using churches as short-cuts where the piazzas were thickest with people awaiting the papal procession and blessing of palms, he brought me in no time to the spot he was making for.

A funny old bridge, spanning the Tiber just outside the walls of the Vatican. 8 arches to it, with the three in the middle higher than the rest, so that the road slopes up and down crazily on both sides. It's made of this pepper-coloured stone.

The Tiber was running real high.

Faust stopped at the first arch.

He stripped his cloak from his shoulders and handed it to me.

'What's this in aid of?' I said.

'Wash it,' he said.

'How?'

'In the Tiber. Like I promised.'

I felt too shagged out to argue with the lunatic.

I leaned over the arch, dangling the cloak, Akercocke thumping about in his cage on my back like some heart about to burst. That first arch is low, like I said, and the river ran high. Even so, it was only a half of the cloak that was meeting the water.

Faust unstrapped the cage from my shoulders.

He set it down on the stone of the bridge as carefully as if it contained some holy relic.

'Right over,' he said. 'I'll hold you by the heels.'

Satan sat down by the cage.

The dog and the monkey considered each other.

I considered running for my life.

'Trust me,' Faust said.

'Why should I?'

'Because you've got to,' said Faust.

I looked down at the deep dirty river.

'I could kill you,' Faust said. 'But I won't. I'm not going to let you drown now. Not after all that we've been through together. Just wash my cloak. Like you wanted. Like I promised you.'

'*Me?*'

'I mean to keep my word,' Faust said.

'You didn't promise *me* you'd wash your cloak first thing you did in Rome! You promised *Helen!*'

'Just be a good lad, will you, and stop arguing?' Faust said.

It was insane. I didn't want to do it, but I did. I got up on the parapet and Faust held me by the heels and I hung right over and dragged his cloak to and fro and round and round in the Tiber.

It came out filthier than it went in.

218

3 Holy Shit

Faust put on his cloak, dripping wet. Now he stank worse than ever.

Holy shit.

(That's what the Tiber consists of.)

And I had no more jam on my person.

To make matters worse, the sun came out. It burned down on the spires of Rome. The cloak started to steam on Faust's back.

'Helen,' I said. 'It was Helen.'

'Who's Helen?' he said.

He wasn't grinning.

He looked really puzzled.

He took a mouthful of brandy and then offered me the bottle.

I drank some. I needed it. Hanging upside-down over a running sewer isn't good for the senses.

'Helen,' I said. 'Helen of Troy.'

Faust sucked his moustaches and stared at me like I was mad. Then he patted my cheek.

'You're an angel,' he said. 'You know that? You're an angel, and this is your bridge.'

'What the fuck are you talking about?'

Faust chuckled.

'The Bridge of the Angels,' he said. 'That's what they call this little construction. The Emperor Hadrian built it.'

'You don't say?'

'I do.'

He pointed across the bridge at this castle on the other side.

'The Castle of the Angels,' he said.

I shielded my eyes from the sun. Sure enough, there was a marble angel perched on the top of the ramparts. It was a small ugly angel with a sword in its paw.

'I guess that's where we're staying?' I said. 'Me, you, and Satan, and Akercocke? In a castle for angels?'

'Not likely,' Faust said. 'The Pope would get wind of it.'

He snatched back his brandy bottle.

He drained it.

Then he chucked it away.

I watched it ride there for a minute or two in the muck of the Tiber. That nice Saracen bottle, gold leaf in the bottom of it, quickly filling with sewage. It sank.

'Hiccups,' I said. 'Hail Mary. You remember our Helen?'

'You were always quite the little Christian underneath it all, weren't you?' Faust said.

'Amen,' said Akercocke.

4   Helen of Nowhere

He's forgotten her.

Helen of Troy, and elsewhere.

Tongue-tisking Helen.

Our Lady of Screeches and Fat Lies and Hiccups.

Miss Shadow Smile.

Sometime page to the antipope and kite-flyer in far Cathay.

Helen who thought me a smart ass.

I miss her.

He doesn't.

She's Helen of nowhere, now.

5   Here Comes the Pope

'Pssst! Here comes the Pope!' Faust informed me.

I heard a great blare of trumpets.

I saw a man on a chair on two sticks.

Faust whisked me away as the papal procession came onto the bridge. We melted into the crowd in front of St Peter's Basilica. Two Germans (one wet), and a dog, and a monkey. I had a good view of the Pope as he came passing by.

He wore white satin robes, with a tiara the shape of a bee-hive on top of his head. His feet were encased in scarlet mules with crosses stitched on them. He looked small on his chair, small and fat. The sticks supporting the chair were covered with red velvet. It took 12 men to carry him, six in front, six behind. They bore the ends of the sticks on their shoulders. They walked slowly and steadily, and they were all the same height, so Pope Paul 3 didn't rock about in his chair.

The Palm Sunday sun was quite hot.

The face beneath the triple-crowned tiara was leathery brown in colour and more or less triangular in shape. It was a shrewd, clever, political kind of face. The half-closed eyes looked like they might be doing sums. The right hand twitched in automatic blessings.

The bells pealed out.

The crowds chanted.

'Hosanna!'

'Holy father!'

'Benedictus!'

'72 years old,' Faust whispered in my earhole. 'Three sons. One daughter. Well, he's had a good run for his money.'

6   There Goes the Pope

People fell on their knees as Paul 3 passed by. Faust fell on his face, but since early morning drunks are not unknown in Rome this aroused no great interest. He pulled me down with him. My cheek was shoved next to Akercocke's cage. That bastard took a bite at my nose. He missed.

'So you still mean to do it?' I muttered, lips pressed to the pavement.

'Long live the Pope!' shouted Faust, in impeccable Latin. 'May the Pope live for ever!'

Roman pavements taste nasty.

Old women were rattling rosaries. Old men were waving crosses, palms, and walking-sticks dressed up in scraps of yellow straw. Children threw marguerites in the Pope's path and then wrestled for possession of the trampled petals when he had gone.

I saw soldiers in peculiar uniforms – puffed trousers and sleeves, yellow and blue stripes over red. They genuflected smartly as the Pope reached the steps to St Peter's.

'Swiss Guards,' murmured Faust. 'New gear. Michelangelo designed it.'

I remembered Justine.

'Very kinky,' I said, in Low German. 'Our Great Work, though. Is it still on?'

The 12 bearers were lowering the chair.

The Pope hopped down.

Quite sprightly.

He knelt.

He kissed the steps.

When he stood upright again he produced this daffodil from his cope.

He blessed the crowd with the daffodil. His voice was like a wasp in marmalade.

'*Benedicat vox omnipotens Deus . . . Pater, et Filius, et Spiritus Sanctus.*'

'AMEN!'

St Peter's Square exploded with thousands of tongues crying the one word of response.

'Nothing's altered,' Faust said. 'I came what I came for.'

'Amen,' said Akercocke.

Satan wagged his tail in my face.

The Pope turned, still bearing the daffodil, and ascended the steps of St Peter's. The doors of bronze swung open. A fanfare sounded. The organ roared out for the papal High Mass of Palm Sunday.

He must be about five foot three.

7   Skulls

Rome was intolerably hot. The sun made my head spin. The crush of the crowd was disgusting.

'Can we go somewhere quiet?' I asked Faust.

He nodded.

The incessant clanging of bells wasn't pleasing him either. Besides which, he'd no brandy.

I followed him through some more side streets. I was carrying Akercocke's cage. Satan slunk at Faust's heels, his tongue hanging out like a piece of foul parchment.

Faust found what he was looking for.

A wine cellar.

I drank half a flask of bad muscat.

The old fuck-up filled the lining of his still-steaming cloak with a number of bottles called Vesuvius. They cost him a packet.

'Vesuvius?' I said.

'When in Rome,' Faust said, 'die as the Romans die.'

The bottles made him even more lopsided.

They clanked as he walked.

We came to this church. It was some sort of Capucine nuthouse. I could tell by the hoods on the monks and their filthy bare feet. Akercocke perked up. His brothers?

'Somewhere quiet,' said Faust.

We went in.

He stalked straight to the altar, turned right, and led me down this staircase.

Another cellar.

No wine.

Only monks. *And all of them dead . . .*

'*Coemeterium Capuccinorum*,' Faust announced. 'They're taking no chances. No burial for these guys. When they snuff it, they just park them down here. They're waiting, you see.'

Bone-paved floor. Bone-inlaid ceiling.

Skeletons packed in neat rows.

Skulls with candles inside them for lamps.

'*Waiting?*' I cried. 'What they waiting *for?*'

'Resurrection,' Faust said.

I was sick.

8   Mithras

'I like the sun,' Faust said jovially. 'Want to go? Care to see something else?'

I nodded.

'Try a sip of Vesuvius.'

I drank more than a sip. I must have done. And that Vesuvius must be powerful stuff.

The next thing I knew I was holding on to Faust's cloak in some street at the side of the Colosseum. Akercocke still on my back. Satan sniffing at previous tributes left by dogs on the wall of this church that was the colour of soft wholemeal biscuits.

We passed into the building.

'Please . . .' I said.

'This is different,' Faust told me. 'Don't fret.'

There was Mass going on in the church.

Faust ignored it.

We dodged in and out down the side aisles, round pillars, then through this small door. We must have descended two layers. Through a dark maze of underground rooms. As we went, the chanting of Mass quite receded. To be replaced by the sound of a river! Rushing waters! *A stream under a church!*

We came out in this underground temple.

Rectangular.

Stars in the ceiling.

Two altars. To the sun, and the moon.

A single statue dominated the temple.

Faust lit a torch and I saw it.

A youth in a conical cap, his cloak streaming as if he was flying, with a sword in his hand and the sword through the brow of a bull.

'Mithras!' Faust shouted. 'Christ's enemy!'

My head swam. I went nearer the statue.

I saw a scorpion cut there, hanging on to the bull's massive prick. Underneath it, a serpent was drinking the blood from the wound. There was a dog too, leaping for the bull's throat. And a raven. A fig tree. A lion.

'What does it mean?' I demanded.

'Mithras,' Faust said. He drank a long toast. 'Mithras! The god of the sun!'

He ran his hands down the sides of the statue.

He stroked the youth's legs.

'They don't know it's down here,' he remarked, glancing up at the ceiling, and winking.

'*What?*'

'You heard me.'

'They've gone and built a church over a temple to some rival god?'

'San Clemente.'

'And they've *forgotten* the other god?'

'People do.'

'So how come *we're* here?'

'Just sight-seeing,' said Faust. 'Do you like it?'

'It's better than dead monks,' I said.

I shivered, remembering those skulls, some with tatters of skin still left on them.

'More Vesuvius,' I said.

When I'd drunk it, Faust said:

'Now you mustn't get me wrong, Kit. I don't worship this sun god.'

'I know that. You just like the sun.'

9   Donkey Ride

I don't know how long we spent down there with Mithras. My Nuremberg Egg doesn't work any more, like I told you. Let's say, we stayed for two bottles. Two bottles of Vesuvius, that is. The stuff tastes like larva. He drank most, but I didn't do bad.

Then we came out into stinking hot Rome.

The weather's gone crazy.

If this spring is like this, then this summer is going to be hell.

Still, I had something else to make me sweat.

Faust lopes off with Satan, and I have to follow behind. Akercocke's very stroppy. That bloody brass cage weighed a ton. I felt drunk. And the sun on my head made it worse.

Faust went through this slum called the Trastevere and out to the big open field at the Porta di Portese. There's a flea-market there every Sunday. Palm Sunday they sell bigger fleas. When I caught up, he was buying a donkey.

I soon got the idea.

What a fool!

The old fuck-up climbs onto the donkey and starts making his way back through Rome. Satan trotting beside him, woof-woofing. Me and Akercocke limping behind.

He followed, I think, the route that the Pope took much earlier. Only he travels that route in reverse. As if to undo what Paul 3 had done? I don't know. I know he was singing.

These kids started chasing us.

Faust was drinking and scattering coins.

The kids ran for the coins, and the hell of it. Like little birds they were, dodging in and out of his path, pulling faces, flapping their arms, egging him on with wild cries.

It was like the Pied Piper of Hamelin.

It was even more like Jesus Christ.

Palm Sunday. When he rode through Jerusalem.

Only nobody shouted *Hosannas*.

Not for Faust.

Not for a crazy drunk German bellowing at the top of his voice something so unmusical that it sounded like a cross between Henry the 8th's *Green Sleeves and Pudding Pies* and the hymn tune from French Johnny's kirk.

I was scared stiff that he'd be arrested.

He wasn't. Maybe because of the kids. Their running and turning cartwheels around the donkey made the whole thing a bit of a caper.

A few priests stopped to stare.

That was all.

10 Watchmaker

I kept a safe distance behind Faust. Near the Arch of Drusus I noticed this sign with a clock on it. A watchmaker's. I took my watch in.

The owner was this guy with an eye-patch. A Roman. Fat, half-asleep, cynical. He wore a turban of some kind of red crape.

'I make watches,' he said. 'I don't mend them.'

But when I dangled my Nuremberg Egg in front of his one working eye, he changed his tune pretty damned quick.

'Leave it here. I'll see what I can do.'

'This is a good watch,' I said. 'The best German craftsmanship.'

'So why has it gone wrong?' he said.

'You tell me,' I said. 'I'll call back tomorrow.'

'Better make it the next day,' he said. 'Holy Week. I'm worked off my feet. Every cardinal in the city's got a clock bust.'

'I'm not a cardinal. And this watch isn't bust. Like you see, it just tells too much time.'

'I could do with more time,' said the watchmaker.

'Ha ha.'

Well, he liked it. That a foreigner could laugh at a joke in Italian.

'Tuesday evening,' he said.

'Tuesday morning.'

'Tuesday morning I'm saying my prayers.'

'Just make my watch work,' I told him. 'Tuesday afternoon will do. Three o'clock.'

I got a receipt.

You can't trust them.

Not watchmen who need to say prayers.

11   Street Arab

When I came out of the watchmaker's, I couldn't find Faust. I wandered about for a bit, feeling lost. Then, between the two towers of the Porta San Sebastiano I noticed a couple of the urchins who'd been playing the game chasing after him. They were counting the scudi he'd scattered like rice at a wedding. They ran when they saw me, no doubt thinking that I'd want it back. I dropped Akercocke's cage. I went after them. I caught one by the hair, and he talked.

'The magician? He's gone! Up the Appian Way. On his donkey!'

'*Magician?*' I shouted. 'What makes you call my friend that?'

The brat scowled.

Then he yelped when I cuffed him.

'I heard the priest say so.'

'What priest? What priest said so?'

The brat shrugged till I hit him again.

'Outside Cardinal Bessarion's house. This friar. He said so.'

'You're lying!'

'Please, sir, don't kill me. It's the truth. You can have your friend's money back. Only – please, sir – don't kill me!'

'Keep the money,' I told him. 'What else did this priest have to say?'

'That we'd better not follow the magician. That we'd better go home.'

227

'But you *didn't* go home? You *did* follow him?'

'Just as far as the gate, sir. I got no home.'

I believed him. The last bit.

Rome is full of such arabs.

Looking into his eyes, I saw a little frightened bastard in the Wartburg, standing fatherless in a great hall full of cobwebs, straining his ears to catch the echo of songs that no one else could hear.

'You fuck me, sir? I do it Hamburg style.'

So much for high romance.

I let him go.

His skinny body had been absorbed like a speck of dirt into the general dungheap that is Rome before it crossed my mind that I should have got the brat to tell me if his informative friar had been wearing a grey habit.

12 Milestone

I found the donkey first, with no Faust on it. It was standing in a brook, as good as gold.

A little further on, I met with Satan. The creature yapped. I saw it had a bone.

For a minute or two, I stood there staring up the road and wondering if the Herr Trickster had gone for ever.

Gone home.

Like Salome.

Gone home. Wherever home is.

Just gone and left me here. Some final joke.

'*Hey,*' said Akercocke.

New word.

One learnt from me, of course.

'*Hey! Hey! Hey! Hey!*'

He made it sound like he was laughing at me.

Then I heard snoring, and at the first milestone was Faust. Fast asleep on his back. Legs asprawl. Vesuvius all over his Tiber-washed cloak.

I knelt down beside him.

Faustus. Fausta. Faustum.

He looked so unhappy I kissed him.

I kissed the old unhappy mess.
On the lips.
But he tasted like nothing.

13 Bedtime

I sat there until it was dark.

I don't think he knew that I kissed him.

I could hardly believe it myself, not sitting there smelling his smell. He must have shit his pants or something.

He was groaning and moaning a lot. I thought I caught one bit in Latin.

Daemones credunt, it sounded like.

Then *et contremiscunt.**

But I could have been wrong about that.

Truth to tell, he sounded and smelt like a pig.

Even Satan was keeping his distance.

At last, Faust opened one eye. He grinned at me.

'My angel,' he said. 'You're still here.'

'I'm tired,' I said.

'So am I, Kit.'

'I could do with a good sleep.'

'You shall have it.'

He spoke kindly. But the words seemed to mock me.

'OK,' I said. 'Where's it at?'

Faust leapt up with amazing alacrity. He did a wild jig on the spot. Then he ran off, cloak flapping, arms waving.

'Follow me!' he called back. 'This is special.'

'Hey!' Akercocke said. 'Hey! Hey! Hey!'

* *The devils believe and tremble.* Bit like *James*, 2, 19, if the old porker wasn't just grunting.

14 In the Catacombs

In the Rome *under* Rome. In the catacombs. That's Faust's somewhere special. Where it's at.

To be precise: the catacombs of San Sebastiano, just past the second milestone up the Appian Way. A labyrinth of corridors and galleries. A subterranean world. A living hell.

It's here in the catacombs that I've been writing these chapters about Palm Sunday, the first day of Holy Week and our own first day in the city.

Down here.

Like a mole in the earth.

It's night as I'm writing.

Night of Monday, 9th April. (Just three days to Devil Day! In other words, Good Friday, the 13th.)

Not that there's difference or distinction between night and day in this spooky maze. I would guess we're about 50 feet below ground. But I looked up an air-shaft just now and I made out the moon.

Lucky moon!

Like a half-eaten cheese.

(I'm real hungry.)

Faust's asleep in a broken stone coffin. He doesn't have company. All these vaults were well-ransacked for relics more than six centuries back. Then they closed them and sealed them. The Herr Genius (but of course) knew a secret way in.

I'm damned if I'd sleep like him, though.

Not in a secondhand sarcophagus, thank you.

There's this chapel just off the main crypt, and I've made my bed there. Akercocke in his cage on the altar. Nice touch. He doesn't like that.

Nothing happened today. We just stayed here. Faust drank his Vesuvius and I crawled around in the tunnels. They're like some dead beehive. Miles and miles of galleries where both pagans and Christians were buried in long low horizontal recesses, tier above tier, like the berths in a ship. Satan caught nine rats and a rabbit. I'd have eaten the rabbit if it hadn't had three eyes.

I found this stucco vault with nice decorations.

Lotus leaves.

Acanthus.

A peacock.

Also a lot of graffiti. The usual pious drivel.

Faust slept. With his hat on his chest.

His stink's got even worse. He must have wet himself. No doubt that's why he's always favoured wearing black. In black, the stains don't show if you're incontinent.

15 Tuesday Morning Blues

Bloody Tuesday. I think that I'll go mad. It's so *boring* down here underground.

When I woke, I lit candles round Faust's coffin.

I whistled.

Then I sang.

I stamped my feet.

Result: The old man just snored the more loudly. He might as well be dead. He won't wake up.

I can tell that it's morning by the air-shaft. I sit under it. I have to see the sky.

I'm not dead.

I'm not dying.

Does it make any sense? To be living in a city made for corpses? That's what this is. The catacombs. They took the bones away. Faust's found his home.

Some home! He's welcome to it!

But can he really have come all this way just to turn up his toes in a rat-hole and wait for his blood to run cold?

Where's the great free spirit gone? Where's the assassin? Would Simon Magus just lie down and die?

Well, fuck Simon Magus.

(I must add that to the graffiti. The theology is orthodox, after all.)

I've got to get out of here, and that's for certain.

I need water.

I need air. I need light. I need food.

I reckon Faust must be in some kind of coma.

I've tried shouting.
I've tried shaking him and punching him.
Not even the Vesuvius makes him move . . .
His eyes open. His eyes shut. He grins. He shuts his eyes
again. He can't wake up.
I pricked him with a needle.
He just laughed. Still fast asleep in his sarcophagus. Just
laughed, and bled a bit, and then stopped laughing.
A sleep like death.
Jesus Christ! *Should I go fetch a doctor?*

16   The Doctor Declined

I got out. I was lucky. Satan seemed to remember the way. I
guess I might have made it by myself, though these catacombs
are complicated. Still, dogs have an instinct for such things.
Even Calvinist dogs.

I didn't, of course, get a doctor.

How do you tell a doctor you've got this buddy lying dead
drunk in a coffin underground who just needs some pills to get
him fit for a little Pope-assassination?

Where would you start?

'See, Doc – it's pretty damned urgent. He's going to hell on
Good Friday at midnight if he hasn't killed Pope Paul 3 by
then . . .'

No.

There's some things you can't tell a doctor.

So I went for my Nuremberg Egg.

Leaving Akercocke down here.

Too bad.

17   No Trouble with a Nuremberg Egg?

I bought apples and meat, bread and wine. I walked along
eating the apples. I sat under the Aurelian Wall. It was
really damned hot. Flies everywhere. Mad weather for
April.

At three I called in at the watchmaker's.

'Nice watch,' he remarked. 'Want to sell it?'

'No. I don't. Have you mended it?'

'But of course.'

'What was wrong?'

The watchmaker's eye went to and fro among his clocks. I noticed the clocks all told different times. 15 clocks, and not one of them near three.

'Impossible to explain,' he said shiftily. 'Very difficult job. Very tricky.' He scratched at his turban. 'Five ducats.'

'*Five ducats!* Just for mending a watch?'

'I'll *buy* it for five,' said the watchmaker.

Now that was a very good price. Five ducats comes out at ten dalers. Nearly twice what I bought it for. Still, I wasn't interested.

'My watch isn't for sale. Your repair bill?'

'Ten ducats,' the watchmaker said.

'I told you. I won't sell at *any* price . . .'

'You misunderstand, sir. Ten ducats. That's the repair bill.'

'Twice as much as you'd pay me to *buy* the thing?'

'That's right, sir,' the watchmaker said.

It was crazy!

And I didn't have ten ducats.

I'll tell you what made the scene worse. I got the distinct impression from the watchmaker that far from it being a difficult job, he'd had no trouble at all. More, that he'd found *nothing wrong* with the watch! His own clocks suggested that he wasn't capable of mending a sundial . . .

What in Christ's name was I to do now?

Go back to the Herr Sleeping Beauty and pick his pockets? Would there be anything left from his donkey spree? The 'leg' money! But what if the street arabs had got it all?

As I stood there, weighing up my chances of grabbing the Nuremberg Egg from the counter and making a run for it, the watchmaker produced this black box.

'A mechanical theatre,' he said. 'Very nice. Very clever. Unique.'

He opened the box. Wound it up.

I'd never seen anything like it.

The marionettes were tiny, just an inch or two tall, and the whole thing worked by wires and clockwork.

'Observe,' said the watchmaker. '*Inferno* . . .'

The little mechanical theatre played for about five minutes, and the subject of its play was indeed a marionette version of hell.

There was a man in a black cape, and a devil in a red cap. The devil came in from the left and touched the man on the shoulder. The man had been reading a book and waving his hands. The devil bowed to the man. The man knelt down to the devil. The devil handed the man a sheet of paper. The man wrote on it. The devil took the sheet of paper and put it in a cupboard. Then the devil waved his cap and a girl came in through the window. The man and the girl got into a bed and the sheets went up and down. Then the man kicked the girl out of the bed and the devil came in with a sackful of gold. The man got into the bed with the gold. Then he got out of bed and grabbed the girl again and the girl got into the bed and the man and the girl and the gold went up and down under the sheets. Then the devil took the piece of paper out of the cupboard and handed it to the man. The girl disappeared back out of the window. The gold fell through a hole in the floor. The devil was waving his cap. The man fell down on his knees. An angel appeared through the window and tried to fight with the devil. But the devil hit him with a stick and the angel went through the hole in the floor. The man was still down on his knees. He grabbed hold of the leg of the bed. Then the clock at the back struck twelve and the devil grabbed hold of the man and the floor opened and you could see that under the floor there was a pit full of fire. The devil dragged the man and the bed down into the pit full of fire. Then the devil came up again and did a little dance and bowed.

'Chinese,' said the watchmaker. 'Amusing?'

I nodded.

Amusing was hardly the right word for what I had just seen, but I didn't know what was.

The watchmaker snapped the box shut. He patted it.

'Very valuable,' he said.

I said nothing.

'Expensive. Extraordinary. *Inferno* . . .'

He had a habit of smacking his lips round each syllable. I notice most Romans do this. Like vowels are some kind of pasta.

I asked casually:

'Where did you get it?'

The watchmaker shrugged. One of his bad clocks chimed seven.

'A long story. Very boring. Unimportant. Would you like it, *mein Herr*?'

I pretended to think for a bit.

Then I nodded.

His one good eye narrowed. He tapped at his eye-patch, as if it contained some great secret. He put one flabby hand on the black toy theatre, the other on my Nuremberg Egg.

'Very well, sir. It's yours! In exchange for your watch, now . . . How's that?'

I was getting a bargain. But why?

Who cares? I just wanted the thing.

'OK,' I said. 'It's a deal.'

19   Quo Vadis?

I scurried back to the catacombs with my prize. I was sweating. I felt happy and excited.

One small thing happening on the way.

There's this little church, close by the first milestone. It's called Domine Quo Vadis. Reason being that it stands on the spot where, according to legend, St Peter, hotfooting it out of Rome to dodge his martyrdom, met an apparition of Jesus marching in the opposite direction.

'Lord, where *you* going?' asks Peter. ('*Domine, quo vadis?*')

235

'To get crucified again!' answers Jesus. ('*Venio iterum cruci-figi!*')

So Peter turns round and goes back to his right death, head down.

Believe it or not. That's the story.

Well, Satan runs into this church and comes out with a bone. He also looks like he's been drinking. Maybe from the font.

A crowd comes out after him. They're shouting. They're mad. An altar boy with a thurible takes a swipe at the dog. Charcoal, cinders, and incense all over the place. Satan's singed. But he doesn't stop running.

We both ran up the Appian Way.

We soon shook the Christians off, and we didn't meet Jesus.

The dog's happy. His bone.

I'm happy. My box.

And so we returned to the underworld.

20   Tuesday Evening Puppet Shows

'Hey, Faust,' I said. 'Here's your story.'

I lit candles.

I opened the box.

I placed the mechanical theatre a few inches from his head where he slept in the coffin. Then I wound up the mechanism.

The marionettes went through their paces.

One of Faust's eyes opened about half way through the first show. It betrayed no expression in the candlelight. But that eye didn't shut. It stayed fixed on the bright tiny figures.

He grinned as I wound the thing up again.

By the end of the second show both Faust's eyes were open. They looked bright.

When the devil took his bow at the end of the third show, Faust clapped. He sat up in his coffin.

'I thought you might like it,' I said.

Faust made me keep winding the clockwork. He must have watched those marionettes go through their antics at least thirty times.

My hand ached.
But I couldn't refuse him.
'Again,' he'd say. 'Just one more time, Kit.'
At last, he seemed satisfied.
He got out of the coffin.
He laughed. Tears ran down his face. But he didn't look happy or sad.
'You *do* like it?' I said.
Then Faust kissed me.
'I love it,' he said. 'It's quite perfect.'

21 Martyr Dirt

'So how do we do it?' I asked.
'Like this,' Faust said.
He buggered me.
There in the coffin in the catacombs.
I swallowed a mouthful of martyr dirt.

22 Thanks

'That's not what I meant,' I said, when he'd come and I wanted to go.
Faust smiled at the candles. He said nothing.
'The Pope,' I said. 'That's what I meant.'
Faust still didn't answer me.
I heard a rat scuttle down one of the tunnels and Satan go after it. I felt sick. I was sore. I despised myself.
I got out of the sarcophagus and washed my behind with white wine. Then I gargled with some of his Vesuvius.
'It must be gone midnight,' I said. 'Two days. That's all. Two days left to Good Friday. *So how do you murder the Pope?*'
Faust's eyes were shut fast.
He'd started to snore. He's always a quick sleeper after sex.
'You bastard!' I said.
I shook him awake.
I leaned over him. I pinned him down by the arms. He

237

smelt vile. He was worse than the martyr dirt. He was grinning, of course.

'Such passion!' he said. 'Don't you love me?'

'I came with you,' I said.

'No, you didn't.'

'I'm not talking about *that*,' I said. 'I came with you to Rome.'

'Thank you,' he said.

Faust shut his eyes again.

I tugged at his hair. His moustaches. That made him take notice.

'Listen,' I said. 'I don't believe in you. You know that. You've known it a long time. I don't believe in your pact with the Devil, your grey friar Mephistopheles, the rest of that shit.'

'Thank you,' Faust said.

'Don't thank me,' I said. 'Just make sense. *You* believe it all, don't you? That's why we're here! God damn it, if *you*'re just fooling, then the whole fucking journey's a joke! And more than the journey. Your whole life. And my life. The lot!'

'But you like jokes,' Faust said. 'Tell me a Luther joke. What about the one where he loses the Great Farting Contest on account of his –'

'Balls!' I shouted.

'I didn't ask what keeps your ears apart,' Faust said.

I hit him.

He looked really shocked. Then he shrugged.

'Very well, Kit,' he said. 'I'll tell you tomorrow.'

'Tell me *now!*'

'Tomorrow,' he said. 'Maundy Thursday.'

'You'll be cutting it fine . . .'

'It's cut,' he said. 'Long ago. The Devil's scissors, remember?'

'Oh fuck off,' I said. 'It's all crap. You've got nothing to tell. I've rumbled your secret, you bastard. Your secret is that you've not got one. No secret. No plan for killing the Pope. Nothing! I used to think that you were mad, but you're not even mad. You're a joker, that's all.'

Faust laughed.

He lay licking his bloodstone.

'You'll see,' he said. 'And if I'm a joker, then you are my best joke, my son.'

He shut his eyes wearily. His fingers were stroking his hat.

'Tomorrow,' he promised. 'Maundy Thursday.'

I stood there and stared at him. I was trembling. I couldn't say why.

'And thanks for the puppets,' he added. 'That joke was on me, wasn't it?'

23   Flies

I crawled to this chapel off the main crypt. Like I said, I've made my bed here. Mosaic floor. A fresco over the tympanum. The subject of the fresco seems to be the Raising of Lazarus. Only, Lazarus looks really *reluctant* to rise from the dead. Wise artist. After all, nobody thought to ask the poor guy if he wanted to.

I couldn't sleep on account of the flies.

I never noticed them before. Now they're everywhere.

Black flies and blue flies and others the colour of the walls of the catacombs themselves, so that you think they're a part of the rock till you hear the rock buzzing.

Buzzzzz.

It's horrible.

Akercocke loves them. He picks off the wings and eats hand-fuls. His jacket's all stained. His bell tinkles.

He catches flies in his hands and holds his hands to his ears, for the music.

Flies thick on his cage on the altar. Like black raindrops. Like a widow's black veil.

I'm writing because I can't sleep.

So we kill the Pope tomorrow?

I wasn't born yesterday!

Here's the Pope of the Flies:

He was crawling right over my page.

I've killed the Supreme Fly Pontiff of the Catacombs, anyway.

'Hey!' Akercocke's saying. 'Hey! Hey!'

24   Reformed Graffiti

Satan's gone. I've looked everywhere, down all the tunnels. The rats must have eaten him. Or he's heading back home to John Calvin.

Wednesday, 11th April.

Late morning, I guess.

Faust's still snoring.

Flies still buzzing.

My night without sleep has inspired me. I thought up a bit of graffiti which I just added in a fair imitation of a first century A.D. hand to the wall of the vault with the lotus leaves:

> *Here I sat, broken-hearted,*
> *Paid a pfennig but only farted . . .*
>   M. Luther

25   Fairy Story

Once upon a time there was a boy who loved angels. He was kidnapped by a wicked magician who shut him up in a tower in a black forest. There was no escape so the boy decided to turn into an angel himself. He worked really hard at turning himself into an angel until one day he woke up and found he had wings growing out of his back. He flew up from the tower and far away over the forest. But the wicked magician had wings too and he came flying after the boy. The magician had black wings. The boy's wings were gold. The magician also had silver scissors. When he caught the boy he cut off the boy's wings with the scissors. The boy fell out of the sky. He fell down a hole. At the bottom of the hole he found his mother and father. His mother was stirring a pot full of soup. His father was 7 feet 7 inches tall. I don't know what the fuck his father was doing. THE END.

26 Another Fairy Story
   (Abandoned after a Promising Beginning)

Once upon a wart.

27 Luther Joke

When Luther was a lad he wasn't so much of a theologian. He never paid attention in Sunday School. This wasn't so bad. The other kids were no better. Well, the bishop is coming. So the Sunday School teacher primes his class. The bishop will go down the line asking questions. First question: *Who made you?* Answer: *God made me.* Second question: *Who were the first man and woman?* Answer: *Adam and Eve.* Etc, etc. Luther is second in the line. His answer is *Adam and Eve.* 'Adam and Eve,' he keeps muttering. 'Adam and Eve.' Fierce concentration. Well, just before the bishop arrives the first boy in the line is excused to go out to the jakes. The bishop comes in and therefore begins with young Martin. 'Who made you, my son?' 'Adam and Eve,' Luther answers, as quick as a flash. The bishop is scandalised. 'No! No! God made you!' 'He didn't,' says Luther. *'The boy God made is outside taking a shit!'*

28 Lie

I have now killed a total of 666 flies.
   A significant number, of course.
   Revelation, 13, 18.
   And the first and last lie in this book.
   What I mean is:
   I'm bored out of my mind down here trying to pass the time making up stories, telling jokes, avoiding Akercocke's staring, shutting my ears to Faust's snoring, and so on and so forth.
   Anyway, I *have* swatted a lot of the bleeders. But still they keep coming. Buzz. Buzz. Fucking buzz.

29   Another Luther Joke (Fishy)

Luther likes fishing. He never catches much, but he likes fishing. Most of his hymns have been inspired by unsuccessful fishing trips. 'All we do is vain, even in the best life' – that famous line came into his head after a weekend without a single bite. It's a fact.

Well, one day he's out in this little boat all on his own on the Bodensee, fishing away, praying and farting, considering the total depravity of mankind, the uselessness of human reason, and so forth, when suddenly he has a vision. The Constipator hasn't caught a fish all day, of course, but all at once the sky goes dark and he sees this tall figure in snow-white robes walking towards him over the water.

It's Jesus.

Naturally, Luther is impressed. The Bodensee is 827 feet deep, after all.

'Lord! Lord!' cries Luther, remembering his *Matthew* 14, 25. He's debating with himself whether to step out of the boat and test if his faith is stronger than St Peter's, when he notices that Jesus doesn't look so good.

In fact, with each stride towards him across the Bodensee, Jesus is sinking.

Slowly.

But surely.

Going down.

Inch by inch.

Jesus is up to his ankles in the water.

Now it's his knees. Now his waist. Now only his head shows above the surface. He has to make a grab for the boat.

'Master!' cries Luther, disappointed. 'You used to be able to walk on water fine. What's the matter?'

Jesus spits out a tench.

Then he tells him. 'Martin,' he says. 'That was *before* . . .'

'What do you mean?' demands Luther. 'What do you mean, Lord – *before?*'

'Before I had these bloody great holes in my feet,' says Jesus.

30 The Very Famous Joke about Luther's Honeymoon

The night that the Constipator got married to Catherine von Bora, who was of course a Cistercian nun until she kicked the habit, they both —
NO!

31 Relief

Faust's awake!
    He's calling out to me:
    'I could do with a drink!'
    Vesuvius bottles lying empty or smashed all around his sarcophagus.
    Release from this bondage at last . . .
    I have something to do.
    A reason for living.
    A reason for leaving.

32 Pursuit

It's better down here telling Luther jokes!
    Jesus H. Christ . . .
    7 bloody grey friars.
    OK. Set this down carefully, Wagner. Too much Vesuvius? OK. But I'm not drunk. I swear I'm not drunk. I was certainly not drunk when it happened.
    When what happened?
    This.
    It was afternoon when I came out of these catacombs to go fetch Faust's booze. Sultry heat. Most unseasonable, unreasonable. The sun like a poached egg over Rome. The Appian Way really crowded.
    When I got to the city the crowds got much worse. The big

build-up for Easter's begun. Thousands of pilgrims, plus hucksters and tricksters from all over christendom. I had to fight my way in through the gate. Once inside, I had to move more or less where the crowd moved. A couple of times the press was so thick that my feet left the ground. I watched out for pickpockets, naturally. Faust had given me the necessary ducats. I didn't fancy having to do this job twice.

I found a wine cellar almost by accident.

I say 'almost'.

The fact is that a drunk woman was thrown out of it right in my path and I fell over her straight down the steps.

Alcoholic predestination rules OK.

I bought the Vesuvius. Many bottles. I strapped them all round me and on me. I had a Vesuvius necklace, a Vesuvius belt, and Vesuvius clubs in my hands. I was wearing Vesuvius armour. I must have looked like a walking volcano.

Give or take the odd crushed toe, bruised rib, and a poke in the eye from a banner with St Christopher* on it, I was doing not bad till I reached this ruined church at the start of the Via di Porta San Sebastiano. San Cesareo, I think it's called. The one near the house where that Cardinal Bessarion lived a hundred years back. The Greek guy who would have been Pope if he hadn't been Greek. Known to his secretaries as Good Queen Bess.

Well, just as I reach these church ruins a grey friar pops out of them.

'That's him!' he cries. 'There he is!'

A perfectly ordinary grey friar.

Bit fat. No shoes. Looking in need of a shave.

'Catch him!' he screams. 'He's a devil!'

The friar's pointing his finger.

I look round.

Just the usual spaghetti of Romans behind me. Men and women. Whores and street arabs. Pilgrims. Tourists. The obligatory nun.

Not a single horned demon in sight . . .

Then the pfennig drops:

The friar's pointing the finger at *me*!

'Hang on,' I said reasonably, in my best Italian. 'I'm a German citizen. I have papers. You can't —'

* !

244

But he could.

Or he bloody well tried.

Screeching some exorcist gibberish in Latin, the friar makes a dive for my person.

I swerved. The fat fool missed me. I ran.

Ran, you understand, insofar as it's possible to run with a cargo of Vesuvius. Quite a handicap. But that Franciscan nut meant business. So I moved.

The bottles were quite helpful in one way. I had a bottle in each hand and I waved my arms like windmills as I went. That caused the crowd to open, give me passage. I headed for the San Sebastiano gate.

I reached Bessarion's house.

The doors flew open.

Three more Franciscan friars!

All beckoning . . .

'Come here, you devil!'

I didn't find their invitation tempting.

I ran on, blindly, till I reached the gate.

With four grey friars pounding at my heels.

And there, at the gate, *two friars more!*

Great brutes.

Like Gog and Magog.

I didn't stop. I hit them with the bottles.

I got one on the skull as he stooped down to scoop me up. The other I got in the balls.

Vesuvius everywhere.

Two broken bottles.

I chucked them over my shoulder as I headed up the Appian Way.

I was panting. I was dripping with sweat and Vesuvius.

I didn't look back. I didn't need to. I could hear bare Franciscan feet slap-slapping behind me. What a game! What a nightmare! Being chased up the Appian Way by a gang of grey butchers!

The last one loomed up in front of me where the road meets a path leading to the Temple of the Deus Rediculus. That's a few hundred yards past Domine Quo Vadis.

I gave him volcanoes.

A swing in the gut with my Vesuvius belt.

By the time I passed the second milestone I was just far

enough ahead of my pursuers to give them the slip when it
came to darting away from the road and disappearing down
the entrance Faust showed me to these forgotten catacombs.

A very nasty experience.

Grey friars! Well, I ask you . . .

7 in all.

New graffiti:

St Francis is strictly for the birds.

33   Broken Puppets

'What kept you?' Faust said.

When I got my breath back, I told him.

He just grinned when he wasn't busy drinking. Still, he offered
some Vesuvius to me – which may or may not have meant
sympathy.

I wouldn't have touched that gut-rot except for one thing.

What the old fuck-up had done down here while I'd been
out friar-dodging in Rome to get him his medicine.

The mechanical theatre is broken.

It won't work any more.

'Kit, I had to do something,' he said. 'I was dying for a
drink.'

So, apparently, he'd tried just to wind the thing up, make it
go, pass the time with performances. But his big stupid hands
got the shakes and he busted the toy.

The key's bent in half. The mechanism's all jammed. The
little figures can't move.

I did do my damnedest to mend it.

No use. So I drank the Vesuvius.

When Faust breaks something it stays broken for good.

34   No Tears for Satan

'Satan's gone,' I said.

I hoped that would hurt him. The way I was hurt by the
puppets.

246

Faust just shrugged.
Then he said:
'I don't need Satan any more.'

35 Small Talk

'*Why* did the grey friars chase me?' I said.
  'How the hell do I know?' Faust said.
  'They called me a devil,' I said.
  'My angel!' Faust said.

36 Slightly Bigger Talk

So I've come in here. To the chapel.
  I'd rather put up with Akercocke, frankly.
  I'd sooner listen to *his* crazy chatter.
  'Hell.'
  'God.'
  'Devil.'
  'Amen.'
  'Hey.'
  'Hell.'
  'God.'
  'Devil.'
  'Amen.'
  'Hey.'
In between mouthfuls of flies.
Sitting up there in his cage on the altar.
  'Hell. God. Devil. Amen. Hey!'
  'Hellgod. Devilamen. Hey!'
  'Hellgoddevilamenhey!'
I'm not drunk.
But I'm worn out.
I think I shall sleep.

37 A Dream

I dreamt a dream. What can it mean? I never had a dream before. I've been missing out, evidently. Dreams are OK. Dreams are fine. *Sweet dreams*, they say. I can see why. This was one hell of a sweet dream all right. I can see why people dream dreams now. This was a very nice dream indeed. I'm going to write it down so I can remember it. Then I can dream it again. I wouldn't mind dreaming this dream again tonight. And tomorrow night. And the night after that. And the next. I'm still a fact man basically, of course. But it's great stuff, this dreaming. It's hot stuff, this dream.

38 Of Fair Women

I dreamt I was here in this chapel in the catacombs and in the middle of the night I woke up and Marguerite and Gretchen were kneeling side by side at my feet.

They were just like they were when they first came to the Tower.

You'd have thought they were praying from the way they were kneeling, but from the looks on their faces you could tell it wasn't prayer they had in mind.

The little twins were naked. So was I.

I saw Marguerite had this feather in her hand.

'Helen's Gabriel feather!' I cried out, in the dream.

Marguerite nodded.

Then she whispered:

'Helen doesn't need it any more . . .'

Marguerite starts teasing my prick with the angel feather. She tickles up and down, flicks to and fro.

Gretchen giggles as she sees me getting big. She reaches out to get some of the action.

Together, one on each side, the twins worked over my prick with that angel feather.

They brushed it.

They rubbed it.

They smoothed and smacked and scrubbed it.

In short, the angelic works. And –

Well, I came.

Marguerite's smiling. She kisses the feather. It's sticky now. She likes that stickiness.

Then Gretchen snatched the feather.

Gretchen sucks it.

Now they masturbate each other, taking turns up their cunts with the quill from old Gabriel's wing.

Both girls laughing.

I spread out my arms. They snuggle up close to me.

One on each side.

Only it isn't Marguerite and Gretchen any more . . .

It's Zuleika and Salome!

'Salome's been naughty,' Zuleika says.

'So's Zuleika,' whispers Salome.

'Salome deserves spanking,' Zuleika says.

'Zuleika should be tickled,' whispers Salome.

I ask them in my dream:

'Who needs it most?'

'I do!' Zuleika cries. 'Kit, tickle me!'

'No! Me first!' begs Salome. 'Spank me, please!'

I found I could oblige the two at once. Zuleika stood naked beside me as Salome lay over my knees. I'm tickling a hot cunt with my left hand as I spank a bare bum with my right. My prick soon gets hard again. Salome's wriggling about on it as I spank her. I'm sucking Zuleika's nipples as I tickle her clit. We all come at about the same moment.

Then Salome rolls off my knees.

She laughs and looks up.

Only it isn't Salome any more . . .

It's Justine, of course!

And the girl standing laughing beside me isn't Zuleika . . .

It's Nadja!

Nadja's fingers that play with my prick.

Justine's lips that love sucking it.

'Hang on,' I cried out, in the dream. 'This is too much! I can't . . .'

I could.

And I did.

249

Nadja's fingers.
Justine's lips.
'He's coming!' cried Nadja, as she squeezed it.
'He's come!' cried Justine, as she swallowed it.
Then this voice says:
'OK, little German.'
No prizes for guessing –
Yes, *it's Jane*!
Justine and Nadja have gone.
Jane stands, hands on hips, looking down at me.
'Kid's stuff,' she sneers. 'Sexy *games* . . .'
So I fucked her.

39   Moral

It's a great life if you don't weaken.
  It's a great death if you don't waken.

40   Reflections

Hell!
      God!
            Devil!
                  Amen!
                        Hey!

41   Maundy Thursday Amnesia

'What was it I was going to do?' Faust said.
  'Tell me,' I said.
  'I'm *asking* you . . .'
  'What?'
  'What it was. What it was I was going to do.'
  'Jesus Christ!'
  'Cut the cackle. Just remind me.'

Re-mind him!

Well, he needs a new head, that's for sure.

'Yesterday,' I said. 'About seven bottles of Vesuvius ago. Yesterday you said you'd tell me today. Your plot. How you plan to do it. What you came to Rome for. The Great Work.'

'Good,' he said. 'I've got it.'

'Right. Tell me then . . . How do we kill him?'

Faust looked blank.

'How do we *what*?'

'Assassinate him!'

'*Who?*'

'THE POPE!'

Faust grinned.

'Funny,' he said. 'I could have sworn that you wanted me to *confess* to him . . .'

42 Toilet

Faust lay licking his bloodstone.

'OK,' he said. 'If you want me to.'

I had opened a bottle of Vesuvius. I was drinking it down in one go. His mind really frightened me. The lack of it.

'That stuff's lousy,' he warned. 'You'll get hiccups.'

Faust fished in his pocket. He took out a little box of butter. Then he grabbed one of the candles, still burning, and poured himself a palmful of hot candlegrease. He added the butter to the grease, rubbing his long hands together. Then he slapped the whole lot on his boil.

Faust pulled himself together in the coffin. He smoothed his cloak. He smacked his black hat on his thigh. Then he put the hat on his head at an angle.

He stood up.

'Let's go,' he said.

So we went.

43 Travel Arrangements

How did we go?

A good question.

I'm sorry I can't answer it.

One moment we were there in the dark of the forgotten catacombs under San Sebastiano. The next moment we were in the Sistine Chapel.

I can't remember moments in between.

That Vesuvius is powerful all right.

44 Modern Art

The Sistine Chapel was stinking with paint.

The Pope had the decorators in.

All these ladders.

Big brushes.

Pots.

'Michelangelo,' Faust said.

'Can't catch me!'

I pointed up at the ceiling. It was done.

'Not the ceiling,' Faust said. 'The altar.'

True enough, there was this guy working away over the altar. He was up on the scaffolding. He looked drunk. He went at that wall like a rapist. He had workmen busy scraping off some nice old stuff. As fast as they destroyed it, he slapped nasty new stuff in its place.

If it was Michelangelo, he should shoot himself.

I don't like modern art.

This was awful.

45 'The Last Judgment'

'He calls it,' Faust said, '*The Last Judgment.*'

'Well, it doesn't look like anything on earth!'

There were all these stupid figures. Muscle-bound. Their heads were tiny and their torsos huge. Michelangelo – if it *was* Michelangelo, and not some drunk imposter – had them all flying about in empty space, without the help of wings, and with no flat surfaces to rest upon.

It wasn't science and it wasn't art.

'Which are the damned?' Faust said. 'And which are the saved?'

'Good question,' I said. 'They all look the same to me.'

Every face on that wall was bug-eyed and full of terror. Every fist clenched to fight. Every body distorted.

Even the angels holding the cross looked like they'd like to kill each other.

And the saints were all out of proportion. For instance, I could make out what I took to be St Peter standing on a cloud. Then there was St Bartholomew* with another team of saints to his right. Bartholomew's team is placed further forward in the fresco than Peter on his cloud, but they were only half his size. That's against the known rules of perspective.

'The Christ is interesting,' Faust remarked.

'He's fat,' I said. 'He looks like Hercules.'

'That's what I meant,' Faust said.

'Well, he's not tall enough,' I said. 'He should be six foot three. And what's he doing with his hand up?'

'Judging,' Faust said.

'Looks like cursing to me.'

'Same thing,' Faust said.

---

* Apostle. Spread the gospel in Armenia. Flayed alive. Emblem: a butcher's knife.

46 Pants

'I should have thought that the Pope would have made him put pants on them all,' I remarked.

'The Pope hasn't seen it yet,' Faust said. 'No doubt you are right, though.'

'It won't make any difference, of course. The guy just can't paint!'

Faust said nothing.

He took off his hat and looked into it.

I lost interest in that crazy 'Last Judgment'. After all, had we crossed the Alps just for art's sake?

(Art?!

I could do better with a brush up my arse . . .)

Faust was standing there in the middle of the Sistine Chapel staring into his hat.

'So how do we do it?' I said. 'You still haven't told me.'

47 Plot

Faust took a host from his hat.

'I'll tell you,' he said.

He told me.

The plot was superb!

Diabolical!

Get a load of this . . .

48 Presanctification

'Tomorrow,' Faust said, 'is Good Friday. Good Friday – which commemorates the death of Jesus Christ. Now, there's something peculiar about Good Friday. What is it? As an Old Wittenbergian, you should know!'

He was holding up the host between two fingers.

254

That gave me the clue.

'No Mass,' I said. 'No communion.'

'Not bad,' Faust said. 'Seven out of ten.'

'Wait a bit,' I said, remembering. 'Let me get it right! Good Friday . . . Yes, in the Roman Church that's definitely the only day of the whole year when Mass is *never* said. It's forbidden, in fact. And communion is very, very rare. Only those who are dying may be given it.'

'Eight out of ten,' Faust said. 'You've forgotten something.'

I racked my brains, scowling at the host. That thin wafer of unleavened bread looked very white against the black of Faust's hands.

Then I got it . . .

'The Mass of the Presanctified!'

'Meaning?'

'Meaning that Mass isn't *said*. There's no consecration of the bread and the wine. But a host consecrated at a previous Mass is eaten. A so-called presanctified host.'

'And who always eats it?'

'The priest. He breaks it into three parts. He drops one part in a chalice of presanctified wine. He eats the other two. Then he drinks all the wine with the other part in it.'

'Full marks!' Faust said. 'The Mass of the Presanctified, which the Roman Catholic Church allows only on Good Friday, is the only Mass in which there is always *one* host and the officiating priest *always* gets it. And tomorrow, at the high altar of St Peter's, Pope Paul 3 gets this one . . .'

'Jesus Christ!' I said.

'You've guessed,' Faust said, grinning. '*It's poisoned!*'

49   A Grain of Monkshood

I looked round nervously.

It was OK.

The painters and decorators had gone.

Opening time, probably.

'Michelangelo' back to the Home for the Blind.

We were all on our own there in the Sistine Chapel.

'Not an arbitrary choice,' Faust said. 'There are a hundred

ways you could kill a Pope. I'm choosing to do it the best way. With his own weapons.'

'What's your poison?' I said.

'Wolfsbane,' Faust said. 'Known otherwise as monkshood. *Aconitum Napellus*. Aconitine. Call it what you like. The names don't matter. The most deadly of all known poisons. With no known antidote.'

'How much does it take to kill a man?'

'One 16th of a grain,' Faust said.

'And what's in that wafer?'

'There is a whole grain here which will kill a Pope.'

50 Smelly Feet

We drank more Vesuvius.

I began to develop quite a taste for the stuff.

'Monkshood,' I said. 'Nice name.'

'I prefer wolfsbane.'

'Wolfsbane is very nice too.'

We sat there in peace. It was good not to argue. The Sistine Chapel is a decent place to sit, if you have enough booze to blot your mind to the walls and the ceiling.

Then Faust said suddenly:

'Do you reckon my feet stink?'

I didn't say anything.

He tugs off a boot.

'Look,' he says, flexing his toenails. 'This foot could do with a wash.'

I was holding my breath.

Faust sucks his moustaches.

'It would be reasonable, therefore,' he says, 'to assume that its fellow is in a similar condition.'

He was drunk.

I was drunk.

What the hell . . .

It seemed a strange thing to me: to start worrying about feet you haven't washed for 7 years when you have a Pope-assassination plot on the go.

He puts the poisoned wafer back in his hat.

'I know just the place,' he says. 'A wash and brush up.'

He stands, unsteadily.

'Come on,' he says.

I followed him.

Faust was hopping. Wearing just the one boot.

He hops into St Peter's.

Lots of people. Some service about to start. The Pope at the altar, dressed in white.

Faust falls flat on his face.

He rolls over.

He gets me to pull off the other boot.

It wasn't easy. I'd had too much to drink.

He had to hang on to a confession box while I pulled.

The curtains open.

This priest looks out. He's startled. It's not every day that confession boxes shake.

'Sorry,' Faust says. 'Spot of trouble here . . . My fault!'

At last, the job is done.

Two bare black Faustian feet.

The priest goes back to his business.

The old fart hands me his boots.

He winks.

'Watch this,' he says.

'What you going to do?'

'Kill two birds with one stone,' Faust said.

51   The Mandatum

To my amazement, the Herr Stinker is not the only guy in St Peter's who's minus his footwear.

Twelve men in a line at the altar.

Old men. Dirty men. Beggar types.

And not a single shoe between the lot of them!

Faust joins the line: the 13th.

I leant against a pillar. My head spun.

One Pope, in white. And 13 barefoot Fausts, in black.

'No more of that Vesuvius,' I vowed.

I must have said the words out loud. These fat-arsed Roman matrons turn round and start shushing me.

Then I remembered:
It's Maundy Thursday.
The Mandatum.

This couldn't be chance. Faust knows the rites of the Roman Church inside-out. He knows what he's doing. He knows what he's up to now. He's crazy, of course. But there's method in all his madness.

See, on Maundy Thursday there's just the one Mass at St Peter's. A host is specially consecrated and carried in procession to a side-altar called the altar of repose. That's the host which they're keeping for Good Friday, the one which only the Pope is allowed to eat. Then they strip the high altar of everything but cross and candlesticks. They they have the Mandatum, this ceremony where the Pope washes the feet of 13 poor men.

It's all to do with what Jesus is supposed to have done at the Last Supper.*

It's called the Mandatum from the first word of the first chant at this particular Mass: *Mandatum novum do vobis* (A new commandment I give you).

Faust has got in on the act all right.

As the 13th man in the line he's right up there next to the Pope.

I watch his hand sneak out while the Pope and everyone else is bent in prayer, eyes shut.

Faust puts the poisoned wafer on the altar. He pockets the ordinary one that's waiting for the magic words.

The Pope stands up.
Bends forwards.
He consecrates Faust's host.
He makes the sign of the cross.
He pronounces the words.
'*Hoc est enim Corpus meum . . .*'
('*For this is my Body . . .*')
Monkshood!
Wolfsbane!
Aconitine!
The Pope holds up the host so the people can see and adore it.

* See *John*, 13, 4–17, etc.

258

A thin white disc of crisp bread about three inches in dia-
meter.

100 per cent pure poison!

The Pope's meal for tomorrow!

52 Umbrella

They carried the poisoned host to the altar of repose.

It was comic, the way that they did it.

A solemn procession.

With the deadly bit of bread in some sort of urn, and the
urn with a white veil draped over it.

Everybody genuflects twice as the damned thing goes past.

And there's this deacon who has to walk backwards. He's
holding an umbrella over the urn. Just in case it rains in St
Peter's and the transubstantiated Christ should get wet.

Then they stripped the high altar.

And the Pope did his foot-washing bit.

As he went down the line, I remembered that abbot at
Monte Oliveto Maggiore.

I shivered. I didn't like that.

When the Pope got to Faust I thought that I'd laugh,
though.

It's like Jesus and Judas all right . . .

Here's Pope Paul 3 washing the feet of his own murderer.

And then kneeling down and kissing them as well.

53 Vigil

When the ceremony's over, and Faust's got his boots back, we
went to visit our handiwork there in a side-chapel.

Lots of flowers and lights.

With the host on the altar.

And old women kneeling in front of it. Mumbling their
prayers. Clicking rosaries.

It's the custom.

They kneel there all night. Shifts of them. A vigil.

Cluck cluck.

Clickety click.

Poor old Jesus won't get any sleep with that racket.

'Good idea, though,' I said. 'Just in case someone switches it.'

'No danger,' Faust said. 'No one will even *touch* the bloody thing. Not till the Pope pops it into his gob tomorrow.'

He yawned.

'I could do with some shut eye,' he said.

54   Trumps

So here we are. Back safe and sound in the catacombs.

The Herr Assassin's asleep in his stupid sarcophagus.

Snoring his head off.

At peace.

Me, I'm in my chapel.

What's the time?

I wish I could tell you. But you can't tell the time by a broken puppet theatre.

It's night, anyway. And I've not taken long with writing down our adventures of Maundy Thursday. A great pleasure to write.

Jesus Christ! Yes!

Faust's clever.

He's mad. But all the same I have to hand it to him. Never let it be said that Wagner didn't give credit where credit was due.

What a plot!

What a caper!

Devilish!

I thought he'd let me down. But he's come up trumps.

Akercocke's rattling the bars of his cage on the altar. He's starving. He's desperate for food. He can't live on flies.

Well, starve away, Akercocke.

Just looking at that monkey makes me think of that host on the altar.

Is the Pope sleeping well?

Not as well as he'll sleep on Good Friday . . .

Good Friday.
Tomorrow.
I can't wait for it. It can't come quick enough.

55   Pope versus Angels

Not that I've got anything personal against the Pope, you understand.

As Popes go, he's no worse than most.

Corrupt, of course. Worldly.

I'm no Luther. I don't give a fart about that.

Old Eye-tie family, the Farneses. All the right friends. Bags of money. This Alessandro's their first Pope, so far as I know. He rose fast in the church. Got his cardinal's hat through the cunt of his sister, Giulia. She slept three in a bed with Pope Alexander 6 and his daughter, Lucrezia. It's common knowledge.

The present Pope's not famous for incest. His 3 boy bastards are thugs, but he's fathered no kids on his daughter.

I've got nothing against the whole office of Pope, if it comes to that. I turned down a basinful of hot anti-Papist porridge at Wittenberg. Too silly for words. There have been 'good' Popes and 'bad' Popes. It's nothing to me.

My mind goes for higher things.

Angels.

Now, if the Pope was an angel, I'd have time for him.

(Just my little joke.)

To be serious:

The pleasure is in seeing something done *perfectly*. Faust's come up with that. Absolute and ultimate perfection.

Angelic.

Incredible.

The perfect Pope-murder.

And even more angelic and incredible because Faust is a fuck-up himself.

56   Maundy Thursday Nightcap

Perfection?

No.

I start to sound like Faust.

Better shut up.

It's *nice*.

That's all.

The flies down here are not nice. The flies are nasty. It's worse than ever, their buzzing. Flies, flies, flies.

It's interesting to note that the Herr Vampire never so much as mentioned 'Mephistopheles' all Maundy Thursday. And no talk of the 24 years that he thinks of as wages for this. His mad mind (when it's not too spaced out or hungover) must be really on the job.

Hey ho.

What the hell does it matter to me?

Only one thing matters: that the Pope drops down dead once he swallows that wafer tomorrow. Faust will believe he's satisfied his 'spirit'. I'll finish my book. We'll go home.

When I write the word *home*, my mind is a blank. Why's that? It's one of those nasty words. Like *father*. Words better avoided.

And yet words are nothing.

I hate words.

I'll be glad to stop writing this book.

The truth is I'm far too excited. My heart's like a clock. Sleep's the answer. I'd dream my nice dream again then.

Things to do. Things to think of. To sleep.

Luther jokes?

Angel names?

Fly-swatting?

Vesuvius!

That's the ticket.

I'll drink just enough Vesuvius to nap nicely . . .

57 Good Friday (11 p.m.)

So he's failed!

The old fool! The stupid great son-of-a-bitch!

How *could* he have failed? How on earth is it *possible* to have fucked-up like that?

Well, he did.

He has.

So it's over.

It's all over.

And now Faust's got nothing better to do than blunder about drunk down there in the ruins of the Forum.

I can see him in the moonlight.

He's stripping off his cloak. His shirt. His bloodstone.

The madman.

He's expecting the Devil's agent to come and claim him in an hour . . .

At midnight.

'Mephistopheles.'

Of course, his 'Mephistopheles' won't come.

There *is* no 'Mephistopheles.'

No one is going to come.

Nothing is going to happen at bloody midnight.

We've got a long ride back to Germany ahead of us, that's all.

58 Good Friday Morning (Early)

'Happy birthday,' he said.

He woke me up.

He was leaning over me.

He was grinning. He was stroking my hair.

'Happy birthday! Happy birthday!'

'Today's not my birthday,' I said.

I should explain: I don't keep a birthday. I don't know the exact day I was born. It isn't important.

263

'Happy birthday!' Faust said.

He started to sing it.

He started to dance round and round.

He grabs hold of Akercocke's cage. Faust and Akercocke go spinning round and round in the catacombs while I'm still half-asleep, a bit groggy with Vesuvius.

'*Happy birthday to you!*'

I should have known then that he'd botched it.

59   Good Friday Morning (A Bit Later)

But I didn't. I didn't suspect a damned thing. How could I? Why should I? I *saw* it yesterday when he slipped that poisoned host in place of the ordinary one on the altar. The plot, like I said, seemed perfect. I had no reason for supposing that anything could possibly go wrong.

Faust couldn't keep dancing for long.

He fell down.

He dropped Akercocke.

The cage lay on its side. I didn't right it.

Flies crawled down Faust's face in his sweat. He didn't swat them. He didn't flick them away.

'Good Friday,' he said. 'It's Good Friday.'

'Yes,' I said. 'It's Good Friday. It's the 13th of April. But it isn't my birthday . . .'

He leered at me.

'How do you know that?'

'I don't know,' I said. 'I just know.'

'You don't know! You just know!'

Faust winked at Akercocke.

'The birthday boy,' he said. 'Your master, Christopher Wagner. He doesn't know! He just knows!'

'Amen,' said Akercocke.

'Amen indeed,' agreed Faust.

He turned his horrible hawk's beak back at me.

'Happy birthday, dear Christopher . . .'

'Just shut up!' I said. 'This is crazy talk.'

Faust looked hurt.

'I'm telling you things,' he complained. 'All the time. I'm

264

telling you things. But you're not listening. How will you ever learn if you don't listen? Look at you! You're ignorant! You don't know when your birthday was! You don't even know who your father was!'

'Devil,' Akercocke says.

I jumped up. I was furious with Faust. I should have hit him. Instead, I kicked Akercocke's cage. It clanged against the wall. It got dented.

'Will you fuck off?' I cried.

'But it's a fact,' Faust said. 'You like facts, don't you?' He pretended to count on his fingers. 'Fact One: You don't know what day you were born into this abortion of a world. Fact Two: You've never found out who your father was.'

I smashed my fist down on the altar.

I must have killed all of 7 flies.

'OK, Herr Know-all,' I said angrily. 'But since when has it had to be *today* that's my birthday?'

'Since one night 24 years ago,' Faust said. 'Another Good Friday.'

He was staring at me.

He was staring at me like he stared all those years ago when I first met him in Auerbach's cellar.

My mouth tasted dry.

'Would you care for a sip of Vesuvius?' Faust said kindly.

60   Good Friday (11.15 p.m.)

Christ! I saw well enough what he was trying to insinuate . . .

I saw.

And I didn't want to see.

I saw what I'm seeing now.

Faust's fantasies.

There he is, down in the Forum, toasting me:

'Kit! Can you hear me? You're the son of my pact!'

Long and lean. All disjointed. Dancing like a broken puppet. In and out among the ruins and the fallen masonry.

61   Good Friday Morning (?About 10)

I drank quite a lot of his Vesuvius as it happens. My mouth
was like the bottom of a cage. There was some taste in it I
couldn't get rid of.

Faust sat silent for a long while.

Hunched and bunched.

Arms wrapped round his boots and his dirty white hair
falling forwards to hide his face.

It was like he hadn't meant to say so much.

I should think so! I should bloody well hope so!

He'd just shown me a new madness, hadn't he?

Faust never made a move. It seemed like hours. I got im-
patient. The Vesuvius, not unwelcome in the circumstances,
had clouded my mind and made for a brooding mood. But
now there was sunlight coming down the air-shaft. Not much.
A trickle, in fact. But enough.

Enough to make Faust's stillness seem really crazy.

Didn't he care?

Didn't he want to watch his plan work?

Didn't he need to see the Pope drop down dead with that
wolfsbane wafer in his gullet?

At last, I couldn't stand it any longer.

I said:

'What time's this Mass then?'

'Noon,' Faust said.

He still didn't move.

'Look, I'm going,' I said. 'Are you coming?'

'If you like.'

He looked up at me. He was crossing his eyes. He was grinning. All as usual, you might say. But there was something
different. The eyes had no mind in them. The grin had no
heart. He was leaving it all up to me.

'If I *like* . . .'

Jesus Christ!

Well, I nodded.

62   Good Friday Morning (Between 10 and 11)

Flies came buzzing behind us as we quit the catacombs. A black cloud. A black plume. Like our shadow.

We had no shadows otherwise.

A hot day.

But the sun masked in mist high above us.

I think it was Akercocke the flies liked. If we hadn't taken Akercocke the flies wouldn't have followed. But Faust made me take Akercocke. The dented brass cage banging up and down upon my back as we walked.

Or maybe those flies followed Faust. His smell. A death smell. Perhaps that's what they feasted on.

They came after us all day, in any case. Wherever we went, the flies followed. I had flies on my face, on my neck, on my hands, on my shoulders. I must have killed hundreds of flies.

We trudged down the Appian Way in blank silence.

The only sound was the buzzing of the flies.

Past the two milestones.

Past the church called Domine Quo Vadis.

Not a word out of Faust the whole time.

We entered Rome by the San Sebastiano gate.

Few people. Deserted streets. An air of mourning.

Then I realised what it was that I was missing. The sound of bells. Rome is all bells at most times. There's always a chime sounding from this church or that. But on Good Friday the bell towers stay dumb. In token of Christ's crucifixion, I suppose. Not a single bell will ring till the dawn of Easter Sunday. They they suddenly unleash the whole lot.

It was eerie.

We passed through the streets. Over bridges.

Faust walked slower and slower. He limped.

Even with Akercocke on my back, I outpaced him. I had to keep stopping and waiting for him.

Down the wide road that leads to the basilica.

I looked back at a clock as we climbed up the steps of St Peter's.

Both hands were on the eleven.

Like one hand.

63 Good Friday (11.30 p.m.)

Faust can't reach me. He just tried. He's far too drunk.

I'm halfway up this broken flight of steps.

The moon's behind the Capitol behind me. There's a temple up there. I think, to Jupiter.

I climbed up here to get out of his grasp.

It was horrible. He kept kissing me and hitting me. One moment, a caress. The next, a clout.

It made no sense.

And taunting all the time.

He's too drunk now to get out of the Forum. He's lost among the ruins. No way out.

He knows where I am, though. He knows exactly where I'm sitting here with Akercocke. With this moon he can see us both up here.

Faust got just a few steps up these steps. Then he fell over backwards. Ha ha.

Now he's taking his boots off.

Can he think that he'll catch me without them?

And with every breath shouting mad shit.

Like:

'How do you reckon Trithemius fell in your lap, eh? And mouldy Mutian?'

And:

'Got hiccups yet, Kit? Fancy another julep?'

And:

'The seven girls, Kit! All gone! All gone home! Justine and Nadja and Jane and Zuleika and Salome and Marguerite and Gretchen ... They were succubae, Kit. You know about succubae?'

Yes, I know about succubae.

They're devils. They're supposed to be female devils that can fuck with a man in his sleep.

What's Faust trying to do?

Frighten me?

Drive me mad?

The old fool! The old fart! Does he dream I'll go crazy like him?

Now he's off.

He's throwing his boots as he runs.

He's off running again through the ruins, across the stones, across the patches of grass and weeds and nettles between the stones.

'Helen! Come down here, Helen!'

That stupid name echoing back through the Forum.

'Helen . . . Helen . . . Helen . . .'

64 Good Friday Morning
(The Adoration of the Cross)

My first thought was:

He is a different Pope!

There, at the high altar, in St Peter's.

A Black Pope.

A Black Pope with his back to us.

Yesterday's Pope had been white. A White Pope. A White Pope on Palm Sunday also.

But this Pope was different.

Black as night.

Then he turned. He was holding this huge silver crucifix up in his hands.

And I breathed again . . .

I saw I was just being stupid.

It was Paul 3 all right. The same man. The same face of pure politics. The same parchment skin.

The face of a man who never considered an angel in his life.

And the voice coming through those shrewd lips was the same voice I'd heard in the square outside, giving the blessing on Palm Sunday. The same voice – not a syllable of spirituality in it – I'd heard here in St Peter's, just yesterday, pronouncing the mumbo-jumbo words of consecration over Faust's wolfs-bane wafer.

A voice like a wasp in marmalade.

Yup.

It was Alessandro Farnese, OK.

It's just that, in black, men look different. And Paul 3 was robed all in black now. Black stole and black chasuble. Black cope.

Clothes change the man, especially clothes like these.

And black's the liturgical colour for Good Friday. For the Mass of the Presanctified.

It's also the colour that's worn for a requiem Mass. That's the only other time the Pope wears black vestments. For a Mass for the Dead.

'Look! He's going to celebrate his own death!' I whispered to Faust.

Faust didn't say anything.

We went and crouched down near the front.

I had Akercocke. That was OK. The Romans take their pets into church. The aisles of St Peter's reek of cat piss. I saw dogs tied to pews. So the cage on the ground between Faust and me attracted no notice.

An hour's tedium followed.

Real pantomime.

They call it:

The Adoration of the Cross.

The Pope stands there waggling this big silver crucifix and people come crawling past us towards the altar. They queue up to kiss it. The crucifix. Not an orderly queue. Lots of pushing.

They did these things better in Germany, before Luther pulled the chain on the lot.

Christ, and most of the riff-raff took off their shoes before planting their lips on the cross.

I can tell you: I wish that Paul 3 had taken a bit of soap and holy water to a few hundred extra feet the night before.

Akercocke got restive during this malarkey. Hunger, probably. The flies hadn't followed us into church.

'Hell,' he said. 'Hell. Devil. Amen.'

It was hardly appropriate to the ceremony. But what with the shuffling and the barging and the spitting (the Romans are great spitters behind pillars) nobody seemed to hear him.

As for Faust:

He was sweating.

Thick gobs of sweat that dripped and stained the stones.

He was sneaking swigs at his Vesuvius all the time.

He looked worried as hell. I don't know why.

The Pope himself looked bored.
I sympathise.

65 Good Friday Noon
(The Mass of the Presanctified)

What happened next I must set down carefully.

The Pope and his acolytes moved in procession to fetch yesterday's host from its altar of repose.

I wondered idly if it would be stale.

The Pope's black cope was removed for him from his shoulders.

He held up the host.

Some spotty-faced boy swung incense all over it.

The Pope stood with his back to us there at the stripped high altar.

His next movements were swift. Almost brutal. There was none of the usual long-drawn-out conjuring. The host was already supposed to be 'done', after all, like I say.

The Pope's movements were swift, but I saw every one of them.

I saw the host taken up in his hands. I saw him holding it aloft before the altar.

I swear he never had a single chance to palm it.

My eyes never left that stupid bit of bread as the Pope prayed three prayers very fast.

1: '*In spiritu humilitatis, Orate fratres . . .*' ('In a humble spirit, brothers, let us pray . . .')

2: An ordinary *Our Father* (but in Latin, of course).

3: '*Libera nos, quaesumus, Domine . . .*' ('Deliver us, O Lord, we beseech thee . . .')

Then he broke the lethal wafer in three parts.

He dropped the smallest part into the chalice of wine on the altar.

He knelt.

He bowed his head.

He said the usual prayer before communion:

'*Perceptio Corporis tui, Domine Jesu Christe . . .*' ('Let the partaking of thy body, O Lord Jesus Christ . . .')

Then he popped two bits of the bread into his mouth.

271

He chewed.

I saw his neck muscles heave as the mouthful went down.

Then he stood.

He picked up the chalice.

He tilted his head back.

He drank all the wine with the third bit of Faust's poison mixed in it.

I saw every move.

I watched.

I waited . . .

Nothing happened.

I couldn't believe it. I watched. I waited . . .

Nothing happened. Nothing. Nothing at all.

Pope Paul 3 looked more bored than ever. That's all.

He was holding his hands over the chalice so a server could pour wine and water all over his fingers and thumbs where they'd been in contact with the bread. That's to remove any crumbs.

Then the Pope drank these ablutions.

He was drying his lips.

He was drying the chalice itself with a small piece of linen.

Faust crashed forwards beside me. He fell smack on his face on the floor.

I ignored him a moment.

I couldn't believe that the poison wasn't working in those Papal veins.

I couldn't take my eyes off the Pope.

The Pope's face.

Alessandro Farnese looked fed up. Pissed off. Like a servant tired of an old chore. He was barely bothering to conceal a yawn of indifference with the back of his hand.

But he didn't look like dying to me.

He didn't look like dropping down dead.

He was muttering a few prayers impatiently.

He was raring to go . . . Scram . . . Skedaddle . . .

I pressed my lips close to Faust's eardrum.

'*How long does it take?*'

Faust was moaning and groaning and mumbling. The wax in his ear looked like egg yolk.

'*How long?*' I hissed urgently. 'How long for the aconitine to work?'

Faust was kissing the stones. He was clawing at them.

I grabbed his hair.

I hauled him up.

'*How long, you old fool!*'

'An instant!' Faust muttered. 'Ten seconds ... Twenty seconds at most ... *One whole grain!* He should be a dead man!'

'What the hell –?'

'Jesus Christ!'

'What's gone wrong?'

'Jesus Christ! Jesus Christ! Jesus Christ!'

'You great fuck-up!'

Akercocke's rattling his cage.

'God,' he says.

Then the Pope gives his blessing.

'*Benedicat vos omnipotens Deus* ✠✠✠ *Pater et* ✠✠✠ *Filius et* ✠✠✠ *Spiritus Sanctus.*'

And Faust's crossing himself!

A man in black staring at a Black Pope.

His hand moving, twitching, shaking, following the lazy crosses traced by the Pope's hand in the incense-laden air.

'Amen!' roared the congregation.

'Amen,' Faust said.

66 Good Friday (11.45 p.m.)

He's torn his breeches off.

He's standing there in the moonlight as naked as the day that he was born.

And he just won't stop shouting.

More mad stuff.

Like:

'My angel! You know now? You're my angel!'

And:

'Can you hear me, my son? Are you listening? It was true, Kit, you see? All, all true! All the time, Kit! Just you and me! Always! It was always just you and me, son!'

And:

'Luther missed you with the inkpot! Luther missed you with the inkpot!'

He was chanting the last bit. He started dancing.

273

Now he's trying to crawl up these steps again . . .
He won't make it. Even Akercocke can see that.
He's falling. Faust.
Fallen.
His face is all bloody.
So Faust's cracked his own skull?
Hey ho. No. No such luck.
I can see his eyes. Still open. Moving.
By the way, I can tell the exact time from the clock on San Lorenzo in Miranda. Nice big clock. And I've a good view from up here.
So Faust's got 15 minutes . . .
Don't worry.
If any 'devil' turns up in the Forum, I'll *describe* it!
'Mephistopheles' in a toga, no doubt.

67   Good Friday (1 to 11 p.m.)

I'll be brief with the rest of this Good Friday.
Faust drank.
He wouldn't talk.
We walked about.
I was drinking too. Vesuvius and other stuff. Funny thing is: it didn't make me drunk.
I was angry with him, see. Really angry.
Anger keeps sober.
And I got angrier when Faust wouldn't talk.
'You buggered it! You fucked-up! You big fool!'
But *how*?
By late afternoon, I could think of only one possible way.
'It was all a bad joke! You never switched that host!'
Without so much as glancing at me, Faust took this greasy wafer from his hat.
He stuffed it in his mouth.
He gulped it down. Then he threw away his hat. He stamped on it.
So it wasn't that.
So what was it?
Christ knows. I don't.

274

What's more: I don't care.

I don't give a shit any more.

All I know is Faust came to the Forum and started this latest little breakdown and I left him for a bit and climbed a tree to look over the Vatican wall.

I saw the Pope taking his ease in the cool of the evening. He was walking in his rose garden. He was listening to this Spanish-looking guy. He didn't pay him much attention.

The Spaniard seemed to be some kind of monk.

Sackcloth and hempen shoes.

A high bald head.

At the same time, he could have been some kind of soldier.

This sword strapped over his habit.

A real eccentric.

He did most of the talking. The Pope sniffed the roses.

Like I say, we're having a forward spring.

I caught just the odd word that the Spanish guy said.

Something about a Company.

Something about a Society of Jesus.

Something about more teeth for the Inquisition.

Nothing of much interest.

Paul 3 looked bored. But he kept nodding his head quite politely. Sniffing roses. Fondling petals. And at last he gave the Spaniard his blessing.

They parted.

The Pope trots off one way. He was looking as fit as a fiddle.

The Spaniard went the other way. I noticed he walked with a limp.

I got rid of those damned flies anyway. They followed the Spanish guy. He was about normal height. 5 foot 6.

68   Good Friday Midnight

Nothing.

Nothing is happening.

No one has come.

No Devil.

Nothing.

Did you want bells?

Some cracked bell tolling *John John John?*
Well, I warned you.
I told you.
No bells till Easter.
No bell for John Faust.
No bell and no Devil.
Nothing.
Nothing at all.
Just Faust and me.

69   Holy Saturday

I did what I was born to do.
　No more. No less.
　I went down the steps to him. I didn't hurry.
　He lay there on his back with the moonlight on him. He'd
had three minutes longer than he bargained for.
　I said:
　'Hey, Faust.'
　He tried grinning.
　He tried crossing his eyes.
　He found he couldn't grin or cross his eyes.
　'You know now,' he said. 'The first words. Now you know.'
　He started laughing.
　'Hey, Faust,' I said.
　'Happy birthday,' he said.
　I said: 'That was yesterday.'
　He started crying.
　I took his neck between my hands. His flesh was hot. He
smelt really nasty.
　'Kit,' he said. 'It was the body of Christ.'
　'Fuck it,' I said.
　I started to twist his neck. It was really easy. He knew better
than to offer resistance to me.
　'Christ,' he said.
　He smiled just once when his face was halfway.
　'Christ have mercy,' he said.
　I wrenched his head right round to face out from his shoul-
derblades.

70   Easter Sunday

It only goes to show how you can be wrong.

I opened the cage when they rang all their damned bells this morning.

Akercocke's nice.

Akercocke's really nice.

Nov '80